CANARD

...CASE 341

CANARD

...CASE 341

A NOVEL

Anthony Williams

AW Book Publishing
Mesa, Arizona

CANARD...*CASE 341*

Published by:
AW Book Publishing
Phone: 727-776-0109
EMAIL: anwillie23@gmil.com

Anthony Williams, Publisher / Editorial Director
Yvonne Rose/Quality Press, Book Packager

ALL CHARACTERS IN
THIS BOOK ARE FICTIONAL

AW Books are available at special discounts for bulk purchases, sales promotions, fund raising or educational purposes.

Paperback ISBN #: 978-1-0879-5554-4
Ebook ISBN #: 978-1-0879-5555-1
Library of Congress Control Number: 2021905313

Acknowledgements

First and foremost, I'd like to thank God. For nothing is possible without Him. Nothing is impossible with Him. In my life, God is always working! "...even when I don't see Him, He's working, He never stops..." I've truly been protected and blessed all of my life by God. In this carnal voyage though, I give honor and thanks to my Mom and Dad who are not here with us anymore, but their echoes still whisper. They protected my siblings and me by forbidding us to be out after dark among other things. I understand that not much good happens after midnight. I now see what they saw way back then.

To my siblings, Willie James Williams Jr. (deceased) – My encouragement. He always told me that I could; Catherine Delores White (deceased) – The reason I'm a Christian today; Evelyn Johnson – Helps me see the flip side of things; Melvin Williams – He is my superhero! I always wanted to be like Mel; Lucille Barnes – My example of patience and calmness in chaos and grace under fire; and Gwen Williams – My mirror. I think we're attached to the collective. Thank you all for your patience and support throughout the years as I ebbed and flowed in my life. I love you all.

To my children Michael Williams – A brilliant individual with tremendous insight, self-awareness and a sponge of knowledge. He inspires and challenges my mind every day; Timothy Williams – Cool as a cucumber, great sense of humor, very observant and a leader among his peers. He makes everyone feel at ease. Not a wicked bone in his body. He always brightens my day. I love you both.

To my best and lifelong friends, Ray and Jay House. I heard it preached that three people are needed in one's life, a mentor, a protégée and a friend. Ray and Jay have been all of those three for me. I love the entire House clan. Thank you, my extended family, for always including me in those weekend getaways.

To Natalie Woods who did a fantastic job with outlining, researching facts and helping me stretch ideas.

To Yvonne Rose and Amber Books. I appreciate your hard work and dedication to this project. Your communication and professionalism are paramount. You made me feel comfortable and treated every one of my concerns with respect and urgency. I am so thrilled that you have maintained the dying practice of picking up your phone and saying…"Hello".

"Special thanks to my good friend Floyd Espinoza for lending an eye…"

There are so many to thank for my life. So if I didn't make mention of you publicly then publicly I say Thank you, thank you, thank you.

Table of Contents

CHAPTER

1

"And I asked God, Father why do we have to search our hearts? I've come to realize that God is concerned more with *why* we do what we do and not primarily what we do. Jeremiah 17:9 tells us that, 'The heart *is* deceitful above all *things*, and desperately wicked: who can know it…?' We search our hearts to reveal to us our hopelessness. For The Lord in us is our hope of glory. I don't know about you, but I'm glad this morning…"

The day started out as any other. Annie woke up five minutes before her parents' alarm and bounced on the foot of their bed until they pried open their eyes. At the precocious age of five, this behavior was still considered acceptable. The limitless energy—a novelty. The bouncing curls—adorable. At the age of six, she might not be so lucky.

After a well-balanced meal of Lucky Charms, she tackled the giant Golden Retriever and dragged him to the front door to fasten his leash. As far as patience went, this dog was a saint, and only slightly less enthusiastic about these walks than young Annie. He stood perfectly still as her tiny hands tugged his fur and fumbled with the clasp. Once it was secure, she turned proudly to her mother, breathless with anticipation and hungry for praise.

"Mama—I did it all by myself!"

Annie's mother, an over-worked under-slept woman in her early thirties, hugged her terrycloth bathrobe tighter around her as she struggled to focus in the early morning light.

"That's great, Ann. Did you bring your bowl to the counter?"

"The *leash*, mama, I did the *leash*."

Her insistence was rewarded with a smile. "You did good, baby girl. Now you just sit tight while mama throws on some clothes and gets her coffee—and then we'll go outside, okay?"

This seemingly innocuous suggestion was met with unbridled rage.

"*No*—I want to go *now*! I put on the leash by myself, so I can take Clap for a walk by myself too!"

It was far too early for tantrums and Annie's mother was far too un-caffeinated to make much sense of the shrill, piercing wail. Why her daughter had seen fit to name their dog 'Clap' to begin with was beyond her. With remnants of last night's wine still churning away in her stomach, she raised her fingers painfully to her eyes.

"Alright," she cut short the hysterics before they could begin. "You can walk him just to the end of the sidewalk, but you wait for me there—do you understand?"

Annie was a blur of speed and self-congratulations, tugging the big dog gleefully out the door and down the front steps to the gate.

"*Antonia*—I said, do you understand?"

Annie's little shoulders jumped just like every kid when they heard their full, unadulterated name, and she nodded so fast her teeth chattered. "Yep!"

And then they were off. A girl and her dog. The whole wide world in front of them. Nothing but horizon. A horizon that stopped by the dumpster at the end of the block—but it was better than nothing.

The little girl skipped joyfully along, swelling with excitement at her newfound independence. Her house was in a slightly nicer section of a not so nice town—a somewhat questionable cul-de-sac made solvent by the fact that it was bordered on one side by the city's only hospital. But the streets were quiet at this time of day—most of the ambulances that streaked past in the night had come to rest; as the meth dealers, inebriated high school kids, and rival gang members had finally stumbled in to sleep.

It was at this lone hour—the hour between waking and sleep—that the neighborhood found a temporary peace. A sixty-minute window for the cloistered inhabitants to crawl inside and lick their wounds. To light a cigarette and take a breath. Kiss their mothers, kiss their kids, and brace themselves before the cycle started all over again.

Thus it was at this hour, and this hour only, that Annie was allowed outside the house alone for even the briefest amount of time. She relished the freedom and eyed the opposite sidewalk jealously. It was beyond her strictly outlined borders, but perhaps she could reach it anyway. She could feign confusion or blame the dog...

A fierce growl interrupted her scheming thoughts and she looked at Clap in alarm. He almost never made that kind of sound—the only time she could remember him being aggressive was when a stranger walked up to her at the playground on her last birthday. The fur on the back of his shoulder blades bristled to the sky and she patted it down as best she could.

"What's wrong, Clap?" She knew instinctively to whisper. A little chill ran down the back of her neck and she was about to high-tail it on home, when she saw a pair of dirtied boots sticking out from behind the hospital dumpster. Curiosity overcame caution, and she inched timorously forward.

At first, her childlike mind couldn't make sense of it. Why was the man sleeping at such an odd angle? Why had he chosen behind the festering dumpster for his bed? And what was the sticky brown substance painted all over his neck?

Spurred on by her newfound autonomy, she was about to creep closer still, when the man suddenly opened his eyes.

She screamed at precisely the same moment that a phone call shattered the silence in a house just two blocks over…

* * *

'I can think of younger days, when living for my life…'

There was a muffled groan from beneath the sheets as a solitary hand reached out and slammed down at the alarm clock. It missed.

'Was everything a man could want to dooooo. But I could never see…'

A pair of eyes appeared to back up the hand, and the second time around, they got their target. The clock went sailing to the floor where the battery promptly fell out upon impact and the glass screen cracked in two places.

A part of Michael was almost smug.

He hated the damn thing. Every time it looped that same song, he would jerk awake with something akin to heart palpitations—something a heart like his could in no way handle. Already he felt the telltale buzz as his pulse jittered and skipped beneath his skin. With a tired sigh, he set his feet firmly on the floor and lowered his head between his knees, waiting for his body to calm down and his mind to wake up.

It had been a rough night. He'd had the dreams again—always the same dreams. The ones where absolutely nothing was out of the ordinary except that he was back where he'd been four years ago. Back in a gang, living day to day, drugs and so many passing women he couldn't for the life of him remember their names.

It was to be expected, in a neighborhood like this. New York City was close enough that it shadowed the fair streets of the little town, but far enough away that they didn't get any regulation. It was a town run by forces, rather than laws.

There were the gangs, there were the drugs, there was the high school (a perfect gateway to channel teens into one of the aforementioned occupations), and then there was the church.

Michael had transitioned rather seamlessly after graduation with most of the rest of his class. In this town, gang affiliation was based more on location than color, and Michael's foster house had placed him squarely in one of the worst ones. But it had to be said, for a while, he didn't really mind it. In fact, after bouncing around from house to house, it was almost nice to get some stability. But with that 'stability' came guns, and deaths, and arrests, and enough dark shadows that they still popped up from time to time in his dreams.

He stopped himself there, before his mind could wander too far down that particular path and picked up his broken clock with a sigh.

The tune had been a favorite of his mother's. Joni Mitchell. It was one of the only things he could remember about her—that she liked that song. She had died when he was only four. He snapped the batteries back inside and rubbed his finger along the cracks. What had started out as a sweet homage had quickly turned into some Pavlovian cardiac episode. Maybe it was time he searched for another…

Thinking over a list of options, he threw on some clothes and breezed down the hall to the bathroom, still rubbing his chest with an absentminded hand. The numbed tingling sensation, which usually faded after the first few minutes, was lingering longer than usual, and for a second, he considered calling his doctor.

At a glance, it may have seemed like a strong reaction to such a minor symptom, but when you were diagnosed at six years old with congenital heart disease, Michael had learned that there were no such things as minor symptoms.

His diagnosis had worsened over the years—no doubt hastened by his post-graduation debauchery and a string of bad foster homes—and had eventually progressed to the point where he'd been granted a place on the UNOS wait list for a new organ altogether. He remembered the day he'd gotten the call. It had been from Ray Price—a doctor at the nearby hospital and the only 'old family friend' Michael had. Price had been an ever-present force in his life since he could remember—sending him envelopes of lunch money in elementary school, attending his high school graduation, fiercely chiding him for his wayward path in the months that followed. The two had gotten so close, that when Price called him a little over a year ago to tell him that he'd made the list, Michael had assumed that the man was playing some sort of joke.

"You can't be serious," he'd said, twirling the phone cord as his heart sped up hopefully, just in case.

"I am serious," Price had answered. "Serious as a heart attack."

Michael rolled his eyes—insensitive medical humor was one of the things he and Price had consistently bonded on over the years, and it had grown increasingly frequent.

"But seriously, Mike—you're on the list. Give it some time, but you're going to get a new heart."

Price was the only one who called him Mike. The only one he'd ever opened up to about his constant, sickening fear of mortality. The fear that one day, this broken heart of his would simply stop.

He'd stopped twirling the cord by now and was staring at the wall with an almost hungry expression in his eyes. "How much time?"

"Could be a couple months, could be a couple years," the doctor answered. "But you're on the list, Mike. It's happening. Now you just gotta hang in there, kid."

"I can do that," Michael had promised, and in the coming year, he'd kept his word.

He went to regular check-ups, took his medicine without fail, and did whatever kind of exercise his team of doctors would allow—working it in each day in little bursts. As a result, his twenty-six-year-old body was in prime physical shape. Muscular, but lean. Tall and sculpted. In fact, if one were to simply spot him from afar—they would assume that he was the kind of guy who could 'handle himself.' The kind of guy you wouldn't want to mess with on the streets.

If it weren't for the ticking time bomb in his chest…they might have been right.

So today, when the strange tingling sensation refused to dissipate, Michael seriously considered calling Dr. Price. He knew Ray would want to know and figured it couldn't hurt. He'd been waiting so long, gotten so close—at this point, he didn't want to take any chances.

He'd actually picked up his phone and started to dial the memorized number, when it buzzed suddenly in his hand. It was the church calling—Pastor Jeff.

"Morning," Michael answered it, pulling on his shoes.

"Michael—good morning! I hope I didn't wake you."

"Not at all, I was just on my way out the door."

"Perfect, then I caught you just in time." Jeff spoke quickly, raising his voice to be heard over a mild commotion in the background. "I was wondering if you could bring your camera with you today to the church. The news bulletin is going to run an article about the pancake breakfast, and I thought it would be nice if we had some pictures of the set-up."

Michael smiled. Jeff was asking incredibly casually, but they both knew that the weekly church news bulletin was a matter of the utmost importance in the Pastor's mind. Something topped only by Friday night football and Jesus Christ. In other words, this was not a request.

"I'll see what I can do," Michael teased, leaving him hanging. "Be there in a few."

He hung up the phone and grabbed his camera bag from where he hid it each night in a little nook below his bed. In the three years that he'd lived in this apartment, he'd only had one break-in (a rather outstanding feat in a neighborhood such as this), and then, it was only a kid looking for some food and spending money. But he loved the camera in question the same way that Jeff loved his weekly news bulletin. It had cost roughly the same amount as his broken-down car, and he guarded it just as jealously—giving it the one and only hiding place in his whole house. 'Rather they take my life, than my camera,' he'd always say.

He swung the strap over his shoulder and headed down the street, waving to the occasional neighbor as he braced himself against the crisp autumn wind.

Not that he had anything to compare it to—he had never left the state—but Michael loved the way New York did seasons. It snowed in the winter, rained in the spring, baked in the summer, and in the fall—on days like today—it *sharpened*. The leaves were brighter, the wind was harder, and the air had a bite. There was a sense of anticipation—a gradual build-up that bottomed out sometime over the holidays.

Screw Christmas and the Fourth—Michael would take a fall day every time.

"Morning Willy," he said as he ducked into a little coffee shop. The man behind the counter looked up with a smile and started preparing the usual brew.

Judging by the size of the shop, it used to be something like a broom cupboard but had been transformed around the time that Bill Clinton was elected president. Now, it operated as half café, half gossip center to the four men whose regular patronage kept the place open. Michael was one of the four. Although quite a bit younger than his three companions, he would regularly sit around the lone checker-boarded table after hours, watching whatever sport happened to be on the three-channel television and speculating tirelessly as to who was going to win the coming election. School boards, state officials, the presidency—it didn't matter. The men had a passion for politics at any level. The second one race was over, they'd move on to the next.

"You setting up for the church breakfast this morning?" Willy asked, pouring the scalding hot latte into a paper cup to go.

Willy, Tommy, Jerry...and Michael.

Mikey, they always pressed. *Michael* stubbornly refused.

Michael flicked the strap on his camera bag as he took the cup with his other hand. "Jeff has me taking pictures."

"Aw, come on now," Willy grinned, "you know Jeff don't care about none of that."

Michael laughed and set his money in the tin. Judging by Willy's increasingly frog-like smoker's laugh, he should be on a UNOS list of his own. But Michael somehow doubted that anything so small, as obvious as untreated lung cancer could do old Willy in. Not with another election race just around the corner.

"Cheers," he said as he backed out of the door, raising his cup in farewell.

The church was only a few blocks away and Michael quickened his pace, taking burning sips of coffee and ignoring the dull ache that had started in his chest.

Probably just the cold, he thought to himself. *Or the caffeine.*

Either way, no time for it now.

The sanctuary was already in full swing by the time he stepped inside. Pastor Jeff had an uncanny ability to inspire unwavering loyalty in the members of his congregation, and according to Jeff, that loyalty had to be regularly proven by shows of support. This support came in all shapes and sizes. Whether it was helping gather funds for uniforms for the girls' softball team, starting a food drive to take to the homeless shelter every October and March, or even setting up for the annual pancake breakfast like today. That unquestioning loyalty was the reason Michael had brought his camera.

"Think fast!" he said with a grin, blinding the Pastor with a flashbulb as he turned around. Normally, he didn't favor the flash—but Jeff had always deserved special treatment.

Jeff squinted and swatted at the air between his eyes, as if he could simply push the green dots in his vision away. "Finally— what took you so long?"

Michael rubbed his chest and appraised the picture he'd just taken. "You called me exactly seven minutes ago. Didn't the good Lord have something to say about patience?"

Jeff twiddled his thumbs and pretended not to have heard. "Anyway, Michael, I'm glad you're here—and thank you for bringing that." He gestured to the bag. "If you want to hold off for just a minute, Sherry and Calvin are dragging some chairs up from the basement and I'm sure they could use some help."

"Sure," Michael said easily, heading to the Pastor's office. He tucked the camera safely away in the desk before jogging down the stairs to help with the chairs.

He greeted several more bustling people as he weaved his way down the familiar halls. It hadn't been that long ago that he'd never set foot in a church. Never listened to a sermon, never closed his eyes in a quiet room to pray. The concept of 'God' was completely foreign to him—something he'd assumed had been either weaponized for whites, republicans, or politicians; or if God was real—He was reserved for a thoughtful kind of person who lived on the opposite side of town. The kind that took vitamins, and washed their car, and remembered to feed their cat.

He didn't think for one second that someone like God would ever be in the same sentence as someone like him.

How things had changed. Perhaps it was a good thing that Jeff had left his church in Minnesota seven years ago to come to the grimy New York suburbs, because instead of being discouraged, he'd taken all Michael's pre-conceived notions and doubts as a challenge. He'd fallen down on his knees in instant prayer—entreating the Lord to change this child's heart. He'd broken them down by force of will—much in the same way that he demanded his now-infamous church loyalty. It was something that he and Michael still talked and laughed about during their weekly dinners.

As Michael descended the last of the stairs, he saw Sherry Bir and Calvin Moreno—two of the oldest members of the congregation—struggling beneath a shared armful of chairs.

"Guys," he said, rushing forward, "let me help you with those."

He took the chairs from them before either one could protest—although to be honest—they looked rather relieved to be free of the burden.

"Thank you, Michael," Sherry exclaimed, sinking dramatically into an old pew pushed to the side of the wall. "Why Jeff sent the two of *us* down here to do this—I'll never know."

"Speak for yourself," Calvin argued, picking up a much smaller armful for himself. "Not everyone is *old*, Sherry. Just you."

She let out a bout of sarcastic laughter, staring at the white wisps of hair still managing to cling to his head, before turning to Michael for support. "Can you believe the way he speaks to me? And in the house of God, too. You'd better be careful, Calvin. Never know who could be listening on the other end. In fact, I'll have you know…Michael? Are you okay?"

She stopped her rant suddenly short and turned to where Michael had frozen abruptly on the stairs. His shoulders were rising and falling as he sucked in rapid, shallow breaths. Beneath the metal loops of the folding chairs, his chiseled arms had begun to shake.

"Michael?" she asked again when he didn't say anything. "Sweetheart, are you al—"

Her voice cut off with a shrill scream as he collapsed in a pile of chairs on the ground. His hands were shaking as his eyes fluttered open and closed. Time started to move in stilted snapshots, lurching forward and then stalling out with every blink.

"My pager," he tried to say, "get my pager."

But they couldn't hear him. In what had to be the worst luck in the world, he was stuck in the basement with the only two people in the congregation who still refused to wear hearing aids.

A minute later, Pastor Jeff came tearing into the room. He'd heard Sherry's scream and fell to the ground immediately beside Michael, propping up his head and patting the sides of his face with shaking, helpless hands.

"Michael," he cried, kneeling down to try to catch the young man's eye. "Michael, what do I do? What can I do?"

"My pager…" Michael's voice had grown faint, and he could feel himself about to pass out. "Call the number on my…"

Then the world went dark.

* * *

The phone call had timed out exactly, so that even though Dr. Price was only two streets away, he didn't hear the little girl scream. It was from a blocked number and he took a deep breath before answering. There was only one person who ever called whose information was restricted. And it was often not a call he wanted to take.

"Ray," the voice said as soon as he picked up.

It was never phrased as a question, never an 'oh, there you are—is that you?' It was a summons. Every time.

"What do you need, Pete?" Price answered, rubbing his eyes. "It's early."

"I left you a little present by the dumpster. See that it gets in the right hands."

The line clicked dead.

Most people would have ignored such a statement—written it off as a prank, or simply crazy. Dr. Price did none of these things. Instead, he stared at the receiver with an almost fearful expression clouding his already-lined face.

Peter…was in New York?

Fortunately, Price was the attending surgeon for the day, and didn't have to wait long to find out what the cryptic message meant. A body had been discovered by a young girl earlier that morning. Well, it had been a man when it was discovered, but it was a body by the time it was brought into the morgue. Nevertheless, time of death was less than two minutes before the doctor came racing into the room and there was still time enough to harvest the organs.

Price was just cutting into the cadaver's chest when he got the call about Michael. The young man's heart had finally given out, and as fate would have it, the ambulance taking him into the hospital was already on the way.

Fate…? Or something else?

For just a split second, Price paused with his hands still in the dead man's chest. He didn't believe in fate. He didn't believe in chance either. He believed in dumpster presents and restricted phone calls. He had been that way for many years.

"Bring him straight in," he instructed the ambulance on speaker phone. "We're in O.R. Seven."

The phone clicked off as he carefully extracted the recently beating heart from the bloodied cadaver.

"Today's your lucky day, Michael," he murmured. "You just moved up on the list…"

CHAPTER

2

The woman watched the whole thing from the shadows. Watched as the little girl and her dog came across the body. Watched as the police and a few curious neighbors quickly crowded the scene, tossing predictions and speculations around like popcorn. Watched, just moments later, as the ambulance streaked past—lights and sirens blasting into the early morning air.

Her eyes gleamed faintly as she backed away from the curb and headed down the street towards the slum on the east side of town. She rubbed the sides of her toned arms to keep warm—shivering a little in her thin, pink dress as her muscular legs pounded the pavement. She hadn't planned on being in New York on the verge of winter, where thin sheets of ice were already coating the inky streets. She hadn't planned on coming here at all. Perhaps she would buy herself a coat...

It wasn't until she stepped out of the shadows and into the sun that a passerby would have given her a second look. Yes, she was striking—with her heavily made up eyes, sheets of long blonde hair, and the tiny satin dress clinging to her powerful frame. But it was none of these things that would have made anyone walking past give a moment's pause.

It was the question. The unspoken question that seemed more and more obvious the longer she walked down the road.

She…was not really a *she* at all. Was she?

A rusted car sped through a red light and almost hit the man who called himself Vivian as he headed to a pawn shop up the road. The slick tires skid several feet and came to a stop just inches away from his gloved fist. The next second, the fist dented in the hood of the car.

"What the hell are you thinking, lady?" the driver shouted, still hungover from a late-night party that had stretched into the early hours of the morning. His eyes struggled to focus as he reassessed the situation. "I mean, that's a nice weave dawg—what, you auditioning for the circus or something?"

Vivian turned to him for the first time and the driver suddenly paused. It didn't seem to matter that this transvestite was on the other side of the glass, that he himself was in a moving vehicle, or that the person in question was wearing four-inch heels. The driver suddenly believed with every fiber of his being that this was…unsafe. He needed to leave. *Now.*

"Sorry, man," he muttered, stepping gently on the gas and easing past Vivian through the crosswalk.

Vivian watched him leave with a steely look in his glittering eyes. He had never liked this town. Never liked, that as the fates would have it, he had to spend any amount of time here. That he had to give it even a second thought. He continued down the road with a sigh, pulling open the door to a pawn shop and taking welcome relief in the state-of-the-art heating system.

One way or another, the dice had fallen and here he was. And by the looks of things, not a minute too soon…

* * *

It had been two days ago that he'd gotten the call. That's how long it took for him to set up this little maneuver and fly halfway across the world to get to this little armpit of a town. He remembered the moment it had happened—the moment his entire life had abruptly changed.

He'd been in Budapest at the time, sitting on the balcony of his little flat, staring out across the river at the Hungarian Parliament. There was a brochure on his bed. 'Things to do in Hungary.' Inside had been slipped a picture of a forty-five-year-old man. Six-foot two. Dark hair. Blue eyes. Approximately two-hundred and ten pounds. Scribbled alongside the photograph were details of his itinerary for the next four days, along with a plane ticket, two passports, and enough Forints for him to purchase one of the many riverboats sailing along the Danube River.

He glanced back at the mattress and sighed. He had been hoping to stay here a few more days—long enough for the heat back in Saint Petersburg to dissipate. He never did jobs in his hometown if he could help it. It was a basic principle, a virtual nursery rhyme. 'Never kill people in the same city where you sleep.' And yet, when the powers that be commanded him to take out a high-ranking diplomatic informant, he did so without question, firing two bullets in the back of her head before driving her car into a snowbank.

When asked for a status report, he'd said she'd obviously died of natural causes. It was said with a careless smirk, nonetheless, he was quick to put in a request for work outside of town. "Was Hungary far enough away?" they'd asked. Yes, Hungary would be just fine.

Except for this man. This—Anico Boros. He had arrived early for his conference, and as such, the schedule had jumped up by several days. It wouldn't be a problem, of course, but Vivian— three days ago, Peter—would have preferred a bit of a cushion.

He pushed abruptly to his feet, striding into the apartment and retrieving a .22 caliber pistol from his nightstand, laying just atop a Gideon's Bible. He glanced at the book as he loaded the gun from memory, his eyes tracing over the worn cover. He'd rented this place through his agency, who rented it through five separate 'third parties.' Those Gideons sure had a long reach.

A minute later, he was out on the streets, his leather coat and dark jeans blending in seamlessly with the people around him. In fact, there was nothing about the man's face that would stand out in a crowd. He had the same haircut as everyone else, the same watch, the same shoes. In the airport on the way over, he'd even picked up the same chewing gum. This was all by design. The perfect formula to become the invisible man. His job required it. It had saved his life on more than one occasions.

The gun was cold against his back, stuck securely under his heavy jacket in the top of his jeans. He almost smiled when he thought of it. It was amateur hour over here. No self-respecting assassin walked around with a gun sticking out of his jeans. But unlike most places in the world, the Hungarian custom was to frisk front before they frisked behind. It was only enough to buy you a split second's advantage, but Peter had been in enough of these rodeos to know that sometimes, a split second, was all it took.

"Elnézést," he stopped a passing boy, "you speak English?"

"Yes, sir?" the child answered, looking up at the man curiously.

Up close he was not as invisible as he was in a crowd. The face was handsome, but hard—the kind of face that would make you look twice. There was a thin scar just above the left eyebrow—the only remnants of a grazing bullet that should have shattered his skull. But perhaps most telling was the eyes. They say that when you killed enough men, their spirits lingered in your eyes. You were a marked man after that. People could just look at you and know. Some people said it happened after only one man.

"There's a man inside that restaurant," Peter said calmingly, smiling to put the child at ease. He held up the photograph. "He's here with the embassy and I've been sent to give him and his wife concert tickets for tomorrow night. I'm not dressed to go inside," he gestured to his casual clothes, "could you bring him to me?"

The child paused, a little thrown by the unusual nature of the request. But there was an undeniable confidence in the way Peter spoke, and like most children, this one was trained to obey.

"Igen—yes. Okay."

Peter tapped him under the chin, and he ran inside, a tiny volunteer to bring the lamb to the slaughter. The assassin's eyes locked on his little back as he slipped past the valets and darted through the front door. He didn't like using children for this sort of thing. In fact, he didn't like using children, period. But this was a special circumstance.

The schedule had changed and his window for taking this man down had drastically shortened. The only time left to do it while still ensuring a minimal amount of possible civilian casualties was here at the restaurant. And after the incident in St. Petersburg…

Needless to say, he wanted to keep the casualties as minimal as possible.

He was still waiting in the alley, shifting restlessly back and forth in the new snow, when there was a sudden vibration in his jacket pocket. His face froze.

There was one thing that could identify him in the milling crowds beyond. There was one thing that assuredly separated him from every other person in his line of work.

He carried a cell phone.

Cursing in a dozen different languages, he ducked behind a cart selling tourist keychains and flipped open the phone. He didn't need to check to see who was calling. Only one person had this number.

"Ray."

He struggled to control the anger in his voice, whilst his eyes kept flickering anxiously to the restaurant. The boy would be out any moment now. With Anico Boros in tow.

"What is it? You know you're never supposed to call this number—"

"It's Michael."

Just like that, the mission was forgotten. Peter tossed the gun in the trash and started heading briskly for the apartment. Anico Boros would live another day.

"What about Michael?"

Halfway across the globe, Dr. Ray Price sighed. "You know he's been on the list for a little over a year now…"

"Yes. And?"

"And I don't think he's going to make it that long." A throat cleared followed by the distant rustling of papers. "I've been going over his scans. Cardio CT's, angios… Peter, they're all saying the same thing."

There was a brief pause.

"And what's that?"

"That Michael's not going to live long enough to get a donor heart. Not with how many people are in front of him on that list."

At first, Peter's mind blanked in horror. Then, as it was trained to do, it started spinning with a million unspeakable possibilities.

If there were too many people ahead of Michael on the list, then maybe those people needed to get out of the way. He could take care of that. There could only be, what—thirty? Forty tops? Over the span of his illustrious career, that was nothing. A drop in an ocean. He would do all that and more for Michael.

But then, as Price began droning on and on about medical statistics and the specific ways UNOS categorized people, his mind began moving in a different direction.

Maybe something a little more direct? Michael needed a new heart. Peter knew many people who wouldn't be needing theirs for much longer. A donor heart could only last a few hours without oxygen before it was considered unviable.

Perhaps, if the timing was just right…

"Ray," he interrupted whatever the good doctor was saying, "what's Michael's blood type?"

This time, it was the doctor who paused. "He's AB Positive…why?"

With almost robotic precision, Peter ran through a list of everything he knew about his son. Six foot four, around two-hundred fifteen pounds. Muscular. Fit. He knew from his countless hours of internet research and two decades grilling Price that both the donor and the recipient had to be approximately the same size and build.

Who did he know that fit that description…?

The answer came to him like a proverbial bolt of lightning. His lips curled up into a smile, and all at once, he found he wasn't overly concerned with the worried ramblings of the doctor. Without changing his direction, he lifted his hand to hail down a cab.

"Price," he cut him off again, mid-thought, "don't worry about anything. Just keep an eye on Michael. I…I have a feeling it will all work out."

He hung up just as a taxi pulled over to the curb.

"Where to, my friend?" the driver asked as he climbed inside.

"The airport."

* * *

In the notorious career of Peter Canard, there were very few things he hadn't done. His list of targets was as extensive as they come, and he'd 'performed' in almost every country, with every method, in every circumstance you could imagine.

There were, however, a few standouts on his list.

For one—he had never been shot. In his line of work, this was almost unheard of, and he had to admit—over the years—

he'd grown almost anxious for it to just happen already and get it over with. He could survive a bullet, couldn't he? He'd survived worse.

Also on the list: he'd never had any repeat performances.

Once he was given a name, that name did not live to see the following month. Or week. Or sometimes, even day. This didn't weigh heavy on his conscience. In fact, he liked to think that he was ridding the world of some of its evils, one by one. The people he was sent after were the worst of the worst, and he dispatched them accordingly. No one escaped. No one lived to tell the tale. Except one man.

Lucius Montana.

Montana was in the same line of work as Peter—only for a different side. And fortunately, on a different continent. While Peter's work kept him mostly in the Eastern European block, Montana stayed primarily in the Western Hemisphere. That is, until one fateful day. A day where Montana was tasked to protect a man Peter was tasked to kill.

Their collision had been brutal but brief. Montana favored the knife—in fact, he was well known for his ruthless tactics—and Peter almost lost a lung before he was finally able to get the upper hand. Montana escaped—barely—while Peter stayed behind to tend to his wounds.

That had been almost five years ago. It wasn't something either man was willing to talk about (Montana's record was almost as spotless as Peter's), but an assassin neither forgave nor forgot. They were always somewhere on each other's radar, peripherally keeping track, waiting for the day when they could finally finish what they started.

That's how Peter Canard knew Lucius Montana was currently in New York.

* * *

The flight landed at JFK on schedule and Peter breezed quickly out of the terminal, having checked no baggage to recover. He hopped into a cab just as fast, eager to get out of the open and out of sight.

He'd had only one demand when he signed up with his agency. One demand that was followed to the absolute. No jobs in New York.

It wasn't even New York City that was the problem, it was a little town outside it. A little hell-hole leeching industrial power on the outskirts. The town where Michael lived.

If Peter accomplished nothing else in this life—for this life was surely the only chance his miserable soul would get—it would be that his son, Michael, would never have anything to do with the shadows that chased his father. If nothing else, Michael would always be safe.

Hence, no bags. Fake passport. Disposable cell phone. Nothing that could trace back to Peter. Because as surely as Peter used his target's loved ones as a way of tracking them down, he knew his shadows would do the same.

Upon Peter's command, the cab headed for a grimy little bar in the heart of Hell's Kitchen. If you blinked, you missed it. But if you lived in the area, it stood out like a red flag. This was the place where all the drug kingpins and their mistresses of the week went to congratulate each other on their vast importance and unparalleled wealth. The place where the seedy underbelly of New York came together to drink shots of Jameson and laugh over Cuban cigars while secretly sizing each other up.

Coincidently, this was also where Lucius Montana was dining tonight.

Peter crouched behind some trash bins at four in the morning, waiting for him to come outside. There would be no children's invitations this time, no limiting civilian casualties, no middle-men. Montana was going to die tonight. And for as long as this particular fight had been coming, it actually had nothing to do with Peter's bruised ego.

Montana was going to die, so that his son could live.

About twenty minutes later, the door to the bar banged opened. A gust of warm air tinted with the smell of whiskey and the faint hint of vomit poured out into the cool night. Peter tensed, every muscle at the ready, as the giant silhouette of Montana lumbered drunkenly into the alley. He'd strategically waited in the darkness between the bar and Montana's car, hoping to catch the man off his guard.

Unfortunately, in Montana's case, that was far easier said than done…

The second Peter eased out his gun, Montana's eyes locked upon him, catching even the slightest movement in the dark. They dilated then widened, as Peter—having lost the element of surprise—stepped out into the dim light.

"Peter Canard." Montana actually smiled. "It's been a very long time. How's the chest?"

Peter's hand came up automatically to the long scar he'd carried since meeting Montana the first time, but he smiled easily back, falling into a casual fighting stance. "It's fine—a distant memory now."

"Distant memory, huh?" There was a small whisky cloud hovering around him. "Then why exactly are you here? I can't remember a time you were ever in New York." Just as casually as

Peter had done, he shifted his weight strategically backwards, readying his muscles to spring.

"I came here to see you, old friend." Peter's soft voice cut through the still night. "You see, you have something I need…"

Without waiting for him to reply, Peter launched himself into the air between them.

With virtually any other opponent, his quick reflexes and raw strength might have done the trick, but Montana was ready for him. He grabbed Peter by the jacket—still mid-air—and sent him flying into the brick wall above the trash bins.

Peter slid to the ground but landed on his feet just as Montana pulled out his signature knife. His eyes latched on to the silver blade, but far from being discouraged, his lips turned up in a little smile. A knife might just be the way to go.

You never knew if a bullet was going to hit the wrong thing and kill you. And as much as he might despise this man, he needed him alive.

In a flash of silver and black, they came together—each growling under their breath and panting as they tried to get the upper hand. Montana knocked Peter hard in the jaw with his elbow, but Peter held firm, turning the knife—inch by inch—towards Montana's chest.

When it was actually touching the edge of Montana's shirt, he seemed to think that temporary retreat was the best option. He kicked Peter's knees and bolted for the front of the alley, but Peter leapt upon his back, bringing him down to the ground.

As he raised the knife ceremoniously over the chest of his enemy, he chanted what had become his customary farewell. Words just as famous as Montana's knife.

"Do you repent and accept the Lord Jesus Christ into your heart?"

Montana's eyes clouded in rage as he spat blood into Peter's face. There was a smile, and the knife flashed in the moonlight before sinking into Montana's stomach. Montana twitched with a gurgling cry, before looking down in astonishment.

"My stomach," he croaked, his head falling back against the wet pavement. "You're really going to draw it out that long?"

"I told you, Lucius," Peter said, swinging him over his shoulder with a painful groan, "you have something I need. And for that, I'm going to need you to stay alive just a little while longer..."

* * *

The trip to Woodlands—the ironically-named pit where Peter had stashed his infant son all those years ago—took a little over two hours. Long enough for Montana to get a good head start on bleeding out in the trunk of his stolen car. Peter checked on him now and again to make sure he was still breathing. In fact, he even pulled over at a convenience store on the fringes of the city and forced some water down his throat.

"Why are you doing this?" Montana panted, glaring with fierce hatred even now at the end. "Even I wouldn't have done this to you. Where are you taking me?"

"I told you," Peter said calmly, "I need—"

"Yeah, I know, you *need* something. You cryptic son of a bitch. What exactly is it you *need* from me?"

Peter screwed the cap back on the water bottle and looked at him calmly. Their eyes met, and for a moment, Peter seemed to be considering.

"I guess I'll tell you…because you won't live long enough to do anything about it." He knelt down beside the trunk as his voice dropped to a low murmur. "I need your heart."

Montana blinked, hands still trying to stem the bleeding. "My…you need my heart?"

"I need to give it to my son. He's sick. And you, my friend, for all the worthless things you've done in your life, might be just the cure."

Much to his surprise, Montana started laughing, choking a little on blood, but laughing, nonetheless. When it finally subsided, he looked up at Peter with a bloody grin. "Oh you see, that's the best thing you could have given me."

Peter's eyes were cold. "And why's that?"

"Because," Montana chuckled again, "because even when I'm gone, I'm going to have the satisfaction of knowing that both you and your son will be soon to follow."

He leaned his head back painfully in the trunk, still grinning away.

"If you think for a second that the people tracking you—the people who are always tracking you, who always track the both of us—if you think for a second that they didn't follow you here, you're crazier than I thought."

Peter was silent, watching as Montana's eyes drifted in and out of consciousness.

"They're going to kill you, and your son," he said again, his voice growing increasingly faint. "One way or another, this heart of mine is going in the ground…"

The trunk slammed shut and Peter stormed around to the driver's seat, throwing himself inside and banging his hands on the steering wheel. As much as he despised the man with every inch of him, Montana was right. He simply voiced the same nagging concerns that had eaten away at Peter since leaving Budapest.

Yes—he could give this gift to his son, this little miracle that could save his life.

…but then what?

Since the day Peter had been handed his first hit list, he'd been simultaneously placed on a dozen international hit lists of his own. That was just the way these things worked. There was no stopping the shadows that lingered constantly behind them. There was only keeping ahead of them, trying to outrun them for so long.

And now he'd brought them here.

He thought of Dr. Price—what he would say if he was here right now. He thought of the man bleeding out in this trunk, how little time he had for Peter to make a decision.

Then he thought of Michael—his dear boy, the most precious thing in the world to him: abandoned at birth. He thought of his son growing up in Woodlands, fighting tooth and nail just to make it through with some semblance of his humanity intact. No father to guide him. No father to protect him. Just a defective heart and a string of bad memories.

Peter's throat clenched as he bowed his head to the steering wheel.

What was he doing here? What did he think this was going to change?

"I know it was you! I saw you take it!"

His head snapped up to see two men fighting outside the convenience store. It was clearly a matter of some 'misplaced' cash, and a vicious back and forth ensued.

"I didn't touch your shit, man! Maybe you should keep better track of your things!"

The first man pulled out a blunt knife and waved it in the air between them. "You think I'm stupid? You think I don't know it was you? Who the hell else is there?!"

Although it seemed so obvious to Peter, neither one of the men seemed to notice the silent woman inching away from the scene. They even bumped into her at one point, but despite the guilty look plastered on her face, no one seemed to give her a second thought.

A little lightbulb went off and Peter's mouth fell open in sudden illumination.

Because she was a woman.

Because who would suspect a woman in a town of hard-hitting men?

As uncomfortable as it was, a plan started spinning in the back of his head. A second later, he threw the car in gear and headed off down the darkened streets towards the hospital, pulling out his cellphone as he flew down the road.

A certain doctor was about to get a call…

CHAPTER

3

Michael opened his eyes to a blur of florescence. There were faint beeps coming from somewhere over his head, and he slowly traced a spider web of wires from his arms to a tall machine standing beside him. As he looked at the machine, the beeping quickened, and his mind made the very sluggish connection.

He was not at the pancake breakfast. He was at…the hospital?

The beeping quickened even more as he tried to sit up. Immediately, two pairs of manicured hands pushed him gently back on the cushions.

"Well good morning, sunshine! You were out for quite a while."

His eyes cleared even more as the faces of two heavily-dolled up nurses came into view.

"I…" He could barely summon the strength to speak. One of the nurses leaned down closer to hear, blanketing him in a waft of perfume. "What happened to me?"

She smiled. "Well, honey, it's actually all good news. You see, you—"

"Trisha! Chrissy!"

The two nurses jumped guiltily, and 'Trisha' quickly let go of Michael's hand—which he hadn't even realized she'd been holding. A new nurse walked into the room, and from the looks of things, this was the one in charge. She'd made absolutely no effort with herself, but she absolutely didn't need to. There was a something regal about the way she carried her hefty body, an undeniable authority in the way she spoke. This woman didn't need frills or cosmetics, she was a queen in her own right.

"I believe the two of you have other patients to round on, isn't that right?" Her voice carried a dangerous warning, and in the blink of an eye, her nervous underlings scampered from the room. Michael's eyes struggled to focus as they vanished, turning instead to the huge African American woman as she leaned over him to check his cords.

"I do apologize for that," she said gently. "It's been a slow day over here, and it seems the word has spread about the dreamboat up on the fourth floor." She smiled and carefully lifted him up, so his back was supported by more pillows.

"I'm sorry," Michael murmured an automatic apology—something about this woman commanded manners, "I don't understand. Why am I here? What happened?"

"Well honey, you fell down at the church. It seems that heart of yours finally gave out."

Michael paled, his eyes flashing around the room with new purpose. "Shit—so what? Am I on bypass now or—"

"No honey, you're not on bypass." She patted his ankle comfortingly as she checked on some more of the tubes trailing out from his body. "In fact, everything worked out for the best."

Michael shook his head weakly, his heavy eyelids dropping shut despite his best efforts to stay awake. "I don't...I don't understand..."

The last thing he heard before he fell asleep were the warm words of the nurse as she covered him up with another blanket.

"You don't have to understand, honey. The doctor will be in soon to explain everything. For now, you just know that you're safe in God's hands, honey. You're safe in God's hands..."

* * *

"Michael? Mike, can you open your eyes for me?"

Still dazed from drugs and blood loss, Michael struggled to do as he was asked. It was like trying to pry apart frozen molasses, but it finally worked. His eyelids fluttered open and shut several times before finally finding their mark. The smiling face of Dr. Price floated into view, shining a light in his eyes and positively beaming.

"Doc?" he asked groggily, trying automatically to sit up.

"Your pupil responses are good...vitals are getting stronger..."

"Doc, what's going on?"

Price pushed him gently back onto the pillows. "You've got to stop doing that, Mike, you're not going anywhere. At least not for a while. We've got to give that new heart of yours a chance to settle in..."

It took a full minute for the words to hit home.

At first, Michael just looked at Price, frozen in shock. Then his eyes drifted up to the ceiling and a little smile lit the corners of his face.

"I have a new heart."

With a booming laugh, Price dropped his clipboard on a chair and sank down beside Michael's bed, clasping his hand tight in his own. "You have a new heart."

It had been an ongoing battle. A fight they'd been locked in together since Michael turned six years old. A constant struggle, both on a moral and physical plane.

Michael had never been comfortable with the idea of taking someone else's organs. How could a person, in good conscience, rejoice in the downfall of another? How could he delight in his new life, when each second of it was bought with someone else's death?

That question had grown in significance and complexity the older he got. There were some days, days in his early adolescence, when he hoped that someone would just kick the bucket already and he could go on living his life. It wasn't fair that this was happening to him so young—let one of the older people take a seat. It was his turn now.

That perspective had changed when he'd entered the church.

Pastor Jeff and he had talked about the question for years now, debating it for hours on end during their weekly dinners. Jeff was of a far different persuasion. Everything happens for a reason—he'd always said. It was all part of God's plan. Just as the good Lord sent his son to die so that we might have everlasting life, so would God send a heart to Michael in his own time—that he might go on living a life dedicated to the Lord. There was no sin in it, Jeff had assured him repeatedly. The sin would be to refuse the gift.

So as Michael lay in bed, staring at the ceiling as the new heart beat away in his chest, he felt nothing but utter joy. Utter joy and gratitude. Without a second's pause, he closed his eyes and began to pray.

A soft knock interrupted him as Pastor Jeff himself came into the room, bordered on both sides by Calvin and Sherry.

"Oh—I'm sorry, Michael," Jeff caught himself quickly, "don't let me stop you."

But Michael looked up with tears in his eyes, a smile still lingering on his face. "Did you hear?" he asked softly, his voice still scratchy from lack of use.

The minister beamed back at him. "I heard. Michael, I can't tell you how…" The words trailed off as Jeff simply shook his head, too overwhelmed to speak. "I heard."

There was a moment's pause, as Michael took in the small army of flowers and balloons trailing behind them and grinned. "Are you guys opening a gift shop of your own, or what?"

"They're from the congregation," Jeff answered, setting a large bouquet of tulips down on the counter, "about half of whom are in the lobby, by the way. After the ambulance carted you off, everyone arriving for the pancake breakfast basically relocated to the hospital."

Michael smiled faintly, still trying to process how his entire world had turned upside-down. "They are? That's so...please tell them all I say—"

"*Oh Michael!*" Sherry fell to her knees beside him, clutching his hand to her chest. She'd always had a penchant for theatrics, and that combined with both her soft spot for Michael and the fact that she'd been present when he collapsed, had worked her up into a bit of a frenzy. "It's nothing short of a Christmas miracle!"

"It's November, Sherry," Calvin said dryly, eying her dramatic performance with distaste.

"A Thanksgiving miracle then! The good Lord Jesus Christ doesn't run on your calendar, Calvin." Her eyes welled with tears as she stroked back Michael's hair. "You gave us such a fright, child. When you went down in the stairwell, I thought we'd lost you—"

"Didn't lose me," Michael said quickly. He'd been present for enough of Sherry's monologues to know to cut them off at the gate. "Here I am, better than ever."

He reclaimed his hand with a casual wince, and Dr. Price took the hint.

"Alright everyone," he clapped his hands together, "it's very nice of you all to come down, but Michael needs his rest now above everything else. I'll let you know when you can come back and see him." He ushered everyone politely out of the room, before returning to turn off the light above Michael's bed. "I'm going to be coming back in a few hours to see if we can get you standing up, alright? In the meantime, you just try to get some sleep. You've been through a hell of a lot."

Michael nodded wearily, closing his eyes as he settled back against his pillow. But before he fell asleep, he looked up with one, final question.

"Ray," he called quietly. Price paused in the door frame. "Whose heart was it?"

For the first time since surgery, a bit of a shadow passed over Price's face. He looked down at his young friend, so weak but so radiant in his newfound second chance, and he flipped off the overhead lights with deliberate nonchalance.

"It came from the Lord, Mike. It came for you just in time."

* * *

Across the hall, the 'lord' the doctor was referring to, was slipping into a pair of extra scrubs. Gone was the blonde wig and the tacky pink dress. Gone were the four-inch heels. The newfound persona of 'Vivian Knight' had decided to go in a different direction.

Gentle black curls cascaded down the sides of his smooth brown skin, skin that had painted with only the slightest bit of makeup. Despite his powerful build, Peter—now Vivian—had always had what people would call a beautiful face. As a man, this beauty translated into him being thought of as handsome. But dressed as a woman, he was simply beautiful.

Oh, if his handlers could see him now, he thought as he adjusted the wig and put on a swipe of lip-gloss. It was not the first time he'd worn women's clothing. Over the last two decades working as an undercover assassin, he'd had to cross-dress on several occasions. But it was the first time he was doing it by choice—and the first time he was doing it to meet his son.

Needless to say, it was not the reunion he had envisioned.

But if this was what it took to keep Michael safe, then this was what he would do.

He smoothed out his turquoise scrubs and pinned on an ID badge he'd swiped from the nurse's locker room. With any luck, Jessica Howard wouldn't even notice it was gone before it was back in her gym bag.

With the confidence of a man who'd broken into countless buildings and assumed countless identities over the years, he breezed out of the supply closet where he'd been changing and headed up to the fourth floor. From the bits of information he'd been able to glean from doctors and nurses outside the break room, the last-minute surgery had been a huge success and the patient was upstairs resting. From the way the nurses were giggling to one another behind their hands, it was also clear that the patient in question was causing quite a stir.

He took the stairs, not the elevator, giving himself more time to figure out what exactly he was going to say. Would the disguise even work? What would happen if Michael somehow recognized him—tapping into his childhood memories and stringing it all together?

That's not possible, he chided himself. Michael was too young when Peter left to possibly recognize Vivian now. Especially in these uncomfortable women's scrubs...

The floor was quiet when he pushed open the door. It was one meant for recovery, and it was almost too easy to sail past the front desk and find his son's room unnoticed.

It was here that he stopped. Through the slotted blinds, he could make out the shape of a sleeping twenty-six-year-old. A handsome young man with a new lease on life, and a bright red scar trailing down his golden bronze skin.

For a moment, Vivian just stared.

How could he have stayed away so long? How could he have left in the first place? This was his son they were talking about. His *son*.

He should have been here. Better yet, should have taken Michael out of this miserable town before it could break him down more than his already broken heart...

He was still staring when Michael shifted restlessly in his sleep. His young face tightened in pain, and his eyes opened and closed in a daze, searching around for someone to help him.

No questions, no what-ifs, no regrets.

Vivian was here now. And it was here that he would stay.

He pushed open the door and rushed to Michael's side, pulling up a chair and taking his hand before he'd even made the conscious effort to do so. Michael stared at him in a drug-addled trance, only half-registering his presence as his mind struggled to focus.

"Are you in pain?" Vivian asked softly, squeezing his son's limp fingers.

Michael nodded with a grimace. "I can't reach the button for my morphine." He tried again but failed with a tired sigh. "I can't really lift my arms..."

"Here, I got it."

Careful not to disturb Michael's position, he reached across the bed and pressed the button to up the flow of medication. By the time he'd pushed it a third time, Michael was already starting to visibly relax. His head leaned back against the pillows, and he sighed again, this time with peaceful contentment.

"Thank you," he murmured. His fingers weakly squeezed his father's and Vivian's breath caught in his chest. "Are you one of my nurses?" His head lolled to the side and he fixed on Vivian's face with huge, dilated eyes. "I haven't seen you yet, I don't think."

Vivian watched the telltale progression of the drugs with a small smile. In his line of work, he was no stranger to the uses and limitation of narcotics, and he knew, without a shadow of a doubt, that Michael would not remember any of this come the next day.

Gripping his son's hand tightly in his own, he leaned forward, and *ever* so hesitantly, stroked back his hair. There was a strange hardening in his chest as he repeated the motion, again and again. It was one of the only times he could remember touching his own child.

Michael's eyes closed with a smile. "That feels nice…"

Vivian's heart leapt, but he maintained a neutral, kind expression.

"Sounds like you had quite the day," he prompted gently, desperate to keep his son talking despite the wave of drugs.

Michael's eyes opened suddenly and latched onto the nurse's face with sudden excitement. "I got a new heart. My old one…it didn't work anymore…"

Vivian smiled at the short, child-like phrases. Any moment now, the morphine would surely carry him off to sleep. Until then, he had no inhibitions. And admittedly a very, *very* limited understanding of what was going on.

"Then it's good that you got a new one," he replied, his eyes soaking in every detail they could. His son was fit and handsome. Enough to make any father proud.

Michael nodded sleepily. "I prayed for one every day…every day I prayed. And now God sent me a new one."

Vivian froze in place, watching as Michael drifted off to sleep. "God, huh? God sent you a new heart?"

"…changed my life," Michael murmured. "It was all I wanted, since I was a kid. I prayed for it and it came, just like that…"

Vivian smiled, stroking back his hair again. "Just like that."

"My whole church is here, they're waiting downstairs." Michael glanced around with a drugged grin. "They brought me balloons…"

"I can see that." Vivian laughed, still gripping his hand. "What were they trying to do? Start their own gift shop or something?"

Michael's eyes widened in unfiltered astonishment. "That's just what I said."

His brow suddenly creased as his eyes traced over the lines of Vivian's face. Without seeming to think about it, he reached out his hand, stretching his fingers to touch it. Vivian caught the hand in his own, laying it flat across his cheek. Michael stared for a moment, before his face softened in a curious smile.

"Do I...do I know you?"

His eyes drooped, and without him realizing it, Vivian kissed his palm.

"Not yet, child, not yet. But you will."

He settled back in his chair, content to just sit for the next few hours and watch Michael sleep—knowing he was safe, knowing he was going to live.

"I promise...you will."

CHAPTER

4

"If you let me sleep for just one more hour, I'll give you anything you want in this world. You name it—it's yours."

Ray Price and Michael Canard were locked in the world's most feeble face off.

The doctor, armed with over three decades of medical precedent and a small army of helpers, stood amusedly by the side of the bed. The patient—pumped full of enough drugs to down a small elephant, languished atop it.

"Mike," Price couldn't help but grin at his young friend's wearied reluctance, "you know that all transplant patients are supposed to get up within the first twelve hours to try to walk. It's critical to your recovery process."

The reluctance was textbook. Crack open a man's chest, take out his heart, stuff a new one in—and it was no wonder he'd be a bit hesitant to go skipping down the halls. That being said, the first few hours after a transplant were vital. There was no avoiding it.

Michael stared up in a pitiful daze, trying desperately to keep his eyes open. "Just one more hour, Ray. I need to sleep. You give me one more hour and I'll give you my car."

Price's lips twitched. "Your car doesn't run."

Michael briefly considered the dilemma. "I'll buy a new one. And I'll give it to you."

There was a brief tittering from the nurses, and even the doctor had to chuckle.

"Clever, kid. Now come on, up you go."

The same head-nurse from the night before took one of his arms, while Price draped the other around his own shoulder. Together—and with some rather choice profanities from the patient—they lifted Michael carefully to his feet.

The entire room seemed to shimmer the second he went vertical. At first, he wavered, grabbing tightly to each of his supporters as two more nurses waited with outstretched hands in front and behind. But after the initial shock, he slowly found his balance, placing less and less weight on those helping him.

"That's great, Mike!" Price exclaimed, genuinely impressed. The diligent physical regime had obviously paid off. "Now let's see if you can take a step, alright?"

Michael shot the doctor another memorable look as his body threatened to shut down in utter pain and exhaustion. Price's eyes twinkled teasingly.

"Oh come on, what's that phrase you're always telling me? Blessed is the man who perseveres under trial, because he—"

"Even God rested on the Sabbath," Michael panted, trying to move his feet.

The encouraging face of the nurse bobbed into view as she shifted position in front of him, helping him take those first, critical steps. He shot her a tensed but grateful smile, though his eyes lingered curiously on her face as he moved carefully forward.

"Where's the nurse I had last night?" he asked breathlessly. The simplest of motions felt like they were sucking the life right out of him. "The one who sat with me?"

The nurse and Price shared a quick look, before she turned back to Michael with a gentle smile. "I'm afraid that was the drugs, honey. I was the only nurse on call here last night—and I had too many other patients to be sitting with you."

Michael's face clouded and he took another step without seeming to realize it. "I could have sworn, I—"

Price chuckled and patted his back. "You're lucky a pretty nurse is the only thing you saw last night. I've had patients on your same cocktail of recovery meds who swore that the mothership had returned to take them back."

Michael laughed lightly before returning his sole concentration to his feet.

They made it half a lap—from his room to the far window—before the buckling in his legs became too extreme to ignore and his little team helped him back. He sank onto his mattress like the walking dead and his eyes closed shut before his head even hit the pillow.

"Sleep well, Mike," Price murmured affectionately, as the nurse tucked an extra blanket around his legs. "You've got a long road ahead of you…"

* * *

Michael may have floated away on a peaceful sea of opiates, but the next morning was a different story entirely.

Considering the patient's rather troubled history, the plan was to ween him off any potentially addictive painkillers as soon as possible. Switch him over to a lesser dosage, and soon after, to a milder drug altogether. This wasn't the doctor's decision, but Michael's. He'd lost too many years of his life to narcotics. Had too many blank spaces, spaces that even today, he couldn't account for.

So in the middle of the night, a nurse came by and turned down the morphine to less than half. She cast him a sympathetic look as she did so, then hurried off to finish her rounds.

He would feel it soon enough. And she was sure she would hear it when he did…

"Helen? Anna? Trisha? Melanie?"

A lone voice rang out from room 402 as he called each one of them in turn.

At precisely six in the morning, he'd woken up feeling like someone had taken a knife and sliced open his chest. And while that actually made perfect sense to his brain, the raw nerve endings screaming all over his skin needed more convincing.

He pushed the button hooked up to side of the bed. "Is anybody there?"

But his calls for help went temporarily unanswered. A four-car collision had just poured into the E.R. and most everyone scheduled for recovery had gone down to help.

"Mrs. Franklin?" he tried the head nurse. Surely she hadn't abandoned him.

But it was to no avail. Gritting his teeth against the pain, he pulled himself to an upright position and paused for a second to catch his breath.

Keep it together, Michael, he told himself sternly. *You wanted this, remember?*

And he had. Some kids had dreamt of playing professional sports, others grew up longing for the perfect car, or for the girl with the braids to finally turn around and notice them.

Not Michael. If one were to have asked him on any given day since he turned six years old, he would have answered the same: He wanted a new heart.

He'd pictured it thousands of times, going over every detail in his mind, shifting it slightly as he aged, occasionally adding on embellishment for dramatic effect.

He'd be going about his usual business—probably pouring cream into coffee or tying his shoelace—something innocuous like that. These moments always seemed to strike at the most innocuous of times. And then, out of nowhere, he'd get the call.

Most people would panic, run a million directions, call up everyone they'd ever known. But not Michael. No, in Michael's imaginings, he was cool and collected. Gathering up his keys and driving himself at a measured pace to St. Andrew's Memorial across town. On days when he was feeling more theatrical than others, he'd even come up with his 'getting a heart' playlist for the drive. It usually included a lot of rap with some power ballads thrown in for balance.

But as much time as he'd spent fixating on the day itself, he had never spent much time picturing the immediate aftermath. Of course, he'd read through the literature. He'd nodded distractedly as his team of doctors and a UNOS representative talked him through everything he should be expecting. Recovery time, physical milestones, activities and foods to avoid. But in the back of his mind, he couldn't have cared less.

He was getting a new heart. That was all that mattered.

Now, in the cold hard light of 'new heart plus one day,' he was rethinking that a bit.

Breathe, just breathe, he told himself as he slowly lowered his feet down to the floor.

He wasn't supposed to be doing this sort of thing alone. Seeing the almost arrogant flash of determination in his eyes the second he saw his goals chart up on the wall, Mrs. Franklin had cautioned him sternly. "Wait for help," she'd said. "Someone will always be around shortly."

But Mrs. Franklin was nowhere to be found, the walls of the tiny room were already starting to feel like a prison, and that goals chart was laughing down at him. Plus, his feet were already on the ground.

A simple walk down the hall. How hard could it be?

Five minutes later, he had yet to make it to the door.

His eyes snapped closed and his face tightened with strain as he wrapped his fingers around the railing on the wall and tried to pull himself forward. This…may not have been one of his best ideas after all. Mrs. Franklin's outraged face floated through his mind, and for a moment, he almost retreated back to bed. But he pushed himself forward and took another step, saying a silent prayer for strength.

He could feel the new heart beating away in his chest. He could see it too. The faint pulsation beneath the angry pink line trailing down his skin. It was strange—it didn't feel any different from the old one. How could it be that not two days ago, this same heart had been the in chest of another? Did the heart find it as strange as he did? Rushed over on ice to wake up in an entirely different body? He found himself thinking of them as two separate entities.

Michael, and his heart.

And of course, that begged the obvious question: Whose 'old body' was it?

Some dead guy, a part of him thought dismissively. *No need to dwell.* But on the treacherous journey from the bed to the hall, Michael found that all he could do *was* dwell.

How had the guy died? Did he have a family? Was his body still here, in some morgue drawer in the basement of the hospital?

He mentally shuddered at the thought. Furthermore, what had the guy done for a living? What kind of wear and tear did this thing already have? Was there some kind of quality requirement for guys who...*or girls?*

What if he had a girl's heart?! Did that matter? He considered it with a sudden frown. He didn't know if it mattered or not, but it disconcerted him none the less. Well, if it had been a woman, she would have had to have been well over six feet tall for them to be a match—

"Michael!"

Michael's head snapped up to see Pastor Jeff rushing towards him from the elevators.

"Thank the heavens," he murmured. "Jeff," he said as the man sped into the room, "save me from my thoughts."

Jeff put down yet another round of gifts from well-wishers and turned with a smile. "I'll do my best. What's it going to be today?"

Michael sighed, gripping onto the guard rail for dear life while trying to act casual all the while. "Well, I've gotten it into my head that this new heart of mine came from some nine-foot-tall Amazonian bodybuilder woman. I'm not sure how I feel about that."

"I'd feel good about it," Jeff said without hesitation. His wife had died of cancer twelve years previous, and while he would never consider attempting a new relationship, he had been known to politely admire from afar.

Michael chuckled, slipping a little against the wall. "Yeah, I bet you would."

Jeff steadied him with quick hands. "Is that kind of thing even possible? Taking on characteristics of your donor? You feeling the sudden urge to put on a skirt and start lifting weights?"

"Actually, since I woke up, all I've been craving is a huge, bloody steak. Think they gave me the heart of a werewolf?"

Jeff shook his head sanctimoniously. "This is Woodlands we're talking about. Stranger things have happened." He placed a hand on Michael's back. "But seriously, why are you up and out of bed already? Are you even allowed to be doing this by yourself?"

"Who are those from?" Michael gestured to the new stack of gifts, shirking the question.

Jeff turned proudly. "Those, my friend, are courtesy of the junior high youth group. They put together a special prayer circle to raise funds and got you different assortments of toffees from that new sweets shop that opened on Seventh and Elm."

"They did?"

Michael spent most every summer coaching kids' basketball through the YMCA and knew most of the middle-schoolers by name. Already, on one of the cards, he could see scribbled, 'Coach Michael.'

"That was thoughtful of them. Not sure if I'm allowed to be eating toffee, but…"

"Oh, you can't?" Jeff feigned oblivion. "Then I'll take some off your hands."

Michael laughed, but as his eyes travelled over the small pile of gifts, he was sincerely touched. Funds were not easy to come by in this town and resources were always scarce. To have the community make such a show of support was a true blessing. One that he didn't take lightly.

"I want to do something for them," he murmured to himself as he gestured around the room. "Everyone's been so kind and supportive, I want to find some kind of way to give back—"

"You do give back," Jeff said, gently squeezing him on the shoulder. "Ever since you showed up at my door four years ago, you've done nothing but give back. You need to let people take care of you for once, Michael. You've earned it."

Michael blushed slightly and dropped his eyes to the ground. He remembered all too well the night he'd shown up at the church all those years ago. He remembered it like yesterday…

It had been right smack in the middle of an autumn rainstorm. He remembered his hair and clothes had been drenched. In fact, it was so abnormally cold that night, that in hindsight, it was a miracle he didn't end up with pneumonia or something. But he had other things on his mind that night. And other miracles that needed his attention.

Just an hour before, he'd been involved in a major drug exchange. Just your typical Thursday night. Each of the five major gangs in town kept to their areas of distribution, but once a week, goods and money would change hands. Michael was usually sent along on these errands because he was known to be quick on his feet, a smooth talker, and a cool head under pressure. Not to mention, when he got out of the car, all six foot four of him, muscles and attitude, it made the other guys think twice about double crossing them.

On this particular exchange, he'd gone with his four closest friends. They didn't have the kind of friendship that Michael enjoyed now—nothing based on shared interests or mutual respect. But they shared a neighborhood, a 'career path,' and a bunch of dark memories that had bonded them together. What with the staggering death rate, membership in these gangs was fluid—but these five had spent more time together than most.

They got out of the car at the appointed spot and waited for the other car to arrive. The storm was only picking up speed the longer they stood outside, and Michael remembered being impatient for the whole ordeal to be over. He was meeting a girl after this, Stacey or Casey or something like that. He already had a bottle of vodka and a box of condoms in his trunk. More romance was seldom required.

When the second car finally did arrive, it didn't take more than a moment to realize that something was wrong. Instead of parking in their usual spot beneath the bridge, they simply decelerated, lowering the windows in what felt like slow motion.

Michael had been the only one to shout, "Get down!" but by then, it was too late. His four friends were riddled with bullets before they had time to register what was even going on.

As the shots rang out in the night, it was like Michael's entire body shut down. Gone were the fabled reflexes, gone was the cool head. He remembered standing there dumbly, frozen in shock, as four or five other people got out of the car.

There was a blur of voices, a gun was pointed in his face.

He actually heard the shots fire. Saw the blast of powder as the bullets were released.

Except…nothing happened.

The next thing he knew, he was wandering aimlessly through a park. He'd left his car where he'd parked it beneath the bridge, condoms and all. Left the keys in the ignition. Stacey or Casey or whatever her name was, would not be hearing from him again. He'd left his four ex-friends, lying in puddles of rainwater and blood. He didn't need to check if any of them were still breathing—he knew at once they were dead.

The only thing he didn't know, was why he hadn't joined them.

There was a break in the trees, and the next thing he knew, he was staring up at the tall steeple of the church. It was an old building, badly in need of repair, but there was still a kind of understated majesty about it, standing proudly on the dingy little street. He must have walked past it a hundred times. Growing up, he'd walked this very street to get to school. But he had never really noticed it until now. Never wondered what went on inside.

He wondered now.

With a compulsion he couldn't control, he found himself half-tripping across the wet pavement, staring up at the tall oak doors as his hand reached out to knock. Jeff had pulled it open before his fingers could touch the wood. He remembered the look on the Pastor's face as he'd stared in shock at the dripping, twenty-two-year-old in front of him. The way his eyes had travelled across

Michael's wild, petrified face with no judgement or reservations—only sincere compassion and honest kindness. The same kindness he'd shown him every day ever since.

Today was no exception.

"Here," he took some of Michael's weight and guided him slowly to the hall, "let's just take this one step at a time, shall we? If you make it to the window...I'll sneak you a toffee."

CHAPTER

5

It cannot be overstated or undersold—the amount of physical, emotional, psychological, and spiritual exhaustion involved in recovering from a heart transplant. There is no image brutal enough to encapsulate it. No metaphor colorful enough to paint it in accurate terms.

Lying in his bed over the course of the next ten days, Michael tried many times to come up with something. A way to give words to his suffering, to pass the horrors and highlights of it along to his friends. Again and again, he came up blank.

He had, however, no shortage of friends upon which to try his ideas.

Not only did the support from the congregation cease to lessen in the days that followed the surgery, it actually seemed to swell the longer Michael was hospitalized. Not a day went by when he wasn't visited and doted upon by five or more concerned companions—each brimming with endless encouragement, most determined to sneak him little cups of coffee.

An unofficial cold war sprang up between Nurse Franklin and the members of Woodlands Church of Christ (WCC). A passive aggressive campaign of subterfuge and plotting on both sides. She would post her subordinates as unofficial lookouts, casually wandering in during Michael's visitations and scanning discreetly for illicit caffeine whilst pretending to be checking the monitors. The members of the congregation, equally cunning on their own end, would place the contraband in little thermoses—either tucked away in their purses and computer cases, or held brazenly in their hands as they pretended the sweet elixir was for their use only.

For his part, Michael would lie helplessly in the middle—seemingly innocent—watching to see which way the cards would fall. While he was fully committed to his recovery and respectful of the limitations it required, he didn't see the harm in indulging now and again. On the other hand, he'd developed a healthy respect-bordering-on-fear of Nurse Franklin and would often make a show of declining in front of her just to get into her good graces. Either way, for the most part, he was just thrilled to be at the center of so much attention.

So it was that the morning Michael was scheduled to be discharged, was an exciting day at the hospital. A small crowd of sobbing nurses and over-zealous orderlies came together with Pastor Jeff and what looked to be no less than twenty members of the congregation to see him off. Nurse Franklin even brought in a batch of home-made butterscotch cookies, tucking them casually into his bag before giving him a motherly kiss on the cheek and telling him to stay well.

Dr. Price looked over his chart for what had to be the millionth time, re-checking every dosage and number with painstaking detail, almost obsessive-compulsively unable to put it down on the off-chance he'd missed something important.

"Ray," Michael had finally said, taking it out of his hands and tossing it lightly on the folded bed, "it's done. I'm good—really." He spun slowly in place, holding up his hands and grinning for effect. "Not a scratch on me. You did great."

Price pursed his lips, but gestured to the tip of the pink scar on Michael's chest, just barely visible over the top of his loosely buttoned shirt.

"That may be, but just remember you *do* have a scratch—a damn big one. You may be feeling fine now, but this was a huge trauma for your body, Mike. You need to keep that in mind these next few months. No extreme physical activity. No greasy burgers and fries. No going down to the center to play ball with the kids, I don't care what you've promised—"

"I won't, I swear," Michael interrupted gently. "Hey—you know me. I'm good about that sort of thing. I'll stick to your little list, alright? I promise." He waved his discharge papers in the air before glancing longingly at the door. "So can I go now? *Please?*"

Price gave a reluctant grin and Michael beamed back in reply. "Fine, you can go. But I'll be stopping by your apartment to check on you in a few days. And you can bet we're going to go down this whole list when I—"

"Yeah, yeah." Michael gave him a brief, one-armed hug before turning around to a huge cheer from the crowd. "Next stop—Burger King!"

"MICHAEL!"

"…that was a joke, Ray."

But the hospital staff and the visiting congregation weren't the only ones keeping a close eye on Michael's recovery. There had been someone else watching too. Disguised as a passing orderly, sticking his head in as a nightshift nurse, even shuffling past the blinds of room 402 dressed as a wayward janitor.

Always watching. Always from the shadows.

It had not been lost on Vivian that—with the exception of three exceptionally talkative old men from the coffee shop—the majority of his son's visitors had been from a church. It had not gone unnoticed that Michael's entire support system seemed to be centered around the humble shoulders of a single man.

As Michael was rolled out in the obligatory wheelchair, Vivian threw a pair of used scrubs into a waste bin as he also headed for the door.

It was time he paid this Pastor Jeff a visit...

* * *

When he passed the first smiling family getting into their van without notice, Vivian breathed a tentative sigh of relief about the quality of his disguise. When he walked past a group of deacons who waved automatically and pointed him towards the office, he breathed easier still. By the time he sashayed up to the secretary's desk to ask if the pastor was in, he was almost a believer himself.

It was official. Peter Canard had been laid to rest. A life for a life, for the one he'd spared in Budapest. He was Vivian Knight now. A single, middle-aged woman. New to town. Looking for friends, a community, something to latch onto. Yes, this new Vivian Knight needed a cause.

And he was here to find one...

"Come on in," a friendly voice called from behind the door.

Vivian walked in slowly, eyes making an automatic, cursory sweep. The office was warm, but poor. Welcoming, but sparse. A reflection of the church itself, no doubt.

The only other chapel in Woodlands was a Catholic parish on the wealthier side of town. It was cold and exclusive—able to keep out the 'dregs of society' through a seemingly endless supply of private donations. This church, on the other hand, seemed to welcome them. A veritable sanctuary, through and through.

Pastor Jeff smiled and got automatically to his feet the second Vivian entered, extending a warm hand across his cluttered desk. The makings of what was undoubtedly another care package for Michael lay unwrapped in the corner, and Vivian found himself smiling in return before he made the conscious effort to do so.

"I'm Jeff Freeman, the minister here at Woodlands Church. You must be Vivian."

They shook and Vivian made a conscious effort to loosen his grip. "Vivian Knight… thank you so much for making time for me. I'm sorry to just drop in like this."

After decades of working undercover, even his voice had adjusted to fit the part. It was low, but smooth. Soft around the edges. Trustworthy.

Jeff gestured to a chair before sitting back himself. "Not at all—I'm always happy to make a new acquaintance. Sometimes Woodlands feels a bit like a closed bubble; it's not often we get people from the outside. So, when did you move to town?"

Vivian kicked back in his chair and examined the minister carefully. Everything about him read like an open book. From his kind eyes, to his honest face, to the way he held back his shoulders—sincere and unassuming.

It was all the things Vivian had been trained to distrust. But at the same time, it was clearly what had so thoroughly enraptured his son. He leaned closer for a better look.

"Just last week." He'd learned in his travels that it was best to infuse a bit of honesty into even the most outlandish tales. It gave them that extra little kick. "I recently lost my husband—he was a soldier in Afghanistan—and there came a day when I...I just couldn't take another second living in that house. I started looking for a new place the very next morning and found myself here in Woodlands. It's...charming, to say the least."

Jeff chuckled briefly, "I don't think it's ever been called that before," before leaning forward gravely to take Vivian's hand. "I'm truly sorry for your loss. I lost my own wife over ten years ago now, but there are still some mornings when it feels like she could walk right back through the front door. I'm not sure it's something a person can ever get over, but I promise, it does get easier. With the Lord's help."

Vivian's eyes teared up and he looked quickly down at the desk. He'd never had any trouble making himself cry. He'd never had any trouble getting people to believe the lies he was telling them. But he had to admit, after hearing the pastor's empathetic story, for one of the first times, he felt a little guilty doing it.

"I'm sorry," he murmured, reaching into his purse for a tissue. "Sometimes it just sneaks up on me, you know?"

Jeff bowed his head with a sad smile. "I know exactly. You take all the time you need."

With a self-conscious flush, the tissue went back into the purse and Vivian stared up intently into the eyes of the pastor. "That's actually why I'm here. Back in Oregon, Tom and I used to attend regular Sunday services. Now I don't know much about your church here, or what exactly you require for membership, but I was hoping—"

"All we require for membership is that you show up with a big smile and an open heart every Sunday morning," Jeff interrupted cheerfully. "You'll find that Woodlands is a diverse community, so we have a rather diverse congregation. We have people of all backgrounds, at all walks of life. I like to think it makes us stronger as a whole. In other words, Ms. Knight, we would be happy to have you."

Vivian's face lit up with a genuine smile. He was beginning to see the draw here for Michael—at least on a superficial level. While he might not believe a word of what this man was sure to preach every Sunday, his spirit of gracious acceptance was at least sincere.

"Well, then I think I definitely made the right choice in coming here today," he beamed, drawing another huge smile from the pastor. "You know, when Tom went away overseas, I got very involved in my church community. Bake sales, fundraisers, outreach programs—you name it. I didn't want it to be a place that I happened to go to for a few hours on the weekend, I wanted it to be...more of a calling. Does that make any sense?"

Vivian had said the magic words. And he had phrased them with the perfect blend of both sincerity and uncertainty to make them shine. Jeff placed his hands upon the desk, looking so abruptly enthusiastic that Vivian found himself almost excited to hear what the man had to say.

"Ms. Knight...I think you're going to be a perfect fit."

Vivian chuckled, then, in a seemingly thoughtless gesture, motioned to the future care package scattered across Jeff's desk. "Like this, for example. I saw people making a 'welcome home' banner in the lobby outside and I've wrapped enough chicken casseroles to guess what's under some of that foil. Sounds like you all just got some good news."

Jeff brightened. "Some of the best news. A young member of our congregation recently had a heart transplant and he was discharged just this morning. I was going to bring these over to his house tonight for dinner."

All at once, Vivian's face turned into a mask of thoughtful concern. "A heart transplant? And you say the person was *young* man?"

"Yes, suffered from congenital heart disease."

Vivian shook his head sympathetically. "That's a hard surgery to bounce back from. When Tom went out on his second tour, I started working with a program helping disabled veterans get the medical attention they required. I was trained as a nurse, so I focused mostly on the physical therapy side of things— helping with recovery. We saw a lot of those same kinds of surgeries. Your friend is lucky he's so young—it will work in his favor."

"A nurse, really?" Jeff was delighted. "Are you looking for a job at the hospital?"

"Actually, no." Vivian pretended to look self-conscious once more. "Truth be told, between the life insurance Tom left me and the death gratuity from the government, I won't need to be working. But like I said, I want to get involved. Take your friend, for example. Please let him know I'd love to help out in any way I can. Those first few weeks can be rough."

It was at this point that Vivian paused strategically and leaned back to watch Jeff think. It had been timed perfectly; this offer to help. Not too pushy, but not half-hearted either. A genuine helping hand. And with the alleged skills and experience to back it up, that hand was more useful than most others.

But of course, Jeff didn't know Vivian. And he clearly loved Michael. It would be natural for him to feel a bit protective, especially given his young friend's weakened state.

Then again…didn't the Lord work in mysterious ways?

"Tell you what," Jeff said with a sudden smile, "what are you doing for dinner tonight?"

"Tonight?" Vivian pretended to be flustered. "Oh, well I…I wouldn't want to impose."

"Not at all! Michael would love to meet you, and truth be told, Vivian, while most of the people in the church would take a bullet for this kid, none of them know the first thing about his physical therapy or recovery. I, for one, would be sincerely grateful if you'd come along."

Vivian's heart soared in his chest, but he maintained a careful smile.

"In that case...tonight sounds great."

*   *   *

If Michael was surprised to see his pastor arrive that evening with a curvaceous African American woman, he certainly didn't let on. Vivian assumed, that growing up in a town like Woodlands, he was used to a rather fluid stream of people coming in and out of his life. But nothing about the hard nature of the town seemed to, in any way, reflect upon Michael. Quite the contrary. His face softened into a gracious smile the second they were introduced, and he immediately limped backwards to allow Vivian into his humble home.

And by humble...

Not since his time spent in the Ukrainian badlands had Vivian seen such a dwelling. Not that Michael hadn't attempted to brighten the place up. The paint was new and light in color. A picture assuredly picked up at a flea market strategically covered what looked to be a spattering of bullet holes in the far wall. There was even a bedraggled looking plant shoved into a corner by the kitchen window to give the place a 'homey' kind of feel.

But Michael was poor. Just like the rest of the town. This much was certain.

Vivian thought guiltily of his penthouse in Saint Petersburg—a place he had bought outright the second he'd made his first kill. He thought back to his various travels around the globe—to places Michael had surely only dreamed of. To the luxuries to which he'd treated himself along the way. A sports car here—a trip on a yacht there.

Nothing too flashy, of course. Nothing to draw the wrong kind of attention. But he had the money to spend, and after he'd amassed a small fortune in savings, he spent it.

That being said, he'd also sent a great deal to Dr. Price to pass on to Michael, he thought with a small frown. Clearly, somewhere between Russia and New York, things had gotten lost in translation. He would have to pay the good doctor a visit and find out what had been going on.

Michael interpreted the stranger's silence correctly, hovering a little self-consciously at the edge of the room. "Sorry it's not…" his voice trailed off in embarrassment, "things kind of got away from me when I was at the hospital…"

"Not at all," Vivian assured him quickly, glancing around the room again, this time with a warm smile. "I was actually just thinking how I wish I'd been able to afford a place of my own at your age. I was still trapped at home with my parents. A fate worse than death."

Michael relaxed with a grin. "Nah—you're lucky to have had the option."

But he glanced around the dingy apartment with a faint note of pride. He even tried to pull out his guest's chair at the table before he was quickly stopped by both Vivian and Jeff.

"Honestly Michael, you've got to take it easy," Jeff chided, dumping a stack of bags on the kitchen counter and unloading a casserole in a huff.

Michael rolled his eyes teasingly and gestured for Vivian to sit. "Maybe I should have been taking it easy before—maybe that's what triggered this whole thing. Ever think of that?"

Jeff glanced back with a sarcastic smile. "You mean, it wasn't your genetic heart defect after all?"

"I'm thinking it was more like your tyrannical dictatorship," Michael answered with a wry grin. "If only you hadn't forced me to take all those pictures…"

Jeff chuckled before reaching suddenly into his pile of bags. "Oh—that reminds me." He extracted Michael's camera and set it gently on the table.

Michael's face lit up as he ran his fingers lovingly over the worn case. A part of him looked like he was itching to unload it right then and there, but he remembered his manners and placed it beneath the table for later.

"Looks like we have a photographer on our hands." Vivian smiled encouragingly, taking in every detail with hawk-like precision. "Is that the Canon EOS-5D?"

Michael's eyes flashed up surprise. "You know it?"

"Used to have one myself."

Vivian struggled to rein in a sudden wave of unexpected emotion. As fate would have it, he used to have the exact same one—he'd gotten it from his father the day he turned fifteen and it was years before he'd been able to put it down.

Long before an endless series of dark hotel rooms and cold mornings waiting behind the scope of a sniper rifle, he'd had aspirations of becoming a professional photographer. To capture a single moment in time and immortalize it forever—the idea had appealed to him endlessly. He'd chosen to take lives instead. But it appeared his son had chosen to take pictures.

He composed himself in an instant, gazing at Michael through a mask of restraint. "So is that what you want to do? Photography?"

"That's what I'm hoping. I've only been doing it for a couple years now, but—"

"But he's incredibly talented and he takes beautiful photographs," Jeff interrupted with unmistakable pride. "He has an amazing eye. You should see some of his work, Vivian."

"I'd love to," Vivian coaxed, silently desperate for the well-meaning minister to disappear and leave him alone with his son. "Maybe after dinner you could show me?"

Michael blushed, but looked pleased. "Yeah, of course. I mean, I take pictures for a living—I work as a reporter for the Woodlands Chronicle—but it's the ones that I take on my own time that I'm the most proud of." His dark eyes flickered excitedly to a series of roughly framed portraits mounted on the hallway wall. "There's actually this—"

"Michael, are you allowed to eat things with a lot of cheese?" Jeff asked suddenly, eying the casserole with concern.

Michael glanced over. "Uh…I'm not sure. No—probably not. Why?"

Jeff's face darkened. "Well, either she doesn't know that, or Ms. Bir is trying to send you straight back to the hospital so she can see that poor oncologist she started stalking…"

Michael and Vivian laughed aloud before Michael pulled himself painfully to his feet. Vivian fought the urge to help, watching tensely from a distance, clearing his face of all emotion.

"That's fine," Michael said easily, limping to the kitchen. "I can grab something for myself and you two can have the casserole."

While Jeff seemed perfectly satisfied with this solution, Vivian leapt to his feet, unwilling to let his disabled son dine on nothing but breakfast cereal.

"Actually, if the two of you don't mind, I'd love to cook a meal for the three of us," he said with a charming smile. "I used to cook all the time back home, and I rather miss it."

"Are you sure?" Jeff said doubtfully, eyeing Michael's cupboards like he wasn't sure what exactly they might find.

"It's really fine, Ms. Knight," Michael said quickly. "I'm good with just—"

"I insist," Vivian said gently, pressing him back in his seat. The words 'Ms. Knight' coming out of his son's mouth didn't sit right with him and he was eager to move on. "I can see we're going to have a difficult time with you. Real independent streak, huh? Always trying to do everything for yourself? Not really the best thing for recovering transplant patients."

He winked, then began moving at lightning speed around the kitchen, setting a pan on the stove and sprinkling in dashes of spices with a master's hand. Six months of cooking classes in Morocco wouldn't go wasted after all. He was making dinner for his son.

Michael laughed lightly, but studied Vivian's profile with sudden curiosity. There was something familiar about this woman. Something he couldn't quite place.

"No…" he finally admitted, "I guess not."

Jeff pulled out a bottle of cider and poured it into three glasses. "I have to say, Vivian, if you can manage to make an edible meal out of anything you find in this kitchen, I'll add it to our list of 'Hometown Miracles' in the church paper."

Michael laughed again and a slow smile crept up Vivian's face at the sound. His hand paused momentarily over the skillet as he breathed a silent sigh of deep contentment.

"Oh, I think you'll find I have more than a few surprises up my sleeve…"

CHAPTER

6

Vivian woke up the next morning overwhelmed with an uncertain emotion he hadn't felt in quite some time. He considered it cautiously as he headed to the vanity in his newfound apartment, taking a seat on the upholstered chair and pulling out a bag of makeup. He debated it warily as he stared up into the mirror at his reflection, turning it over hesitantly in his mind.

He thought it was…joy?

His face broke into a wide smile. Yes, it was joy. Pure, unadulterated happiness. The kind that he hadn't known since—well, since Michael was born.

He'd seen his son a grand total of five times over the span of his life. The first was at the hospital, the day he came into the world. Michael's mother—a beautiful brunette who could have been the best thing that ever happened to him—had already decided to ban him from seeing the child after stumbling into the dark truth about how he spent his time.

It had been just three days before she ended up giving birth—a week early. They had been sitting in the freshly painted nursery in their new townhouse in Washington D.C. Just two soon-to-be parents, terrified and ecstatic all at the same time. Joni had decided she wanted to wait to find out the sex, so the room had been doused a gentle shade of yellow. "Yellow is still technically a girl's color," Vivian—then Peter—had argued. But honestly, painting his lips a deep shade of burgundy, who was he to judge now?

There had been a knock on the door. Nothing sinister. They'd been getting nursery deliveries and well-wishers for weeks. When Joni wandered down the hall to answer it, Peter hadn't given it a moment's pause. It wasn't until she stumbled back into the nursery, a loaded gun held to her throat, that he'd realized something was wrong.

Vivian's eyes darkened, still staring in the mirror, and he refused to let himself think any further. That had been the day when everything changed. When his idea for a fresh start, a clean slate with a home and a family had vanished before his very eyes.

Joni had formally cut him out of her life before the gunman had even finished bleeding out on the yellow floor. He'd snuck into the hospital afterwards to find out that he'd had a son, and then four more times in the months that followed.

At first, he hadn't been able to stay away. It was like swimming against the current. Every single bit of it felt wrong. These two people were the most important things in his life. How could it be that the best thing he could do was, for all intents and purposes, abandon them?

Fortunately, he'd gotten counsel from a childhood friend. His only friend. A young doctor who was just starting to make a name for himself in the big city.

Peter met with Ray Price once a week in a crummy diner, in the middle of the night.

Although the two men sitting across from each other in the booth couldn't have been more different, Peter and Ray had actually grown up together. Their parents had relocated to the same town in the same month, moving in just two houses apart. Instantly bonded as 'the new kids in town,' the boys had sat together that first morning on the bus into school, and had been inseparable up until high school graduation. At that point, their paths had firmly diverged.

Ray had graduated with honors and transitioned seamlessly to Yale as an underclassman before moving on to Columbia and Harvard for med school. He'd been offered his pick of residencies and fellowships and had selected the most prestigious one—

making a name for himself as one of the youngest and most promising cardiothoracic surgeons on the east coast.

Peter...had gone a different route. After high school graduation, the military had come calling. He joined up first with the marines, before being quickly selected for black ops. It was instantly apparent that he excelled at killing people, just as much as his friend excelled at saving lives. But when his talent and enthusiasm carried him too far over the line, the government cut him loose—leaving him with no friends or loyalties, just a horrifying skill set and the desire to please. Needless to say, by the time the 'other side' found him, he was already well on his way towards becoming one of the most ruthless assassins of his time.

When he had met Joni, all that had changed. He had walked away from his old life without a second's thought—determined to put it all behind him and start fresh. He put the guns in a locked box hidden deep in the closet and got himself a desk job. He was a marketing analyst now. An occupation he couldn't care less about and didn't fully understand, but it put food on the table. After Joni got pregnant, they needed a believable way to make ends meet.

Due to an ultrasound that revealed a slight peculiarity in the baby's heart, Peter had called up his old buddy, Price, only to learn that he was currently practicing in the same city—Washington

D.C. Price met with Peter and Joni the next day, and agreed not only to deliver the baby, but to stay on as a specialized pediatrician.

And so, Peter and Ray's friendship picked up right where it had left off. It wasn't the easiest pairing. There were dark gaps in the middle—gaps that Price wouldn't ask about and Peter wouldn't speak of. But as long as the shadows that followed him were kept at bay and those guns were locked securely in the closet, Price was willing to forgive and forget.

When Joni died, just four years later, it was Ray who'd given Peter the news. He'd been in Bosnia at the time, in a near constant state of shell-shock, and the doctor had been forced to repeat it four times before Peter believed it could be true.

Michael. It was his only thought now. *What would happen to Michael?*

"I name you god-parent," he'd said immediately, trusting that his good friend, who hadn't let him down all these years, wouldn't start now.

"I can't do that, Pete," Price told him sadly. "You're not on the birth certificate, you're not his recognized legal guardian. Hell—I'm one of the only people in the world who knows you even exist. You can't name me guardian; you have no authority to do so."

Peter's mind raced a thousand different directions. "Then I'm coming home," he insisted swiftly. "I'll come home…and do a DNA test. Whatever it takes."

"Pete…" there was a long pause, "…you can't come home. It's not your home."

It was at that moment that something vital to Peter simply shut down. Of course it wasn't. And he'd been a fool to think he could just step back into his son's life after stepping out. There was a reason he had left all those years ago. That gunman who'd shown up at their house that night, he wouldn't be the last. As long as Peter was in Michael's life, he'd be in constant danger.

"I don't know what to do." It was almost a whisper, said in heart wrenching tones as Peter clutched the phone tightly in his fist. "I don't know how to be a father to him, if I can't…"

"I'll put in a request for him to be moved to the Upstate New York foster system," Price answered, quickly masking the emotion in his own voice. "Because of his unusual medical history—and because I'm the specialist on the case—that should be allowed."

Peter frowned. "Wait…why Upstate New York? Why wouldn't you both be in—"

"I'm moving to Woodlands," Price said abruptly. "I took an attending position at the hospital there…I'm leaving next week."

Peter blinked. There was a two-car fender bender outside his window, but he didn't even notice.

"Why the hell would you move to a place like Woodlands, New York?!"

Price sighed. "Because, instead of killing people for a living, I prefer to save lives. Because the program there is wildly underfunded, so maybe I could do some good."

"And why didn't you tell me?!"

There was a pause.

"...because you kill people for a living."

It was Peter's turn to sigh. "Ray, you can't do this to me. Not now, when—"

"It's already done," Price interrupted. "I'm sorry, Pete. I really am. But I understand how the circumstances have changed, and I don't want to leave Michael. If you like, I can put in for him to be moved with me. He'll go to a family there in town."

Town—it was a generous name for it. Peter closed his eyes and bit down hard on his lip.

Joni is dead. Joni is dead. He chanted the words over and over. Then, *what would Joni do?*

It would be a hard life—that much was sure. One with no benefits or frills. One where the only way to get by was to pull yourself up by your fingernails. And even then, it was a gamble.

It was no place to send a child. Let alone a child with no family. A child relying upon the notoriously mercurial charity of others.

"Please," Peter murmured, eyes still closed, "tell me there's another way."

"I'm sorry, Pete," the doctor replied, "this is the way, the only decision. It's up to you…"

It's up to you…

Those words would serve to haunt Peter for the next twenty-two years.

When he'd arrived at Michael's house last night, it had been even worse than he'd feared. Not the poverty—that much he had expected. But the little things, the things that no one without a specific kind of training would know to look for.

Michael sat facing the door. In fact, no matter where he was in a room, he was always turned ever so slightly towards it. It was an ingrained behavior. One that spoke to fear and abuse. An instinctual self-protective instinct that he doubted the boy was aware of himself.

The visual sweep Vivian did of Michael in the hospital, Michael did to Vivian at the house. It was the same cursory analysis that Vivian had been trained to do himself. The guarded sizing-up of every new person. Michael might hide it beneath his smile, but again, there was wariness beneath the trust. The kind of scars that didn't fade easily.

That was what growing up in Woodlands had done to him. That was the decision his father had made. The only decision he was allowed to make. And it had almost crushed him.

But he was here to get a heart.

It was perhaps the only brightness Vivian could see. In a world full of grays, there was at least this one shining spot. Michael was alive because he was placed on the list by Price here in Woodlands. He was alive because Price had called Vivian in Budapest.

He was alive…and that had been his father's decision too.

The smiling became easier now, as Vivian's heart soared once more. He thought back to how excited Michael had been at dinner to meet someone new. How he'd never tried curry before. How he'd bolted to his feet the second they were finished eating to show Vivian his prized photographs, hanging up on the wall.

Beautiful pictures. The kind that didn't belong in a town like this. Finding the rare good in a place full of darkness and capturing it in a single moment of blinding light.

They had prayed before the meal—Vivian had made special note of that as well. It had been Jeff who had done it, but Michael had followed along fervently with his eyes closed. When the pastor was finished, they had chorused the 'amen' together.

Vivian didn't know what to make of it. Over the years of imagining what kind of reunion he might—in his wildest dreams—get to have with his son, he never once pictured that there would be three people at the table.

Him. Michael. And God.

To be frank…he wasn't sure there was room.

*   *   *

Michael's head was spinning from dinner last night. It had been quite some time since anyone new had come to town—let alone joined the congregation—and he hadn't realized how starved he was for new blood, until it was sitting there in his kitchen.

But that wasn't the only thing that struck him about Vivian. He had the strangest feeling that somehow, he had seen her before.

Of course, that was impossible. He knew all about her recent move to the east coast, how she'd been married to a soldier back in Oregon before.

And yet…there was something there. He just couldn't quite place it.

He smiled as he remembered Vivian's enthusiasm about his photography. No new people in Woodlands, meant no new eyes he could show his pictures. To have someone fresh who not only knew about photography, but instantly identified his camera? It was the dream.

They'd talked for at least another hour after the meal was finished—long after the remains of the forgotten casserole had cooled. Jeff had watched the back and forth with a fixed smile, but Michael got the feeling he was letting his mind wander out of boredom as the two of them went back and forth, again and again, about all the ins and outs of his hopeful profession.

But not only was Vivian knowledgeable and complimentary, she was critical as well. After giving each piece a painstaking examination, she found several ways to make them better—little improvements Michael would never have known to do himself. She had an almost instinctual-seeming understanding of which lens and camera settings to use for different story telling effects. She also showed him how the entire focus of the piece could be changed by shifting just the slightest angled degree or changing one's point of view entirely to better utilize the ambient light.

They were basic lessons, but ones that he'd never had. Growing up in Woodlands, it wasn't like photography classes were offered on the weekends. In fact, minus the members of the congregation and a few people throughout the community, no one he knew was aware of the fact that he even had a camera. He'd come to understand the hard way that loyalties only stretched so far. He might have known a guy since they were in second grade, but if that same guy needed money for meth and he knew that his friend happened to own a super expensive camera...things could get dicey really fast.

He'd gotten by so far on nothing but passion and a good deal of raw talent (a good eye). Now, after spending some time with Vivian, he was hoping to learn a little more. She'd agreed to go out 'shooting' with him sometime. She'd seemed strangely amused by the request, but he'd let that go. Her willingness to help seemed real, and he wasn't one to pass up an opportunity to learn.

Of course, that wasn't the only way she wanted to help...

His face fell a little as he peered out at the street from the seat on his front porch. The second the three of them had started dinner last night, it became abundantly clear why Jeff had brought her along. She was a nurse, one who was apparently skilled at helping people in exactly his situation—people who were recovering from major surgery. Jeff had hoped that she might be instrumental in helping him keep up with his physical therapy in the first difficult weeks.

The thought...didn't exactly sit well with him.

It wasn't that she was a woman, he'd decided. It was that she was a stranger. He'd been through enough strangers in his early life to be happy, he didn't meet many now. Conversational starvation aside, he wasn't one to trust easily and didn't relish the thought of letting someone new get in such close proximity—especially when he wasn't exactly at his best.

An elderly couple walking hand in hand strolled past on the sidewalk and Michael lifted an automatic hand to wave. They were the only old couple he knew that was still together. All the rest had either divorced well before they grayed or had lost a spouse to some Woodlands-type tragedy. Tragedies that were so common by now, that it was this couple that was rare.

They waved back as they hobbled along to their apartment two blocks down. The McCutchens—Michael knew them well. He went over to their house every winter to get their heater working and ever summer to battle the air-conditioning.

The smile was still lingering on his face when a blue car pulled up in front of his house. Determined not to let his wariness show, he pushed to his feet with a wince he couldn't quite hide and lifted his arm to wave. Another wince.

How was it that he couldn't remember? He'd just gotten sliced in half. He had to be delicate with himself.

The door open and Vivian stepped out of the car. Her face burst into a huge smile the second she saw him, and for a moment, Michael found himself almost overwhelmed with an uncertain emotion. He smiled back before he'd meant to, and before he realized what he was doing, he was heading down the front steps to meet her.

As his eyes swept over her face, that same strange feeling gnawed away deep in his chest, coupled in part with the feeling from earlier. He didn't know what it was.

But he'd felt it before…

"Hey there," she greeted him warmly. "I see you're still being an idiot and doing things you shouldn't." She waved ostentatiously to make her point and he grinned.

Maybe it was trust…

CHAPTER

7

"Excuse me ma'am, you'll have to stow your purse either under your seat or in the overhead compartments for landing. Excuse me, ma'am? *Ma'am?*"

Vivian looked up with a start into the expectant face of a female flight attendant. That *ma'am* was meant for him. He was a *she*. He'd have to start remembering that from now on.

With what he took to be a very coquettish smile, he tucked the leather handbag neatly below his chair, smoothing out his skirt and casting a superior look around the first-class cabin.

Aside from the occasional pronoun slip, he was getting better and better at this whole 'being a woman thing.' The disguise was sheer perfection. He'd yet to have a single person give him a second glance, and by now, he'd tried it out on at least two different continents.

The makeup was flawless, the wig—sublime. The voice? A low feminine purr.

It was so convincing that even poor Anico Boros had no idea who he was looking at while the infamous Peter Canard fired three bullets into his face.

It had to be done. Even if it meant a hasty excuse followed by a last-minute trip to Budapest. For while Vivian Knight was designed to disappear without a trace, Peter Canard had a reputation to protect. Mr. Boros had been living on borrowed time. It was time to face the music.

Budapest wasn't the first of these little trips. Before Hungary had been São Paulo, followed by Rome. It was a necessary evil, Vivian told himself. One that he was doing for Michael's protection as much as his own.

How could Peter Canard be in New York City if he was just reported strangling a diplomat's father in Italy? How could the world-renowned assassin be traced back to his only living relative if he was halfway across the world?

Yes, it was best to create some distance—if only the illusion of distance—in order to keep both he and his son safe. And if he could make a little money in the process? All the better.

The plane touched down and he breezed through the terminal to the long-term parking garage to collect his car. Just moments later, he was flying down the interstate towards home.

In the seat of his car sat a tiny box filled with three different lenses he'd purchased for Michael's camera. It was better than the alternative: 'My father killed a diplomat in Rome and all I got was this lousy tee-shirt,' but not by much.

For the cost of three little bullets, he had just received what was tantamount to a small college fund. He wanted to buy Michael a new apartment. He wanted to buy him a car that didn't have a fender held on by electrical tape. He wanted to take him out of Woodlands altogether and start a new life for them.

But in the absence of all of that, since that was strictly prohibited to him, a few lenses for his son's camera would have to suffice.

About an hour later, he pulled into his driveway actually feeling quite proud of himself for the idea. He could picture the look on Michael's face as he opened it. It was a nice enough gift that it would mean the world to him, without being expensive enough to raise any red flags.

He was still smiling to himself when his porch light snapped on with a sudden *click*, shattering the peaceful darkness.

His body moved before he told it to—acting on sheer instinct, moving with no hesitation muscle-memory precision. He spun around in a low kick, catching the intruder behind the knee-cap and felling him to the ground. There was a loud curse as the shadowy figure crumpled to the cement, but before the noise could alert the neighbors, Vivian picked him up by the back of the jacket and threw him inside the house.

The man was still trying to get himself together when he lifted his eyes to look straight up the barrel of a gun. Vivian was standing calmly on the other end, a dark fire simmering deep behind his eyes as his finger tightened on the trigger.

Then everything froze.

"Ray?"

There was a gasp.

"Pete?" Another gasp. "Pete, is that a gun?"

Vivian rolled his eyes and stuck the pistol back in his jacket. "You know, for a doctor, you're not the brightest of the bunch. Yes—it's a gun."

Price was astounded, mouth still wide open as he pulled himself shakily to his feet, rubbing the bruised skin behind his knee. "Why did you pull a gun on me? You kick very, *very* hard, by the way. You could have actually broken something…"

"That's kind of the point. And why the hell did you sneak up on me? Don't you know better than to drop by unannounced on someone with my…disposition?"

"Well, I had to come talk to you. I never got a chance to thank you for that little present you left me behind the dumpster,"

Price huffed. Then his eyes grew wide and he stared at his friend like he was seeing him for the first time. "Peter…why are you dressed like a woman?"

"It's a long story…" The assassin jutted up his chin. "And it's *Vivian*."

* * *

Two hours later, the doctor had yet to make sense of anything *Vivian* was telling him.

"I just don't get it, Pete," he murmured, rubbing his temples. "You left all those years ago to keep Michael safe. Why the hell would you risk coming back now?"

Vivian took a thoughtful sip from his beer, patting his lips in a feminine way without seeming to think about it. "Michael needed a new heart. I knew a man who could give it to him. But the men Montana worked for live close—too close. I couldn't be sure that they wouldn't trace his body back and make the connection. At first…I was going to stick around to make sure that didn't happen." He gestured to his curls. "Disguised, of course, so as not to raise suspicion."

"I really want to take a picture of this, by the way."

"If you do, I'll shoot you."

"I'll put it up on my mantle. Right next to my copy of *The Feminine Mystique*."

"Right through the throat. Spare the world of your incessant talking."

Price chuckled, then frowned. "Wait, you said at *first* you were going to stick around...'"

Vivian sighed. "That was the plan. But I couldn't just watch from the shadows. I tried, Ray, I really did. But how can I just stand by on the sidelines without..."

"...without getting to know your son. I get it, I really do. But this," Price gestured to the full persona of Vivian Knight—from the new handbag, right down to the shiny pistol, "this isn't going to work, Pete. This isn't a long-term plan."

"I'm going to be careful," Vivian promised softly. "I'm not going to let anything happen to him. Everything's going to be fine."

Price gave him a long stare.

"You have blood on your blouse."

* * *

For the first time in what felt like years, Michael wasn't excited to go to his weekly Bible study. If it weren't for the fact that he was leading the damn thing, he might skip it altogether.

He didn't know exactly why he was feeling this way—maybe it was the stress of getting out of the house so soon after the surgery. Maybe he was in minor withdrawal from his pain medication. But to be honest, it felt like something different.

It felt like an inconvenience.

Even more than that, he was feeling inexplicably rebellious.

When both Pastor Jeff and Calvin Moreno had called him up that morning asking if he needed a ride to the church, he'd told each that the other was already taking him.

In reality, he was going to attempt to get there on his own. His first solo mission since his release from the hospital.

Somewhere, Nurse Franklin had begun to cry, and she didn't even know why...

He'd started out with great ambition, bundling up against the cold November afternoon and walking purposely out his front door. But that walk soon became a limp. And the limp soon became a haggard cry of regret.

Only his pride kept him going. The same fierce pride he'd had since childhood.

That and the fact that he didn't know how he'd physically pull himself back up his steps.

Panting with exhaustion, he had just made it to the end of his street when a blue car slowed to a stop beside the curb.

"Hey there, Shawshank. Where do you think you're going?"

Michael chuckled painfully and staggered to the side of the car as Vivian rolled down the window. "Bible study. I'm one of the speakers today."

"Uh-huh." Vivian surveyed him critically. "So tell me, is this Bible study scheduled for tomorrow, because I don't see you getting to the church before then."

This prompted a rueful grin. "Could you just unlock the door already?"

A tricky seatbelt and a few grateful sips of water later—they were on their way.

"So what's this Bible study all about?" Vivian asked curiously, watching his son out of the corner of his eye. The unopened present sat half-covered in the back seat, but somehow, he sensed this wasn't the right time.

Michael actually suppressed a sigh. "It's actually meant specifically for the ailing members of the congregation—as a sign of community and support. What with me just coming through the surgery and all—Jeff thought I'd be a good speaker."

Vivian considered this thoughtfully. "Sounds like he's trying to make you a poster boy for something you never wanted in the first place."

There was a split second's pause as Michael looked over in surprise. His dark eyes scanned his father curiously before he nodded. "That's exactly it."

Vivian nodded knowingly before shooting him a sympathetic smile. "On the other hand, it sounds like you had all the 'community' in the world when you were in the hospital. Maybe it wouldn't hurt to give back a bit—show them you appreciated the effort."

Michael flushed guiltily and dropped his eyes to his lap. "No, you're absolutely right," he murmured. "And don't get me wrong—I do appreciate it. More than you know." He stared out the window at the passing cars with another sigh. "It's just...turning out to be harder than I thought...trying to manage this on my own."

A hard knot seized up in Vivian's throat, but he kept his eyes on the road. "Well, it looks like you have a good support system to help you—"

"That's not what I mean."

The answer was short and clipped, revealing a whole sea of resentment underneath.

Vivian was barely breathing as he was forced to ask the obvious question. "Where's your family, Michael?"

Michael spoke in an almost robotic voice, as if he'd answered the cursory question so often, said the words so many times, they hardly held any meaning anymore.

"My mother killed herself when I was four and I'm an only child. As far as I know, no aunts or uncles to speak of."

If it weren't for his years of training, Vivian would have crashed the car.

Joni had killed herself?

That lump in his throat was making it hard to breathe. When Price had told him about her death, all those years ago, he'd said that she'd slipped on some ice and fallen from her second story apartment. He'd said she'd snapped her neck and died instantly. All this coincided with both the hospital and police report that Peter had been quick to obtain.

But a suicide? Could it possibly be true? How could Ray not have told him?

Michael gazed impassively out the window, oblivious to the impact of his simple answer.

"And…" Vivian could hardly make himself continue, "your father?"

For the first time, Michael's face showed a flicker of emotion. A flash of anger hardened his handsome features before settling in his eyes.

"Let's just say, he wasn't around."

They rode the rest of the way to the church in silence. Michael was in no mood to talk, and Vivian couldn't think of a single thing to say. He felt as though his own heart had been ripped out and tossed from the car somewhere on Second Street.

As they double-parked against the curb, Michael glanced at Vivian with a sudden realization. "I'm so sorry, I forgot to even ask—did we have a session today?"

It took Vivian a moment to catch on. "Oh—your physical therapy? No," he thought of the present in the back seat and decided to leave it in the next trash bin—it would never be nearly enough, "no, I was just stopping by."

"Oh," Michael stalled a second, before glancing at the sanctuary with something close to dread, "well…would you like to come in with me?"

The second he said the words, he followed them up with an entreating smile—drawing an instant smile from Vivian in return. A smile that faded slightly as his eyes strayed past Michael to the steeple.

"To your Bible study?"

Now who was stalling?

"Today is more like a confessional, followed by a prayer. It can actually be sort of…therapeutic."

Vivian's eyes leveled on his son, before he finally nodded. "Sounds good to me."

Ignoring Michael's proud reluctance, Vivian helped him climb out of the car. He had overstrained his body trying to walk over, and now, even the slightest movement was causing him an excruciating amount of pain.

"Are you sure you're up for this?" Vivian asked with concern as he took one of Michael's arms and laced it around his shoulder, helping him up the front path.

"I'm sure," Michael panted, keeping his eyes locked on the door. "You were right, in the car. These people did a whole lot for me this last week. This is the least I can do to give back."

On that note, the two of them headed into the church.

Although Vivian had only been going for the last two weeks now, he was greeted by name and semi-swarmed the second he came in the door. The eager crowd only dispersed when they saw who their newest member had arrived with.

In a matter of seconds, Michael was the belle of the ball.

He handled all the attention well—Vivian thought, knowing how surely uncomfortable it made him. He seemed to be a lot like his father in that he didn't like to ask for help. He valued his independence and chafed when it was taken away.

"Michael, I'm so glad you made it," Jeff said warmly, slapping the young man on the shoulder, oblivious to the extra pain it caused him.

Vivian ground his teeth together in muted frustration. If only he could take Michael to the 'company doctor' in Switzerland. She'd have him good as new in no time—

"Yeah, well," Michael forced his grimace into a smile. "Time to get back on the horse, right?"

Jeff nodded. "Time indeed."

"Shall we begin?" Michael called over the commotion.

With surprising efficiency, the room settled quickly into a circle of folding chairs. The smell of stale cookies and lukewarm coffee wafted through the little room, setting Vivian's teeth on edge as he took a seat on the opposite side as his son.

"The theme of today's meeting is gratitude," Michael began seriously. He spoke with an ease beyond his years, completely untroubled by the dozens of riveted eyes. "Now, I know that may seem like the last thing on our minds, given our present life narrative, but it's important to think about it none the less. We're all a lot better off today—sitting here in this room—than we have been before. And while it might not seem like it right here in this moment, we all have endless things to be grateful for."

He leaned back in his chair with a wince and took a deep breath.

"I'll begin. As most of you know, I only joined up with the church a few years ago. Before that, there was no structure to my life, no center. I lived day to day, trying to keep myself in the moment because I had no idea if I would even have a future."

Vivian was sitting on the edge of his chair, hanging onto every word.

"I was on a lot of drugs. I was mixed up with some people I shouldn't have been. For all intents and purposes, my life was already over..."

His eyes clouded for a moment, and he bowed his head before continuing in a low voice.

"The church saved me. Inviting the Lord into my heart saved me. Even though I recently had to invite him into a new one," he joked. The room laughed loudly before giving him their undivided attention once more. "I'm *grateful* for that. For each day I survived. For each step I took. Because they all led me here. To be sitting in the house of God with a fellowship of believers. I'm grateful for each and every one of you."

There was a loud 'amen' and another man to Michael's left started telling his story.

The ring of chairs shifted their attention as well, but Vivian was stuck on Michael. His eyes welled up with unfamiliar tears as he fixated on the young man. A man who had been through so much and who had done it all alone. A man who, even now, sitting there with a line of stitches holding together his chest, was publicly proclaiming his gratitude for every breath and dedicating them to a higher power.

A strange feeling began stirring deep within Vivian's chest, and without seeming to think about it, he turned his attention to the new speaker as well. Here was another man escaping a broken life to dedicate himself to the Lord. He was followed by another, and then another.

Finally, when the last volunteer had spoken, Vivian found himself standing up with the rest of them—chorusing a loud *amen* to the heavens.

Perhaps there was more to this Bible Study than he'd originally thought...

* * *

Michael and Vivian were quiet on most of the drive home that night. Each one lost in his own thoughts. Thoughts about the future, thoughts about the past. Thoughts about this crazy, broken down world and their own places in it.

"Thanks for the ride," Michael said quietly as they pulled up in front of his apartment.

Vivian's head snapped up and he spoke without thinking.

"Michael, how did you find your way to the church?"

Michael paused with his hand already on the door, staring back in surprise. "What do you mean?"

It wasn't meant to startle, and it wasn't meant to pry. But sitting there in the car that night, with a thousand chorusing voices echoing in his head, Vivian found that he had to know.

"You said you had a...a different life before." He stared intently into his son's dilated eyes. "How did you...? I mean to say—what changed?"

Michael stared at him for a long time in silence, and for a moment, Vivian was worried that he'd gone too far. Then he finally began to speak.

"I was in a shooting." He dropped his head and closed his eyes, reminiscing as if it happened yesterday . "It was a drug deal gone wrong—happens every day around here. I remember I...I saw the gun pointed at my face. I saw the guy pull the trigger. I actually smelled the powder as the thing went off."

Neither man was breathing, and a sudden stillness filled the tiny car.

"Then…" Michael, his eyes still closed; a small, radiant smile crept up his face. "Someone was talking to me. I was talking back. It was like I was standing somewhere above my body, looking down on the whole thing. I knew I had to make a decision. I could choose to go back to my old life, end up like my friends. Or…I could choose to go a different path."

For a moment, his face tightened in a helpless sort of confusion. Then he shook his head.

"I know how that sounds," he murmured softly. "And I know what I'd be thinking if someone said it to me. To this day, I don't know what really happened. When I came to, I was wandering through the park and found myself walking up the steps to the church. Jeff found me there…and the rest is history."

After he finished talking, it was quiet for a long time. Such a long time, that eventually, Michael peeked at Vivian out of the corner of his eye.

"So now you think I'm crazy, right?" he joked nervously. "If you want to cancel our physical therapy sessions and get me into *actual* therapy instead—I'd understand."

But instead of playing along, Vivian looked up with a steady smile.

A kind of calm he hadn't felt in a long time completely enveloped him, and as he stared at his long-lost child, resurrected from the grave by a power beyond all comprehension, he realized that he, too, had a choice to make.

"Michael," he began with a smile, "I have a present for you…"

CHAPTER

8

The two men touched down at JFK just as the clock touched midnight. They had no bags between them, only a single briefcase that the shorter of the men gripped tightly as they made their way through customs. They moved in sync, never looking at each other, yet turning with perfect synchronicity—like a pair of sinister birds.

They were styled so as not to raise alarm. Designed to avoid suspicion. They cut through the bustling clouds with silent efficiency—just another pair of dark trench coats heading out onto the icy New York streets.

The taller man lifted a hand and a cab swung up against the curb as if they were connected by an invisible wire. As the two men slid inside, the driver did a double take in the rear-view mirror. There was nothing overtly alarming about the two gentlemen sitting behind him, no single characteristic to which he could attribute his feelings. But a strange chill had enveloped him from head to foot the second they stepped inside.

He forced his eyes back to the road and made them stay there, vowing to himself that this time—*this* time—was the last time. Tomorrow he would march into his supervisor's office and finally hang up his keys for good. It was a promise he'd made to himself every week since May.

"Where to, gentlemen?"

For the first and only time in the last twenty-four hours, the men shared a quick glance before the shorter one leaned back against his seat, sliding his hands thoughtfully across the briefcase perched on his lap.

"Woodlands."

* * *

"Just one more rep, Michael—come on, you can do it!"

Little beads of sweat ran through Michael's hair as he ground his teeth together, pushing to the heavens with all his might. Vivian was standing in front of him, ready to catch the weights should anything go awry.

"One more rep—you got this."

There was a mighty gasp, and Michael lifted the iron beam safely into the stand. The second it was secure, he collapsed onto his back, panting with utter exhaustion. Vivian nodded approvingly, scribbling this latest progress into a notebook on the kitchen counter before kneeling down to take Michael's pulse.

"What were you, a drill sergeant in another life?" Michael joked as he opened his eyes to see Vivian's toned arm stretching across him. "You've got muscles as big as mine."

Vivian chuckled softly, but swatted him upside the head. "Let me tell you a little secret, that's not the kind of thing you ever want to say to a lady."

Michael pulled himself slowly to his feet with a wide grin. "Yes ma'am."

They had been training together for about three weeks, working steadily through the recommended physical therapy sent home with Michael from the hospital. Dr. Price had stopped in each Friday to check up on him and was blown away by his progress. Michael beamed with pride, but modestly attributed most of it to Vivian's enthusiastic persistence.

Perhaps a bit too enthusiastic, he thought to himself, limping over to the kitchen to pour himself a glass of water. He didn't think anyone had ever pushed him so hard.

"So how about it?" Vivian asked briskly. "Want to do a lap around the neighborhood?"

Too enthusiastic indeed!

"I can't," Michael answered with scarcely concealed relief, "I've got Bible study."

"Oh," Vivian paused, then brightened at the thought, "mind if I come along?"

Michael picked up his jacket and a worn Bible from the table. "Be my guest. And, uh, think there's any way you can give me a ride back after?"

"Nah, I think I'll leave you there," Vivian teased, picking up his keys. "Make you walk back as penance for skipping your cardio today."

"Hey—the Lord calls," Michael raises his hands innocently, pointing at the clock, "what am I supposed to do?"

"Your cardio."

Not ten minutes later, they were back in the basement of the church.

They had been going together every week. Vivian—with an increasing enthusiasm; and Michael—with an increasing apathy he attributed to his post-surgery fatigue.

Today was no exception. Vivian settled himself excitedly in the circle of chairs, eager for the message to begin—while Michael glanced around the peeling basement walls with a slightly claustrophobic sigh. His new heart beat impatiently in his chest, and even while he turned his Bible to the appropriate page, he found himself glancing almost absentmindedly toward the exit.

For the second time in his life, he had cheated death—snatched from its very jaws the moment it was to take him away. For the second time, he had a new lease on life.

Possibilities. A future. Things he'd never planned on and didn't deserve.

And how was he spending his time?

Trapped in a mildewing basement.

Pastor Jeff caught his eye from across the room, tapping his watch with an encouraging smile, and Michael was quick to put away these dark thoughts.

Who had given me the new lease on life, anyway? Who had sent me the new heart?

God—that's who.

So stop whining, you little ingrate, and be thankful for what you're given.

But Michael couldn't help but think, staring around the same sea of faces he'd seen for the last four years, smelling the same stale coffee as it steamed a wet trail up the dank wall…

He wasn't sure God was anywhere near this place.

"Proverbs chapter two, verses ten through twelve tells us: 'When wisdom enters your heart, and knowledge is pleasant to your soul; discretion will preserve you, understanding will keep you, to deliver you from the way of evil...'"

Michael cleared his throat and gazed around the room.

"Now, what does that mean to us on the day to day?"

Vivian watched the sermon unfold with a glow of paternal pride. In the beginning, he'd merely come along to these little gatherings to hear Michael speak, but as had been increasingly frequent as of late, he found the words hitting a little too close to home.

He'd always believed in a higher power. Even when he was jetting around the world, sending people to an early grave, he'd always given them the chance to repent. He'd actually become rather known for it. But believing in God was one thing—believing that God would have anything to do with *him* was another.

But that's not what Michael was saying in Bible study. It's not what Pastor Jeff preached every morning from the pulpit. According to them, even the darkest sin could be forgiven. Even the deepest of stains could be removed from one's heart through the blood of the Son.

It was actually rather fitting, Vivian thought, *blood for blood. A cleansing of the spirit, by the Spirit. And according to the experts, all he had to do to attain forgiveness, was ask?*

He lifted his hands and bowed his head with the rest of the group as they came together in prayer. The words they chanted—ones he'd already come to know by heart—seemed to resonate within his very soul, taking root in a way he was only partially aware of himself.

For one of the first times in his life, he was so preoccupied, he didn't even notice the black Sedan drive slowly past the window...

* * *

Vivian left the church that night feeling rejuvenated and refreshed. He still might not completely believe the fresh start being preached from the pulpit—but he had to admit—even the possibility of one was an intoxicating prospect.

Complete rebirth upon complete surrender.

His mind was still weighing the pros and cons as he dropped Michael off at his apartment and headed straight back out to the grocery store to pick up something for dinner. It had only taken a few days for him to discover that his son had both the kitchen and the eating habits of, well, a twenty-six-year-old. While normally, the laws of etiquette wouldn't allow Vivian to intervene, he was using Michael's physical recovery as an excuse not only to spend absurd amounts of time with him, but also to introduce him to things like vegetables and vitamins.

The trip was brief, limited to pizza and salad. He was just walking back out to his car, arms laden with brown paper bags, when it happened.

He saw them.

Perhaps it was because they blended in so well, that they stood out to him so easily. An expertly perfected camouflage punctured by two pairs of strategically darting eyes. Perhaps it was because in a city of evening transition, they were the only two things standing still.

Either way, it was their uniformity that betrayed them.

If these two men were really 'from the hood,' then why were they surveying the streets like they were seeing them for the first time? Why was one of them carrying a briefcase that still had the torn remnants of a baggage tag from the airport? And why would two men, wearing two thousand dollars' worth of shoes between them, be standing in a grocery store parking lot in a town like Woodlands?

Vivian almost had to smile as they spotted him coming out of the store and slowly made their approach. To remember the ratted hoodie but forget the shoes? Rookie mistake. He was willing to bet they were both wearing ties beneath those hastily purchased sweatshirts.

Ties and guns.

The smile faded slightly as he shifted the bags in his arms and planned out his move. It had to be said that even though there were two of them, he didn't feel the slightest trace of fear. Truth be told, he was a little insulted that whoever it was these men represented would only think to send two of them after him.

After over twenty years in the business? Show a little respect, damnit!

"Can I help you gentlemen?" he drawled when they got close enough, offering each a sweet smile. The sudden initiation caught them both off guard, and they paused a split second before the taller of the two stepped forward with a polite smile of his own.

"I'm sorry to bother you ma'am," he tried his best for a New York accent, "we just got into town and we're looking for a good friend of mine—I was wondering if you'd seen him."

He shuffled around in his pocket for a moment, before pulling out a crumpled picture.

Vivian blinked in shock at his own reflection.

This...could not be happening. Could it?

It took every bit of his years of training not to crack a smile.

Instead, he frowned thoughtfully at the photograph, trying absentmindedly to remember where he had been when it was taken. "No...I don't think so," he murmured in his velvety new voice. "And it's a pretty close-knit town. I'm sure I'd remember."

Disappointed, but determined to be thorough, the other man stepped in to help. "You're sure? Anyone new come to town? Sometime the last few weeks?"

Vivian stepped back and put his hands on his hips. "You two cops or something? You know, you have to tell me if you're cops. I heard that on TV somewhere…"

It was almost too good for words. The kind of moment that made Vivian wish he had a friend he could share it with. 'Hey, remember that time those two guys showed up to kill me, but instead, they thought I was a woman, so they came asking me for help?' Maybe he'd call Ray…

"No ma'am," the first man started backing away, followed quickly by his associate, "not cops. Thank you for your time."

Thank you for your time? Yeah—rookie mistakes. The words 'please' and 'thank you' hadn't been heard in Woodlands since Teddy Roosevelt was president.

They vanished around a corner without another word, melting seamlessly into the dark night. But Vivian remained standing there long after they were gone, staring at the side of the building as if he could still see them.

They might have picked the most circuitous approach possible—literally canvassing the neighborhood—but it wouldn't be long until they stumbled into something. Despite its medium size, Woodlands did indeed operate like a small-town community.

New arrivals were scarce, and the gossip mills ran twenty-four seven.

Vivian couldn't believe his disguise had worked so completely. Tonight, it had saved the three of them from what promised to be a grisly blood bath. Next time, he might not be so lucky.

He would have to act preemptively, he decided. Track the bastards down and silence them before they stumbled across the wrong person and blew his little charade to pieces.

All his instincts told him to go after them right then. Leave no witnesses. Leave nothing to chance. Drop the pizza and take off running.

But a stronger side of him had one agenda, and one agenda only.

Get to Michael.

Now, more than ever, it was important that he stay close. There was no telling where those two might show up next…

He headed to his car the next instant—his mind utterly preoccupied with this one, paramount thing. The engine revved and he sped out of the parking lot without stopping to look for oncoming traffic. Without noticing his purse strap was stuck in the door.

Without seeing how the shorter of the two men, glanced over his shoulder with a slight frown…

CHAPTER

9

"Get down!" a loud voice screamed through the rain.

It took Michael a moment to realize it was his own.

There was a deafening shower of gunfire, followed by four soft thuds as what used to be his friends dropped without protest to the ground. Then his legs stopped working.

He watched in slow motion as a strange car slowed to a stop, and a pair of heavy black boots jumped out onto the wet pavement. There were other noises—shouts, instructions. He vaguely realized that his own car was being searched and ransacked by a pair of faceless shadows, but he had eyes for only one thing.

The dripping gun pointed at his face.

'This is it,' he remembered thinking. 'It all ends today, and what have I done…nothing.'

A disembodied finger squeezed the trigger, and a burst of powder shot into the air.

Then four more times.

The sound of it echoed off the wet streets and in the spiraling chasms of Michael's mind.

He waited to fall. To feel the warmth of his blood seep slowly from his chest. To feel any pain, for that matter.

But all he heard was a voice—a warm voice calling from somewhere far away...

"I can think of younger days, when living for my life—"

...what?

"—Was everything a man could want to dooooo. But I could never see..."

With a mighty roar, Michael destroyed the wretched alarm clock once and for all. It fell to the floor, shattering in a million pieces, as he bolted up in bed like someone had given him an electric shock. Little shards of plastic still stuck to his fist, and he pulled them absentmindedly from his skin, not noticing as little drops of blood fell noiselessly to the floor.

A hundred, rain-drenched images flashed behind his eyes. The same images that had nightly haunted him since he was twenty-two. He could smell the powder. Feel the cold rain dripping down his back. By now, he knew the dream so well, rehashing it was almost a part of his morning routine—as muscle memory as something like changing the coffee filter, or screwing the top back on the toothpaste.

But this morning was a bit different.

This morning he didn't feel the same pangs of loss that he customarily did. The same horrific adrenaline spike that had sent his old heart racing for the hills.

This morning he felt almost...nostalgic.

He sat there, still as a stone on the mattress—trying to make sense of the feeling. If he was being honest with himself, it almost felt like he wished he was back there—wished he had a chance to do things differently. To snap out of his involuntary freeze, and fight!

A rush of blood flooded his mouth, and Michael glanced down quickly to realize that he'd bitten though his lip in the excitement of the prospect. That, and his finger was bleeding all over the bed.

Skipping his morning prayer entirely, he raced down the hall to the bathroom to get cleaned up—watching the deep crimson swirl together with foamy toothpaste as it ran down the rickety pipes.

Yes, something was different today—he could feel it.

And furthermore...it felt kinda good!

His very steps felt lighter as he dressed quickly and headed to the front door. He didn't give a second glance to the doctor-recommended breakfast list, taped to the fridge. He paid absolutely no mind to his 'only leave the house with a trusted friend' speech as he grabbed his keys and stuffed them into his coat pocket.

He was going to the park today—alone. He was twenty-six years old, in the prime of his life. No one could stop him.

Only the blinking light on his phone gave him pause. There was a new email waiting and very few people had this account. Knowing he'd be unable to fully concentrate unless he knew what it was, he stifled an impatient sigh and flipped it open to see the message.

The graphic design on the heading made him pause yet again. It was from a seminary college he'd been considering in Michigan. They'd finally scheduled an appointment for him to talk with an advisory counselor about the ins and outs of his application. It was the email he'd been waiting for since before his collapse on the church basement steps.

His finger hovered over the screen, as a wave of indecision shook him to the core.

He should reply—that's definitely what he was supposed to do. The Michael he'd come to know and trust these last four years would immediately reply. The prospect of going to seminary—although a dream he had entrusted to very few—was one of the only things that kept him going on days when his life in Woodlands threatened to be more than he could take.

It was his way out. His better tomorrow. And all he had to do was type a simple reply to the administrative office to find out the status of his application.

Except…he didn't.

Without a second thought, he was out the door. The park was calling—a few hours of unsupervised, unchaperoned, irresponsible alone-time beckoned. And there was nothing, not an email from seminary—not even a personal eCard from Jesus Christ—that was going to get in his way.

There were a few warning signs—a few *this is your body telling you that you've pushed it a bit too far* hints, but Michael staunchly ignored them as he made his way the seven blocks down the street to the park.

Vivian would be proud, he rationalized strategically, racing around corners and waving to people as he went. *He was certainly getting in his cardio now.*

By the time he reached the park, he was panting like he'd run a full marathon and there was a light sheen of sweat across his forehead. But he had *made* it. That was the important thing.

He gazed around proudly, soaking in the familiar sights he'd been so long deprived.

He saw the kids playing basketball, the old women sitting in a line on an old park bench—gossiping like the world was about to end. He saw the perpetually broken-down ice cream truck, piloted by a man he suspected was homeless and had just set up permanent residence by the park.

He breathed it all in like a man newly-released from prison—free of the bars that had caged him. Free of the cautious leash his broken heart had kept him tethered to since childhood.

It was actually a full minute before he realized the one thing in the utopic landscape that didn't belong. Like one of those magazines where you circled the thing *wrong* with the picture.

Michael had never before seen the two men in awkward sweatshirts.

He approached them with the confidence of a man he had long since put to rest.

This park was set in the middle of a rather rough neighborhood that had historically threatened the childlike tranquility of its unassuming ways—with its jungle gym and sluggish ice cream truck. But there were those, like him, who had grown up on these tufts of green and would defend them now for the second generation with an almost irrational fervor. If there was one good thing you could say about Woodlands, it was that it protected its own.

Two unfamiliar gangsters lurking near the edge of the playground? Surgical recovery or no—Michael felt he had an obligation to help.

"Excuse me," he jogged purposefully over, ignoring the stabbing pain that was starting around his incision line, "can I help you?"

The men looked up in surprise, but then strode quickly towards him, closing the distance gap in a matter of seconds.

"Yes, actually. Thank you," a man with twitchy hands and a European-looking haircut answered him. "We're looking for a man who's new to town." The photograph popped up without further preamble. "He's around six-feet, thin scar above the left eyebrow..."

He let the image simmer for a few seconds before he offered the half-hearted reassurance.

"He's one of my oldest friends. I'd heard he'd moved here and would be very grateful for any information that could lead me to his whereabouts..."

Michael had been in enough drug busts to know when he was being lied to, and the men had 'interrogated' enough hostile witnesses to know when they were being blown off.

"I've never seen the guy before in my life." Michael almost sneered, an uncharacteristically aggressive attitude boiling to the surface. "But I have been coming to this park since I was about seven years old, and let me tell you, there's no room here for people like you. I don't know what your deal is with this guy, but you need to take it somewhere else. Do you understand me?"

The words were unexpectedly bold—the threat, thinly veiled—and the two men raised their eyebrows in an identical motion of surprise. The shorter of the two—the one clutching the briefcase—looked the impertinent stranger up and down twice before taking an innocuous step backwards.

There was something strangely familiar about this kid— something oddly jarring.

They'd certainly never met before—that much was clear. But there was something about the way he carried himself, something about the fire that burned deep in his eyes. It was almost as if the man had seen it somewhere before.

This time, it was the three men in the park who were too distracted to see the sapphire blue car slow to a stop on the edge of the grass. Too engaged to notice the shapely woman inside lower down the window and gawk at the distant conversation taking place.

Had they had their wits about them, they might have found it curious indeed, the way she stared with open-mouthed horror at the close proximity between the three.

But alas, no one left the park the wiser.

The two gentlemen turned on their heels and headed back towards downtown, while Michael marched triumphantly back the way he'd come—the neighborhood hero, defender of the meek. Even if no one here was old enough to realize it...

He strode across the lawn back towards his house with a smile he didn't even attempt to contain. He knew he'd woken up that morning with a sense of purpose. It seemed he wasn't that far off base, after all.

Only the blue car idled where it had abruptly stopped, lingering suspiciously at the end of the greenery with a clear view of the playground within.

Vivian drew in quick, short breaths.

His son had been talking with assassins, his son had been talking with assassins.

Assassins that could have ended his young life without a second's thought. Assassins that were circling ever closer, like the perpetual tightening of a noose.

Assassins that were here looking for his father.

Well no longer, Vivian thought with dark decision. These men were his. They would regret ever coming to Woodlands...and they would regret it tonight.

* * *

There was blood...everywhere.

It clung to the curtains, to the tablecloth, to the fabric fibers of the carpet.

Vivian had tried his best to be neat. He'd tried to rein in his anger and snuff out the lives of the two offending men as unobtrusively as possible. But his rage had gotten the better of him.

The beginning of the evening was nothing but a blur.

When he'd sought the two men out, cornering them behind an old pawn shop, it was almost as if they'd been waiting for him. They watched the blue car pull up with a look of the utmost anticipation—their hands drifting almost absentmindedly to their holsters. What they hadn't counted on was the level of raw, primal skill lurking just behind the starched panty hose.

In what only took a few seconds, Vivian had disabled them both and stuffed them into the trunk of his car. Waving kindly to an elderly member of his Bible study, he pulled out onto the street and sped off back to his humble apartment with no one being the wiser.

He couldn't just kill these men, after all. Things were different now. There were mitigating factors. There was the church, the home-owners association, Michael...

He'd have to torture them first to find out everything they knew.

Five hours later, he was standing in the midst of what looked to be a used set on a Quentin Tarantino film.

He eyed the viscera dripping slowly down his new wall-paper with distaste—he knew he shouldn't have used a gun. But the shorter of the two men—in true Napoleonic fashion, the more vicious of the two—had pushed all the right buttons.

"You know, it only took us three weeks to find you," he'd panted past the clothes hanger Vivian had been using to discreetly strangle him. "Do you really think we're going to be the only ones?"

At that moment, the phone had rung.

Glancing ironically around the blood-spattered house as his new Nancy Sinatra ring tone bounced through the halls, Vivian tightened his grip—choking silent the man's windpipe—before answering.

"Hey," Michael's voice rang cheerily across the line. Still glowing from his 'win in the park,' no doubt, Vivian thought regrettably. "Do you have a sec? I had a question for you…"

"Of course," Vivian held the clothes hanger even tighter, wiping his shirt with distaste as the man spat out a mouthful of blood, "what's on your mind?"

"Well I know it's a bit short notice…but I was wondering if you'd like to come with me to the annual YMCA camp for the weekend. It's pretty much everything you'd expect: hiking, swimming, campfires—along with some ministry and one-on-one connections with the kids."

There was a long pause as Michael reined in his excitement, and Vivian reined in a man whose life was dimming before his eyes.

"Do you think that's something you'd want to do? It's just for two days…"

The clothes hanger broke through the skin and Vivian kicked the man heartlessly down to the floor. He crumbled in breathless defeat as Vivian put his heel squarely atop his back, positively beaming into the phone at the invitation.

"I'd love to—thank you for inviting me, Michael."

"Brilliant! I'll pick you up at nine."

The line clicked dead.

For a moment, Vivian basked in the long-awaited euphoria of having a weekend away with his child. But then the man slowly bleeding out on his floor had the gall to speak again.

"I knew it," he gasped, unable to stop the tide, "that's your son. That's your—"

A simple bullet stopped his voice forever.

"Yes, it is," Vivian answered slowly, watching the smoke spiral from the silencer. "And no one's going to lay a finger on him."

*   *   *

There are certain calls that no one wants to get at two in the morning. 'Could you come over here and help me get rid of these two bodies?' was one of them.

"Honestly, Pete!" Dr. Ray Price held a hand over his nose as he waded through the bloodshed to put his medical bag down on the kitchen counter. "Talk about over-kill."

Vivian rolled his eyes. "There is never an excuse for assassin-based puns. How many times do I have to tell you that?" His friend seemed momentarily incapable of answering and Vivian's eyes swept over him before he added, "Why did you bring the medical bag?"

Price glanced almost helplessly at his satchel before giving his shoulders a weak shrug. "I don't know—habit, I guess. Usually when I get called to a crime scene, it's to try to work some sort of life-saving miracle..."

Vivian snorted at the words 'crime scene' but let it go.

"Well, in this case, this really was a life-saving miracle. Michael's life," he added quietly, casting a dark look over the mangled bodies. "They were talking to him in the park this afternoon. It was only a matter of time before they connected the dots."

Price purposely tuned him out, kneeling beside one of the corpses and looking at the patterns of head trauma in shock. "Did you use…a waffle iron on this one?"

Vivian shrugged his shoulders with a sign. "I'm a domestic housewife now—what do you expect? And actually, those things are surprisingly efficient—"

"I don't want to know," Price cut him off, holding up his hands and closing his eyes in the same instant. "Now, you called me here for corpse disposal. I'm assuming you have some kind of plan in mind…?"

"Oh no," Vivian waved a dismissive hand, "I can do that fine on my own. I was actually just wondering if you wanted to split this pizza with me. I was supposed to have it with Michael today, but…" he gestured to the broken bodies, "well, things came up."

When Ray didn't say a word, he pressed his luck.

"It's already thawed…?"

Closing his eyes in a grimace that spoke volumes, Ray jerked his head quickly away from the pieces of men littering the floor.

"I'll eat with you—but only because I'm an idiot who made the asinine decision to befriend a complete psychopath. And I'm not doing it in this room."

Vivian bit back a smile. "Where are we supposed to—"

"We'll eat out on the porch."

Ten minutes later, the bodies were stuffed neatly into several bags, and the doctor and the assassin were sitting on an old hanging bench—swinging slightly in the breeze as they chewed thoughtfully on pieces of pizza.

"You know, Pete," Ray choked down a slice of pepperoni, "I don't know why—I know it doesn't make any sense—but I kind of thought that time had passed when I'd get a phone call from you that could still shock me."

Vivian considered this for a moment, before jerking his head inside. "*This?* Surely after all these years, you can't consider *this* to be—"

"No, no, I mean…" Ray waved the slice between them, "you can cook?"

Both men chuckled softly, but it settled differently on their faces when they were done.

Vivian looked like a man free of a great burden, a man who'd successfully delayed the demons chasing him. If only for a little while.

Ray looked like a man fixated on the second half of that statement.

If only for a little while…

"Pete, you know you can't stay here, right?" Ray ignored the flat look Vivian shot him and pressed forward. "People are just going to keep coming after you—and that will inevitably lead them to Michael. This isn't the last time we're going to be having this pizza—not by a long shot."

Vivian's face fell, but the image he projected to the world was strong and sure. "I can protect him."

Price sighed. "Pete—it's me. Be serious for a minute. You can't protect him forever. Eventually, someone's going to get through. Wasn't it you who told me that your life was basically a bad personification of Russian roulette? A question of statistics and timing?"

Vivian glanced back towards the house with a wry smile. "Fortunately, I've been amassing a great deal of good karma since then."

Again, both men chuckled. But this time, it was Vivian who looked unsettled.

"I can't leave him again. When I left the first time, it broke him."

Ray patted his friend on the shoulder, only vaguely aware that he was one of two people on the planet allowed to make such a casual gesture. "He pulled himself through—it made him stronger. You need to have a little faith."

Have a little faith…

The words echoed back in Vivian's mind as he took a sip of his beer.

If you had asked him three weeks ago, the phrase would have meant nothing—just a kitsch saying used by a slew of well-wishers to anchor the Hallmark season.

Now…? They struck a little too close to home.

Nevertheless, there were truths here he still needed to uncover, and a life that meant more than anything this world or the next had to offer.

There was no going back. He'd known it from the minute he'd stepped off the plane.

"I can't leave him," he repeated slowly, his eyes locked on the road. "I won't."

CHAPTER

10

"I'm telling you, if you get on the interstate now, instead of waiting for the 81 crossover, we'll shave about an hour off our time ..."

All the blood had been scrubbed off the walls by the time Michael got there, the next morning. The bags of bodies had been properly disposed of. After Vivian hastily threw away what looked like the remains of a tooth, he opened the door to have a latte shoved in his face.

"Morning sunshine," Michael had said with a beaming smile. "You ready for camp?"

They had proceeded outside only to have Vivian stop short as he saw the 'car' Michael had parked by the curb. At least, he thought it was a car. It looked a bit like one of those boxes that moved up and down a ski lift—only on wheels. At least...he thought they were wheels.

"Is that electrical tape?" he asked curiously, kneeling down by the front bumper.

Michael nodded with a happy smile—he couldn't be prouder. "I got this thing the day I graduated high school. It was used then, so I've had to fix it up over the years—a couple of home remedies—but it still runs great."

He patted the hood fondly and Vivian felt sure things might fall off.

"I thought you didn't..." he stalled, feeling far more fearful about a three-hour ride in the car than he'd been at any point during the previous evening. "I thought you didn't drive anymore, that your car didn't run?"

"Oh, it runs just fine." For just a moment, Michael's face clouded. "I just haven't driven it...for a while."

For four years, to be exact.

Truth be told, the car had been sitting in the exact same spot under the bridge where Michael had walked away from it that rainy night. The keys were still in the ignition, but for whatever reason, no one had thought to either move or steal it. It must have had something to do with the torrents of what looked like blood and brain matter splashed over the tires.

It had actually been Dr. Price who had the thing towed to Michael's house a few months after the 'incident.' Michael had been content to let it sit there forever—a forgotten relic of his old life—but Price was convinced the goodwill of the city wouldn't last much longer, and the car would soon be towed at the owner's expense.

Since then, it had sat idly in Michael's driveway, eroding slowly under seasons of rain and rust. Price had never encouraged him to drive it—for obvious reasons—and Michael had never shown the slightest inclination of wanting to fix it up.

Until now.

"But she's a beauty, right?" He hit the hood again and one of the bolts connecting a tire rolled away down the street. "I actually took a walk to the park yesterday, and after you bailed on me for dinner," he winked good-naturedly, "I decided to see if I could get it to run. Turns out, these things never die!"

"Oh Michael," Vivian sighed, absentmindedly calculating how little the whole thing would sell for sheet metal. "I knew the Woodlands education system was a bit lacking, but I never realized they skipped over such basic terms. You see, the word 'beauty' actually implies a level of—"

"Shut up," Michael laughed, giving him a playful shrug. "She'll get us there just fine."

After tossing overnight bags in the back seat, both climbed into the decrepit vehicle with no further comment, Vivian casting a wistful glance at his own car as they pulled away.

Two hours later, they had yet to break down—although the engine had started emitting an intermittent low-pitched wail, like an orca caught in a blender.

Michael pretended he couldn't hear it, answering Vivian's navigational suggestion about the crossover with a scoff.

"And how would you know?" he teased lightly. "Do you come up here every year?"

Vivian sat back in his seat with a fixed smile, realizing his mistake. The last time he'd been to a place without studying all the access and escape routes had been an Olive Garden at his high school graduation dinner. After all this time, it was second nature to him. The second he knew he was going somewhere new, he'd pull out all the relevant maps and memorize them.

"What's Grand Rapids Seminary?" he changed the subject, pulling an unopened envelope from atop the dash.

"Oh," Michael sounded almost glum. The letter had come with the email and had received the same sort of attention—this time, tossed carelessly into his car. "It's a, uh, a school I was considering in Michigan."

Vivian raised his eyebrows in surprise. "To become a minister?"

"Yeah, something like that."

"Well that's wonderful!"

For so many reasons. Not only would Michael have a guaranteed profession with provided housing for the rest of his life—but it would get him out of Woodlands. Probably out of New York all together, and permanently off the radar of anyone who might be straying too close.

Michael didn't say anything, just pursed his lips and nodded, keeping his eyes on the road. Vivian recognized the 'end of the conversation,' but felt the need to keep going. Based on everything he knew about his son—everything he had witnessed firsthand—this should be a cause for celebration. The letter hadn't even been opened.

"Is that…something you're not as interested in anymore?" he asked lightly, trying to keep it casual.

Michael opened his mouth to answer, but thought better of it—pausing a moment before he finally said, "One way or another, I think I might have to put it on hold for a while." He gestured to the long scar running down his chest with a rather hard look in his eyes.

Vivian considered this for a second, before continuing cautiously, "Looks to me like you got a second chance at things. Like God spared you for a reason." He tucked the envelope securely in the center console.

Michael sighed softly. "Yeah…that's one way of looking at it."

Vivian was right—Michael knew this. He knew it clear as day. And yet, truth be told, since the surgery, he had been seeing things…differently.

What he once thought of as a heavenly coincidence—that a heart came to him when he needed it most—he was beginning to see as divinely unfair. Why did he need a new heart to begin with? Why had *he* been cursed with a genetic defect when he was the one bending over backwards to live his life on the straight and narrow, in a town full of gangsters and thugs?

Seminary—once the light at the end of the tunnel—was now a burden weighing on his already troubled mind. He'd begun to openly resent the time commitment of his weekly Bible study, and he couldn't remember the last time he'd called up Jeff for one of their prized theological debates.

His apathy frightened him, and the bitterness buried deep within set him on edge. What was happening to him? How could it be stopped? More importantly…did he want it to stop?

"You hungry?" he diverted, pulling off into the parking lot of a diner. "We could get some lunch?"

Vivian studied him for a moment, before picking up his purse. "Sounds good."

Anything to get out of that wheezing car.

* * *

The man had been staring at the phone for hours.

The room around him buzzed with a million rushed conversations. Squawks of Russian, Ukrainian, French, Slovak, and English ricocheted off the walls. They bounced around the clearance-protected doors and echoed from the floor to ceiling map on the far wall.

It was this map that held the room's attention. It looked ironically festive, peppered with a sprinkling of little red and white lights—blinking on and off.

Each light represented a problem, and a corresponding solution. The second a white light went out—a call would come in and the adjacent red light would be paid and relocated. If one were to squint close enough at the map, they would see exorbitant sums of money scribbled next to them, all in a variety of international currencies.

It wasn't often that they lost a red dot. They were trained to last. In fact, it had only happened a single time in the last two years. Three weeks ago.

Since then, the clamor in the room had crescendoed to an uneasy swell—escalating with each passing day without contact. The men and women who occupied the room paced closer and closer to the map, their faces flashing with the light of the dots. There was a hole where one should be. A giant gap in an otherwise perfect system. Right in the heart of New York.

While the anxious crowd stared at the map, the man stared at his phone.

It would ring. It always rang. And then everything would go back to normal.

* * *

"I swear to you, this has never happened before."

Michael and Vivian stood on the side of the road. There was no one in sight. Nothing but trees for miles. Trees, and an increasing cloud of smoke wafting from the hood of the car.

Vivian took off his jacket. "I somehow find that hard to believe."

Michael raised his phone apologetically, searching for a signal. "It's going to be fine. I'll just call for a tow. We're almost to the camp, in fact, I'd be surprised if we don't see some people that we know driving this way before long."

"I thought you said we were coming a day early to help set up."

Michael bit his lip. "Yeah, I did say that…"

Vivian rolled his eyes and stifled a smile. It wasn't wise to do this—he knew that full well—but they had no other choice. At this elevation, they weren't going to find phone reception until there was a break in the trees, and it was unlikely anyone else would come this way for hours. They'd have to fix the problem themselves. Even if it meant breaking out of character…

"Hold this," he handed Michael his jacket and rolled up his sleeves.

"What are you going to do?" Michael frowned curiously.

With a pair of skilled hands, Vivian lifted the hood of the car. "When my husband died, all these kinds of problems fell to me. I had to learn all sorts of things I never knew before."

A waft of steam blew into his face and he hastily blotted his makeup. Of course, he'd never done it in lipstick…but who was counting?

"It's just a simple oil leak," he said with authority, tightening up a valve and closing down the hood, "burning around the combustion chamber. Try it now."

Without a word, Michael slid back into the driver's seat. The engine started up without a hitch. His eyes shot to the window, fixing on Vivian as the smoke between them slowly cleared.

"There—good as new!" Vivian called, not seeing the peculiar intensity of his stare.

Michael's brow creased, but he flashed a quick smile and waved him inside.

"…good as new."

* * *

They reached the camp just before nightfall, dragging in their bags precisely as—three thousand miles away—the phone finally rang.

The man answered it in a heartbeat.

"Lucius," he began with relief. A picture of the two men clinking beers stood in the corner of his desk. "I was beginning to—"

"Montana's dead," an unfamiliar voice replied shortly. "This is Yates, his case commander. We received confirmation this morning."

A chilling silence followed this proclamation.

The man's hand tightened on the phone to the point that the palladium began to crack.

"How?"

"It appears to be a knife wound to the stomach. We obtained hospital records, and then the death notes from the morgue."

A hitched breath. "Are you sure it's him?"

"Six foot four, built like a tank, reeking of rye whiskey? Yeah—it's him."

This time, the pause was much longer.

The man on the other end instinctively knew not to break it. He had been in the room with the map before. He knew the man holding the phone.

"When?"

"About three weeks ago. I sent a team out from Liverpool. They arrived a few days ago, but we lost contact after they headed towards a suburb called Woodlands. When they failed to make their third check-in, I activated standard retrieval protocols to locate them, and called base." There was an almost nervous pause, after which he added, "All according to procedure."

He wasn't an idiot. He knew Montana was one of their greatest assets. Despite his heavy drinking and a penchant for underage girls, he had delivered a series of consistently astounding results over the last fifteen years. He was the kind of disappearance that warranted a thorough investigation. Not to mention, he'd heard rumors that Montana and the Director shared a familial connection...

"A knife to the stomach, you said?"

The voice came out low as a growl, but was still enough to cut through the noise of the room. Everyone froze in place, only the blinking lights indicating any sort of movement.

"Yes, sir. I believe…"

The phone cracked still farther.

"You believe *what*?"

"I believe it was his own knife."

The man sat back in his chair. His eyes flickered once to the picture on his desk before roving across the faces of his frightened employees to the map.

He'd been doing this long enough to stay objective. There weren't many people on the planet with the skill to take Montana out. There were even fewer with the inclination to try.

With almost unnatural precision, his eyes travelled to a solitary white dot—blinking innocently on and off in Western Russia.

No, there were not too many people who would attempt such a feat…

"Your orders, sir?"

The man's mouth narrowed into a wry smile.

"Call off your retrieval squad—your team is dead."

The room held their collective breath as the man on the other end spluttered, "Call off the...? I mean, understood."

"Woodlands, you say? In New York?"

"Yes, sir." You could almost hear the poor man sweating on the other side.

The wry smile turned into something sinister. Something sinister indeed.

"I'm sending in a new team." This time, his eyes flashed to a red light blinking deep in the heart of South America. "I think this one's going to take something special..."

CHAPTER

11

"Do NOT put that in the fire—that is poison oak! Wash your hands!"

Michael and Vivian wandered through the YMCA campground like two lost extras meandering through Middle Earth. Gone were all suburban conveniences. Gone were things like electricity, common sense, and soap. It was bare bones out here. A true wilderness experience.

And the kids of Woodlands were *loving* it.

Vivian chuckled to himself as a raucous group of them barreled past, heading off to go 'fishing' at the 'lake.' In reality, it was a grimy little water hole that contained nothing but broken beer bottles and a slew of slowly deteriorating condoms. He wondered if they realized it was basically frozen through.

"Tell me again why this is done in the middle of December?" he asked with a smile, watching as the rag tag bunch galloped down the forest path, a bunch of tattered scarves trailing out behind them like shivering adolescent flags.

Michael grinned, following his line of sight. "Well, we'd love to come in the warmer months, but the church's donations can only get stretched so far. Plus, St. Augustine usually books the full camp in June and July, so we come out here around Christmas."

For many, the icy winds and sub-zero temperatures might be a sticking point, but these kids couldn't care less. They had heard about the concept of 'camp' from the wealthier kids across town—seen it unfold with their own eyes in so many movies and television shows. And while it was easy to be indifferent, even aggressively so in the moment, the term festered.

Now was their turn. Their moment in the sun.

No matter how ironically absent that sun might be.

Vivian nodded thoughtfully, still watching their gleeful retreat. "You came up here when you were a kid?"

It was a throwaway question—one asked only to bolster his cover. He knew full well that Michael had gone to camp since he was six years old. He'd sent Dr. Price money to pay for it. In return, Price had sent him a picture of a young Michael sandwiched on a log between a group of other youngsters at the nightly bonfire. Already tall for his age, he was missing two teeth in the picture. There was a giant scrape on his knee, another on his chin, and he was smiling his little head off like Christmas had come early.

Vivian had stared at the picture for a full minute, memorizing every detail in his newly acquired Austrian flat. Then he took out his lighter and burned it.

Had the photo ever been found, that would have been the last year Michael went to camp.

"Yep," Michael stuck his hands deep in his pockets and looked around, "ever since I was a kid. I looked forward to it all year. Didn't even realize it was church sponsored until I grew up. They don't really advertise and all the prayer groups and things are optional."

"Coach Mike!"

The pair was interrupted by a little string-bean of a kid. Freckles, braces, and stretched absurdly by adolescence, he darted past various groups of people before sliding to a stop in front of Vivian and Michael. Before either one of them could warn him not to, he caught Michael in a huge hug.

Vivian's first instinct was to drop the thirteen-year-old where he stood, but Michael just bit his lip in a grimace and pulled gingerly away.

"Spence!" He grinned tightly, ruffling the kid's mop of curls. "Take a look at you—you're almost as tall as me!"

"Five-eight," the boy said proudly, looking Michael up and down. "I heard you were in the hospital for a while, so I didn't think you'd be coming." He lowered his voice as if they were talking about something scandalous. "They said they took your heart out."

Michael laughed. "Yeah, but it was on purpose—so we're all good. Spence, I want you to meet of friend of mine." He turned to make the proper introductions. "Spencer Throll, this is Vivian Knight. Vivian goes to my church now, she just moved to town."

Spencer's eyes widened. "Why would you do something like that?"

It was Vivian's turn to laugh. "I had my reasons. And as it turns out, I'm rather enjoying my stay in Woodlands."

Spencer shot Michael a look before his face cracked into a grin. "Enjoy it while it lasts, lady. Hey Coach Mike—you think you're up to play a little ball?"

Michael's eyes travelled from his young friend to a group of children eagerly waiting on the frozen basketball courts—the one in the middle holding a ball. The corners of his mouth turned up wistfully, but before he could make any promises his body couldn't keep, Vivian put a casual hand on his arm and pulled them tightly together.

"I'm afraid Coach Mike is *not* up for that quite yet," he said with a stern glance at his son. "But you kids go have fun."

Spencer raised his eyebrows and looked between them. "Are you...?" He grew instantly uncomfortable and turned to Michael instead. "Is she your mama or something?"

Michael laughed again, clear and loud, while Vivian's blood froze in his veins.

"No, she's not. She's just making sure I follow the doctor's orders, that's all. You guys go kill it. Make me proud."

Without a glance behind him, Spencer shot back towards his group—armed with the coveted inside scoop that no, Coach Mike was not dead. And yes, he had indeed lost his heart.

"You really think you're up for playing a game of basketball?" Vivian said in that same stern voice he found himself slipping into whenever he tried to talk sense into Michael. "You really think that's a good idea? Don't make me call Dr. Price. He'll come down here and kick your ass. And then, my dear, I'll send him back to the hospital and do it again myself."

"You know what?" Michael's eyes sparkled as he chuckled to himself. "I don't doubt it."

For the second time that morning, Vivian's heart skipped a beat. Was there more to Michael's words, or was he just being paranoid? Before he could think of a roundabout way to ask, Michael clapped him on the arm and gestured to a trail up ahead.

"What's this?" Vivian asked as they started up the climb.

It wasn't a hard hike, but it looked to be a long one—cutting through the thick foliage as it wound its way gradually up the mountain.

Michael gestured to the top with a small smile. "It's my Everest. If I can make it to the top, I'm going to pronounce myself cured."

Vivian shook his head, slowing down a bit to match his son's speed. "A virtual master of medicine, you are."

Michael grinned. "You know, I always thought I'd make a good doctor. When I was a kid, I stole a bottle of vitamins from the supermarket and scattered them for the birds."

Vivian shot him a look, unable to tell if he was kidding.

They climbed a bit further before he finally asked, "So what made you decide to be a minister instead? Did the birds die?"

Michael's eyes grew thoughtful as he continued at a measured pace. They'd only been going to half a mile or so, but already, he'd broken a light sweat.

"It was Jeff, actually. He first mentioned it about a year ago. Said I spent all my time leading youth groups and Bible studies anyway—said I might as well just go for it."

"But now you're not so sure…"

Michael shot Vivian a sideways glance, before letting out a sigh. "You know, the first time I walked into a church was the worst day of my life. No competition. I was out of my mind, couldn't even speak. But the second I stepped inside, I felt better. It was like turning on a light—stepping into warm water. Instantaneous, overwhelming relief. I waited for that feeling to go away, but it never did. Every time I stepped into a church, or a Bible study, or a meditation—I felt exactly the same way."

He paused for a moment, staring straight up the mountain path.

"Until now."

Vivian looked at him, but despite all his years of training, he found he had absolutely no idea what to say. They were off the reservation here—in about every way possible. It wasn't in Vivian's nature to 'surrender' himself to a higher power. Although he sometimes considered it, he'd always imagined himself more…working alongside. A silent helper doing the good Lord's dirty work here on earth. He couldn't image the feeling of exquisite relief Michael was describing in giving oneself up to God.

That is…until now.

"It'll come back," he heard himself saying, clapping Michael softly on the shoulder. "It was only a few weeks ago that you went through a major life trauma. You can't expect everything to just go back to the way it was. It's normal to have questions, to have—"

"Doubts?" Michael finished for him, glancing from the corner of his eye. "Because it's more than just going through the motions, reciting empty words, it's..." He ran his hands back through is hair and suddenly shook his head. "I don't know. I don't know why I'm even talking about this. We're at a church camp, for crying out loud." He forced a laugh.

Vivian laughed graciously along with him, dismissing the conversation and moving quickly on to another.

But no matter how hard he tried to push it from his head, how hard he tried to reconcile it with rationalization after rationalization, he couldn't get a looping image out of his head:

Michael, dazed with drugs, smiling up at him from a hospital cot. Sliced open from chest to stomach, but *still* praising God for sending him a new heart.

What the hell happened...?

They made it about halfway up the mountain, before Michael admitted that he had to turn back before his legs gave out. Praising him for the effort, Vivian changed the subject yet again and they talked about anything and everything as the sun sank over the trees. Although Vivian tried several times to gently steer the conversation back to the seminary, Michael seemed much keener to talk about Vivian's life—particularly, Vivian's life before Woodlands.

The growing list of inexplicable skills had not been lost on Michael, and he turned out to be just as verbally manipulative as his father as he latched onto the subject and refused to let go.

They were still laughing and bantering back and forth when they heard the screams.

* * *

The pain and fatigue were instantaneously forgotten as Vivian and Michael flew the rest of the way down the mountain trail. The high-pitched wailing was soon joined by the thundering of a dozen pairs of feet as the people still lingering in the camp took off towards the lake.

The real lake, Vivian realized with dread. The one too deep to have frozen through more than just a few delicate inches. The one that no child should have been allowed near.

He and Michael got there right as another crack flew up the ice. Spencer and eight or nine of his friends were standing in a panicked circle on one side of the frozen water, while half a dozen campers burst suddenly into sight at the other.

Only one person was standing in the center, her foot stuck in a wide and growing crack, as it spider-webbed across the rest of the lake. Her blue eyes streamed over with icy tears and her pink fingers were shaking as she balled them into helpless fists.

If she moved, she was dead. If she didn't move, she was dead.

It seemed all there was left to do...was wait.

"Oh my God..." All the color drained from Michael's face as he skidded to a stop beside Vivian. "Elsie..."

Vivian looked out to where the girl was standing in the middle of the ice. Judging by the wedges of ice pushed up in little rings around her and the guilty faces of her friends, she had most likely edged out there on a dare and the others had fled when they heard the ice begin to break. Caught in a rift at the center, she had not been so lucky.

A quick look around proved fruitless. There were no objects he could use to balance out her weight or pull her back in. And between the temperature of the water and the frosty air around it, the little girl wouldn't stand a chance if she were to go under.

Unless...

Vivian closed his eyes with a silent sigh.

He'd spent the last twenty years of his life in St. Petersburg. When he wasn't there, he was jetting around the Eastern Block ending lives. He knew how to handle himself on the ice, dangerous as it might be. His training had prepared him for just about everything.

He just…didn't know how to do it without raising suspicion.

"Elsie?" he called loudly, silencing the rest of the group before he took his first tentative stop onto the lake. "I need you to hold perfectly still, okay?"

A hand caught onto the back of his coat.

"What the hell are you doing?" Michael demanded in a hiss. "You can't go out there, it's going to—"

Vivian tugged himself free. "Someone has to get her."

"Then it's going to be me."

Michael ripped off his coat and took a step forward, and Vivian sighed again. With an apologetic grimace, he shoved Michael hard on the chest—felling him down into the snow. He landed with a sharp gasp, clutching at his incision site as he stared up at Vivian in shock.

"Sorry kid," Vivian murmured as he quickly paced out of reach, "doctor's orders."

The rest of the journey was a series of carefully placed steps and hushed gasps from the crowd. By now, the entire camp had gathered and was collectively holding their breath—no one more so than Elsie, who was watching Vivian approach in silent tears.

When he got close enough to speak to her, his face broke into a reassuring smile.

"It's Elsie, right?"

Her head wobbled pitifully upon her tiny neck, as every inch of her shivered. "My foot—it's stuck in the ice. I'm afraid if I move it, everything will—"

"You absolutely should not move it," Vivian said in that same steadying voice, his eyes scanning the cracks around her sneakers as he expertly inched his way forward. "No, I'm going to need you to stay very still and do exactly as I say…"

There was another deep groan from the bottom of the lake and both of them froze where they stood. A little spider-web of fissures shot up around them, and Elsie sucked in a scream.

It's too much weight, too much weight, Vivian chanted to himself, as the gravity of their predicament was suddenly made clear.

The air around them went suddenly quiet, and for the first time in his life, Vivian found himself saying a silent prayer.

Then the ice exploded.

A sea of frozen water shot up around them in a wide arch as the lake rushed forward with a loud hiss. The hiss was echoed with a loud cry from the beach and a high-pitched scream as Elsie's tiny arms shot into the air.

It was muscle memory. No time for hesitation. No time for regret.

The world moved in slow motion as Vivian darted forward and Elsie slipped out of sight.

He caught her by the arm just as her body hit the water, lifting her like a doll, slinging her effortlessly across his shoulders.

Then the race was on.

No longer did he carefully balance his steps, no longer was he peripherally monitoring the crowd. As the ice in the center of the lake shattered and split behind them, he flat-out sprinted for shore.

He reached it just as the space where they had been standing cracked in half with a loud *screech* and vanished beneath the waves. Collapsing onto the ground on the far side, he pulled the little girl out from beneath his arms and stood her up straight in front of him.

"Are you alright?" he asked a little more forcibly than was necessary. She just blinked at him with her over-sized eyes, like a waterlogged doll, and he shook her shoulders. "Elsie—are you okay?"

It was then that he realized the entire lake was dead quiet.

With a feeling of muted dread, he lifted his eyes up to see the whole camp staring back at him. There wasn't a movement or sound. Just the rapid rise and fall of shoulders and a hundred little clouds of silent breath.

Michael was standing nearest to them, but although Vivian caught his eye, he seemed as speechless as the rest of them. His eyes had dilated to their fullest extent and he was staring at Vivian with his mouth slightly ajar.

For the first time, Vivian wondered how the whole incident must have looked from shore.

He mentally kicked himself for risking his cover just to save the life of one little girl. Then his eyes landed back on Elsie and he kicked himself again for thinking such a thing.

Eventually, he did the only thing that popped into his head. And if you had told him what it was a month ago—there was no way in heaven or hell he would have believed you.

Taking a deep breath, he lifted his hands in the air and closed his eyes.

"Thank God!"

At those words, the stunned camp sprang back to life.

In an instant, a hundred people were gathered around him and Elsie, patting them down, embracing them in warm arms, trying to make sure they were alright. Their collective disbelief turned to divine gratitude as they swept the little girl off her feet and rushed her back to camp for a warm shower.

The other kids in on the prank were fiercely reprimanded and led away by a pair of stern-looking chaperones as the rest of the campers rushed off one-by-one, each of them completely euphoric and overwhelmed by what they'd just seen.

The only one who didn't move was Michael. In fact, he didn't so much as blink.

As the crowd of people flooded past them back to camp, he stayed still as a statue, staring at Vivian with that same expression as when he'd fixed the car.

After what seemed like a very long time, Vivian took a step towards him.

"Michael?" he said tentatively, bracing himself for whatever came next.

Neither of them spoke for a moment, before Michael finally picked up his jacket from the snow. His eyes locked on Vivian for a split second, before he gave him a smile that chilled him down to the bone.

"Thank God."

CHAPTER

12

The man was born in Etapa, a small undeveloped town in the rural plains of Northern Bolivia. It was nestled on the bank of the Rio Madre De Dios. The man had many memories as a child, watching river boats drift lazily past on the wide, brown waters.

It was here that he learned to hunt and to fish, mimicking the older men from behind the slats in his wooden fence. It was here that he learned to smoke and drink—hiding his first cigarette in the muddy riverbank when his mother came calling. It was here that he took his first human life—a seventeen-year-old boy who had raped his older sister. The man was barely ten at the time, but it was in that moment he learned a vital lesson.

You didn't need to have age or size on your side to win your battles. You simply had to be better than your opponent.

For a physically stunted child with a speech impediment, it was music to his ears. From that moment on, he dedicated his life to being *better.*

He worked harder, ran faster, and studied longer than anyone else in his town. By the time he was eleven, he'd set up an improvised 'gym' in his backyard—a haphazard collection of tools and 'do it yourself' projects he'd collected on his long nights scavenging the streets. Some of these tools were books—any and all books he could get his hands on. Language books to sharpen the tongue, books on mathematics to sharpen the mind. Other 'tools' included a pair of rusted ballasts to be used as weights. An old chain he'd dragged from the boatyard to be used for climbing. An assortment of knives and other crude weapons to be practiced with daily.

The work was relentless, but the boy had an unusual fire inside him—a volatility that gave him intense focus but made him unsafe for play.

The day he turned fourteen, he declared himself a man, ready to test his skills out in the world. He hitched a ride to the city, went to the first bar he found, and picked a fight with the biggest man there. The seasoned fisherman didn't last two minutes against the strange young instigator who'd tapped him on the shoulder with a stammer. Neither did his five friends.

The story made the local news. A shocking headline. 'Local Boy Kills Six.' No one could explain it. The few people who had borne peripheral witness said that, aside from the actual killing, the child had shown exceptional manners—waiting for all six men to finish their drinks before escorting them outside.

It wasn't enough to get national traction, but when the same thing happened in two more bars the following nights, it bumped up to international news. 'The Bolivian Bandit' they were calling him—one of the first underage serial killers the country ever had. Of course, he hadn't stolen anything to warrant the 'bandit,' but when it came to selling papers, alliteration was key.

The headline caught the eye of a bored-looking drone in an office, who passed it up the ladder until it ended up in a strange room with a large map covered in blinking lights.

The Director himself flew to Bolivia to meet with the boy. Raw talent combined with a complete lack of conscience was rarer than one might think. He embraced the child like family. Then it was back to Germany, for exhaustive years of training and a complete mental wipe.

What took most agents six years, took the boy two. When he was finished, he returned to Bolivia—living in secretive isolation in a villa just six miles from the town where he grew up.

Despite all the distance he had put between them, he was never able fully to let the town go. The motacú palms and balmy afternoons by the river had a hold on him that no amount of schadenfreude could ever replace.

But while Bolivia might be home, Germany was family. So when the Director called with a special assignment—a personal favor—he was on the next flight.

He browsed through the file in the jet on the way over. Case 341. Peter Canard.

There was a list of aliases, several blurry surveillance photos, and most importantly, whatever bits of credible information on any and all active cases his agency could put together. As a rule, this intel-gathering usually only managed to glean about twelve percent of an agent's actual working history. Even so, Canard's took up the better part of forty pages. Pages the young man read with great interest as the jet broke through the clouds over Brussels.

As they touched down on the runway, the man put the file back in his bag and stared out the window with a rare smile. Finally, some fresh blood. A bit of competition. A new opponent to help him answer the age-old question…*who was better?*

* * *

"Which is better?"

Vivian held up two boxes of graham crackers with a rather distressed look on his carefully made-up face. He had been assigned a single contributive job at the weekend camp, and the perfectionist in him was terrified of blowing it on a technicality.

Michael glanced up from where he was breaking bits of chocolate and looked between the boxes with a faintly amused grin. "Have you never made s'mores before?"

Vivian bristled defensively. "I'm sorry, not all of us had a Norman Rockwell childhood."

"Yeah," Michael snorted, "'cause I definitely got that in Woodlands."

Vivian ignored him, holding up the boxes and waiting for a verdict. One claimed to have more flavor, but according to his research, the other was statistically more popular with kids.

"They all taste the same. Just put them on a plate." Michael slid a stack his way.

Vivian did as he was instructed, now directing his obsessive-compulsive focus to the arrangement, all the while shooting Michael inconspicuous looks. Finally, when the comfortable silence became too much for him to bear, he set the boxes down with a loud *thud*.

"I think you should go to seminary," he announced, smoothing down nonexistent wrinkles in his skirt.

Michael looked up in surprise, his hand paused over a pile of marshmallows. "Why is that? You want to get rid of me that bad?"

"What else would you do if you stayed here?" Vivian countered, coming around the table. *Besides get killed?*

Michael stared off for a second, before he shrugged. "I was actually thinking about switching to full-time over at the paper. They offered me the position weeks ago, but I'd been postponing until I heard back from Michigan. Now I'm thinking I might take it."

Despite his rather urgent desire for Michael to leave the city, Vivian couldn't help but pause. He'd read some of the articles Michael had written for the political circuit. They were well-researched, insightful, and as unbiased as one could be whilst still having an opinion.

"Tom asked you to work politics full-time?" he asked with a hint of pride.

Again, Michael looked surprise. "You know Tom?"

Vivian froze. Of course he didn't know Tom. But decades' worth of training didn't just go away the second he decided to play Susy Homemaker. From the moment he'd learned his son worked for the local paper, he'd done his research—involuntarily memorizing every employee, statistic, and area of distribution the company ever had. He could tell you Tom's license plate and the names of all four kids—but no—he didn't *know* Tom.

Luckily, he was saved a reply as Michael absentmindedly dismissed the question and moved on. "Yeah, he offered me full-time. But instead of politics, I was actually thinking the crime beat."

A stack of unfortunate graham crackers shattered under Vivian's hand as he looked up with admirable nonchalance. "Why crime? I thought you loved politics."

"I do, it's just..." After another moment's consideration, Michael suddenly put both hands on the table, staring across with intense focus. "Do you remember I told you I went for a walk in the park a couple of days ago?"

Vivian remembered the day all too well, in person. He slowly nodded his head and Michael continued.

"Well there were these two guys there—just your average thugs—waving some picture around of a guy they were looking to jump. In a park full of kids, right?" He picked up the slab of chocolate and began breaking it into smaller shards, with perhaps a little more force than was required. "It just gets under my skin. And that's not nearly the worst of it. This entire town is just riddled with guys like that—most of those kids will probably grow up to join them."

"I think that's why camps like this are such a good idea," Vivian redirected gently. "It keeps them off the streets and the church gives them that sense of stability—"

"But why not go right to the source?" Michael asked heatedly, an unexpected and unprovoked rush of blood coloring his skin.

Vivian proceeded carefully, gauging his son's every reaction.

"Michael, you'd be working at the paper to report the news. Not to influence it." There was a pause. "What...exactly are you suggesting?"

For a split second Michael stared across the room as a very peculiar expression darkened his face. Then he shook his head quickly and continued on with the chocolate.

"Nothing. I'm suggesting nothing."

* * *

From Brussels, it was straight back to the jet and on to New York. The Director had been very clear. This was a flight risk, and a dangerous man. Extreme caution must be exerted so as not to spook him, lest he vanish forever. However, once the target was attained, extreme creativity must be used in his elimination. The Director had said this last part with a smile, knowing full well his young friend would understand. They shared a similar love of destroying things. While others found it necessary, they found it engaging—therapeutic, even.

This Peter Canard was slated to receive the best of the best.

He hopped in a rental car from JFK and headed straight to Woodlands. He'd looked at a map of the town on the flight over, as well as the open case file on the missing agents first sent to retrieve him. Everything relevant was committed to memory. Everything irrelevant was also committed to memory, lest it become relevant on some later date.

On the way there, he stopped at a local hardware store and picked up a bundle of rope, some masking tape, a plastic tarp, a pair of pliers, and as unlikely as it seemed—a traffic cone.

Yep. Case 341 was going to be one for the books.

* * *

"Each life is precious; the Lord tells us. Each life is a gift."

Pastor Jeff opened his arms wide, staring around the circle of faces before him.

"It may be easy for us to disregard this. For us to wake up in the morning and fall into a mindless routine. For us to label people as 'expendable,' even if we don't realize we're doing it. The homeless man sitting on the side of the road, the addicts passed out behind the rec center on Seventh. Even you. It may be easy to look in the mirror some days and think, 'Even I'm expendable. What would it really matter if I was gone?'"

Michael's eyes followed Jeff's as they flickered around the camp. The local high school had recently done a suicide prevention assembly after one of the sophomores had jumped off an overpass into oncoming traffic. This little sermon was designed to casually coincide. The fact that Elsie had almost fallen through the lake only bolstered its claim.

"But you're wrong." Jeff smiled. "Matthew six verse twenty-six tells us, 'Look at the birds of the air, for they neither sow nor reap nor gather into barns; yet your heavenly Father feeds them. Are you not of more value than they?'"

He walked around the circle, looking at no one in particular and yet looking at everyone at the same time.

"God created the birds. Painted the wings on the butterflies. Knows every blade of grass on every mountain in every country in the world. And you—human beings who move, and think, and breathe, and commune with Him through prayer—you think *you* can slip through the cracks? That no one will care if *you're* gone? That GOD won't notice?"

He came to a stop in front of the unlit bonfire, holding up a long match.

"*Each* life is important. Each life is precious."

The match dropped into the center, and an explosion of flames shot into the sky.

"Each life…is a gift."

* * *

The fire must have been over twenty feet high. The heat produced by the accelerant was enough to remove any physical evidence from the car. It was a process the man did every time he travelled. Even mindless, routine necessities like rental cars and hotel rooms had to be carefully handled. Some of the greatest names in the business had been taken down by chance coincidences—random discoveries of DNA that snowballed to catastrophic effect. He would not be one of these.

The hardware clerk, too, had been a mindless necessity.

Normally, the man would never have grouped so many possibly suspicious items together in one shopping trip, but time was of the essence here, and he didn't have the luxury of taking all the precautions he'd liked. When the clerk—a student at the local community college—had made a poorly timed joke about, 'all he needed now was cable ties and a good lawyer,' he'd taken her behind the store and shot her in the head.

What was left of her was vanishing now in the car, as well as any stray hairs or accidental fingerprints he might have left behind. The last thing he tossed in was her license. It held up for only a second, before a sudden hole appeared in the picture of her face, slowly spreading its way out until every trace of the girl was gone.

The man watched the flames shoot high into the sky before he started walking slowly across the deserted field. The faint lights of Woodlands were just visible on the horizon, and if he kept up a brisk pace, he would be there well before morning.

* * *

The amber light from the coals danced in Vivian's troubled eyes. The s'mores had been distributed and were being happily gobbled down, but he was too fixated on Jeff's sermon to take much notice.

Each life was precious… Each one was lovingly made by God…

It was strange, he realized. He had been programmed to be a walking encyclopedia—to never forget a thing. Roads, taverns, politician's dogs—he remembered all of them by name. The day he'd gotten his first list of assignments, was one of the proudest days of his life. He'd torn through it like the world was on fire, eliminating each one was a casual squeeze of his finger.

He'd been programmed to remember *everything*…but that list? That oh-so important list?

He couldn't remember a single name.

A strange tingling came over him as he bowed his head to the trembling flames, like a giant hand was curving him over, blanketing his whole body. His fingers started trembling and for the first time in his life, a great feeling of accountability settled on him like a weight. That conscience, which had been stamped out of him in his own version of Brussels, drew its first breath in years.

God had made these people...and he had killed them.

There was no more explanation needed than that. No amount of rationalization or bargaining would ever make it anything better than it was. It was murder. He was a murderer. A murderer of all the Lord's precious things...

Across the fire, Michael was also looking into the flames. But in his mind, a very different battle was waging on.

If every life was precious to God, then why were murderers allowed to roam free? Gotten off on some technicality and then released back into the world to blend in with the rest of society, like nothing had ever happened? If each creation was so important, then why were some allowed to die? Thoughtless acts of thoughtless violence. The kind that a place like Woodlands saw every day. The guys at the park, the drug-dealers beneath the bridge, the fact that no even vaguely-supervised child was allowed outside alone after seven in the evening?

Something had to be done. *Somebody* had to do something.

And if that somebody wasn't going to be God...then why not him?

'Vengeance is mine, sayeth the Lord.' He could almost hear the opposing council raging on in his mind, rallying against what sounded a lot like vigilante justice.

He leaned in towards the fire as the beginnings of a plan began to take hold. Something that couldn't be reasoned away with logic or prayer. A compulsion he felt deep in his bones.

Vengeance is mine.

But what if the Lord needed a little help...?

CHAPTER

13

"So Michael, what is it exactly that drew you to our seminary?"

Anchored to the ground in a stiff little folding chair, Michael shifted uncomfortably in his seat. He felt like he was under a spotlight. The ceiling fan creaked with every turn, there was a high-pitched hum coming from an old printer perched on the desk, and the relentless glow from the fluorescent lights made him feel like he was trapped in some kind of time loop.

Everything about the place was perfectly staged. Even the politely smiling caseworker, who he had seen check him out on his way in here.

What a sham. It took everything in him not to wink.

"I'm sorry," he answered distractedly, flashing a quick smile, "what was that?"

196 | ANTHONY WILLIAMS

The woman—easily twenty years his senior—smiled indulgently back, leaning back in her chair whilst pretending not to drink him in with her eyes.

"There are seminaries all over the country. What was it that attracted you to ours?"

He ran his fingers quickly through his hair as he tried to think of a suitable response.

Jeff had set up this meeting for him. And had called three times just to remind him.

"This is so exciting, Michael!" he had exclaimed, no doubt thumbing through the brochure on his side of the phone. "And to think…all the way over in Michigan."

All the way over in Michigan. Right. Just three states away. What a stretch.

"Uh…I've been following Pastor Kent for quite some time, and when I heard about the residency he took in Grand Rapids teaching…"

Fortunately, autopilot took over and the words flowed out of him without him really having to think. But truth be told, when the question was put in front of him just like that…he couldn't think of a single thing in the world drawing him towards the seminary.

What had his reasons been before? In the weeks before his heart transplant, he hadn't been able to sit still just thinking about it. He'd talk anyone's ear off for hours at a time. The men at the coffee shop had instituted an unofficial ban of the subject.

But now?

"—two year and a four-year program." The woman was delivering a return speech of her own, prattling on about some logistical technicalities as her eyes soaked in every detail of his face. "Now, which would you say you were more interested in? Your file doesn't say."

His heart picked up speed as she flipped absentmindedly through a manila folder in front of her. There was a thin sheen of sweat on his forehead and his skin seemed to jump with every deafening tick of the second-hand clock.

It had to be close to a hundred degrees in the little office. And how was that buzzing printer not bothering anyone else? He couldn't even hear himself think—

"I'm sorry," he got suddenly to his feet, startling her as he towered over the tiny desk, "I know you're only in town for a few days, but would it be possible for us to reschedule?"

She stood up as well, staring him up and down in concern. "Yes, of course, dear. Is everything alright?"

Pull it together, Michael!

He took a deep breath and his face melted into a charming smile. The one he used to flash to get out of turning in homework on time. The same one that had gotten him into the beds of more women than this admissions counselor could shake a judgmental stick at.

It didn't fail him now. Already, he could see the tiny facial muscles worrying the woman's brow begin to relax as the corners of her lips turned up in automatic reply.

"It's one of the kids I mentor. He's getting out of juvenile detention today, and I really wanted to be there to pick him up. Show of support, and all…"

The woman visibly melted. "Oh, well that's…that's just wonderful. Not about his arrest, of course," she floundered, unnecessarily smoothing down her hair. "But it's good to know that he has a support system waiting for him. That's exactly the kind of thing we look for when considering applicants."

Michael pretended to look surprised, like the thought hadn't occurred to him, before thanking her again for her time and sweeping out the door. He almost threw in a kiss on the cheek, but he didn't want to push his luck so soon after resurrecting the legendary smile.

The cold air revived him the second it hit his face, and he breathed in deep gulps of it as he jogged quickly down the steps.

He didn't know what he'd tell Jeff when he asked how the meeting went. Right now, he didn't care. He was free of that dismal little office, back out on the streets—the world at his fingertips.

A world that was a lot bigger than the space between New York to Michigan…

"Mikey?"

His hand shot out to grip the railing as his feet stumbled on the stairs. He knew that voice. And only one person in the whole world had ever called him *Mikey*.

He turned around, a look of sheer astonishment on his face. "Alex?"

She looked exactly how he remembered. Long curly hair, smooth brown skin, seductive little smile. Her body was tiny, but with curves. Curves that, since they'd met in the sixth grade, she'd delighted in presenting to the world in a series of low-cut dresses and mouthwatering tops.

Today, she didn't disappoint.

She was his first crush. His first kiss. His first…well, a lot of things.

His mind flickered back a million miles a minute to a life he'd actively forbidden himself to think about. To a world that, four years ago, he'd made the decision to leave behind.

And there were reasons for that, Michael.

His time with Alex, or Alexandra Morales—as the rest of the world knew her, hadn't always been a good one.

They had fights. Huge, epic fights. The kind where she'd end up throwing a beer bottle at his head, and he'd end up punching a hole in the wall. They made up for their passionate battles with other passions in turn. Emotional whiplash became such a cornerstone of their relationship, that eventually, it was easiest to turn emotions off all together and live solely in the moment.

It was life on the edge of a razor—you never knew which way you were going to fall, but you couldn't well stay where you were standing.

And while Alex might have been what he'd once call his first love, she was a lot of other firsts too.

She was the first person he knew who overdosed. She was the first person who drove him to the ER when he overdosed just two weeks after. She was his first pregnancy scare, and the first girl he'd ever gotten into a fight for. The first person he saw every afternoon when he woke up still black-out drunk, stuck to the top of his mattress.

She was the person he'd been planning to cheat on that night under the bridge. The night when he'd stared down his own mortality from the wrong side of a gun.

"Alex," he said again, shaking his head as if to clear it. "I can't believe you're..." a quick recovery, "it's so good to see you."

They embraced in a rather awkward hug. There hadn't been many of those in the six years they were off and on dating. There was screaming, and screwing. With not a lot in between.

"What are you doing here?" he asked as they pulled away. His eyes flickered up to the building she'd just walked out of. Juvenile Holding. "You work here now?" She did look even more dolled up than usual—although the black skirt she was wearing stopped mid-thigh.

She shook her head. "Carly. I came to pick her up, but they say she won't be ready for another few hours."

Michael nodded quickly to hide his surprise, offering a simple, "Oh."

Carlita was Alex's younger sister. She'd only been about five-years-old the last time Michael had seen her, and to be honest, like most others, it was a night he barely remembered.

"Geez, Carly," he continued, running his hands back through his hair as he pictured the rosy-faced toddler. "I can't believe she's even old enough to—" He stopped himself immediately, eyes darting nervously to Alex.

Much to his relief, she was smiling. Rather mischievously, actually. "What? Like you and I weren't already regulars in that place by the time we were her age?"

A faint blush colored Michael's cheeks and he grinned down at the cement.

"Yeah, I guess."

He'd come to terms with the fact that his life before the church had been an absolute misery. He just hadn't run into too many people he'd known before to remind him. And that wasn't by coincidence, it was by design. A very careful, preemptive design.

"Well, listen," he was suddenly a bit nervous to be spending any more time around Alex than was absolutely necessary, "I've got to run, but—"

"What the hell is that?!"

Before he knew what was happening, she had slid her fingers inside the base of his v-neck shirt, tracing them lightly down the bright pink scar and taking a step forward to see even further. He pulled in a quick breath as her perfume wafted over him. The same scent she'd been wearing since they were fifteen. His skin shivered in excitement and remembrance beneath her hands, and for a moment, he lost all track of what he'd been saying before.

"I'm sorry," he automatically apologized, frozen in place, "hmm?"

She smiled. A smile just as cute as his was charming. They'd used them together many, many times. "Did you finally get a new heart, Mikey? After all this time?"

For a second, all the playful banter was gone. The smile turned sincere.

Despite all the theatrics, fighting, and sex, they had been friends before they'd been lovers. Two young kids confiding in each other on the front porch steps of the Y.

She told him all about her series of abusive step-fathers, shuddering as she showed him every bruise and scar. He'd told her about the ticking time bomb in his chest—the thing the doctors denied, but he knew was eventually going to kill him. The first time he'd told her, she'd taken his hand. He remembered feeing strangely proud—hoping someone he knew would happen to walk by and see them.

"I did." He beamed back at her. "Just a few weeks ago, actually."

"That's incredible!" she exclaimed, taking his hand once again. Then she raised a pair of delicate eyebrows and cocked her hips. "So…you probably still can't go out and do anything fun, huh? No drinking, running…no sex?"

It never failed to startle him. How blunt she always was. And how transparent.

"I can do all those things just fine," he grinned, playing along. "But no, they're probably not…doctor recommended."

They both laughed until they were just smiling at each other in silence. Neither one had taken a step back to correct the proximity she'd created in seeing the scar, and neither one seemed at all inclined to. It wasn't until she lifted a tentative hand to his chest, that Michael suddenly recovered himself and pulled away.

"I've gotta go." He was breathing much faster than usual; the smell of that damn perfume was making his head spin. "I'm having a friend from church over for dinner—"

"Mikey? It's noon."

He stammered and blushed again, but she smiled even wider—not the least bit put out by his attempts to dodge her. Quite the contrary, she seemed to rise to the occasion.

"But yeah—that tracks. I told everyone when you disappeared that you'd gotten a new girlfriend," she teased. "The Christ."

Why wouldn't his face stop blushing?! He used to be so much cooler than this!

"It's not like that," he said half-heartedly, forcing his eyes to stay above her chin.

"Perfect!" In the blink of an eye, she linked her arm through his and began leading him away down the steps. "Then you can take me out to lunch—until Carly gets out of holding," she added when he opened his mouth to protest.

He stared down at her, a million excuses racing to mind—a million reasons not to go.

Then he smiled. "Lunch it is."

* * *

What should have been a simple outing, turned into a very drawn out affair. Alex had this way about her, that from the time they had met—made Michael forget any and all prior commitments the second she walked into the room. He and every other man in a ten-mile radius.

He watched thoughtfully as their waiter gawked openly at her breasts, hands fumbling all over the table as he attempted to clear away their drinks. She'd had a whiskey sour; he'd had an iced tea. A fact that had stirred up more than a little controversy between them.

"Alright Mikey, I let you off the hook the first time, but now you have to get a drink. And by a drink, I mean something they don't serve at the retirement home down the street." She and the waiter shared a conspiratorial grin. "So what'll it be?"

Michael's spine stiffened as his fingers drummed nervously on the table. The last time he'd had a drink had been four years ago, the night his friends were killed. The last time he'd had a drink, he had vowed would be the *last time* he had a drink.

But as usual, something about being with Alex made him forget all that. What was the harm in a simple cocktail? He'd just come from a seminary meeting, for crying out loud. He was the poster boy for rehabilitation. Why not treat himself a little?

Anticipating more resistance, she leaned innocently across the table, giving both Michael and the star-struck waiter a generous view down her blouse. "Shall we have your regular? Rum and coke—no coke?"

He held out for only a second more, before surrendering with a smile. "Sure. Well, actually—let's make it whiskey. Jameson."

She chuckled in surprise as the waiter rushed off to make it so. "Rye whiskey? When did that happen?"

He leaned back in his chair, feeling considerably more relaxed now that the first line of defense had been broken. "Actually, I don't know. Just feels right."

The drinks arrived on a wet tray, and the two of them clinked glasses as the waiter vanished into a pool of jealousy and lust.

Alex's eyes sparkled at Michael over the rim of her glass as she waited for him to propose a toast.

"To you," he indulged her. "Still making me do things I don't want to do."

She laughed again—a dangerous, sparkling sound that warmed his blood whilst raising the hairs on the back of his neck. "It's an art form. I could teach a class."

Five minutes later, they were through their third round. Ten minutes later, their fourth. A couple minutes after that, she was straddling him in the back seat of her car with her shirt off.

"Actually, I don't know if I should be doing this," Michael panted as she ripped off his shirt as well. The words were slightly slurred, all his former tolerance stripped clean away from lack of use. "As I remember it…you can get a little rough."

They shared a grin, both remembering years of bruised lips and long scratches raked across their skin. Then she shifted strategically in place and his head fell back against the leather.

"Don't worry baby, I'll be gentle." She tossed back her messy curls and slid gracefully off of him onto the floor, flashing a wicked smile as her fingers skillfully unbuckled the top of his pants. "In fact, all you have to do is sit there."

The windows had fogged beyond visibility, and she'd parked on the far end of the lot. No one was going to see. No one was going to know.

He said a silent prayer for strength, glanced at all the exits, and then watched as her head disappeared below the chair…

* * *

There wasn't a sound in the kitchen as Vivian stared unblinkingly out the window. His bags from camp still sat unpacked by the front door, and aside from the one window in question, all the curtains were drawn tight.

How could things have spun so far out of control? How could things have gotten away from him so fast?

When he'd first arrived in Woodlands, his son had gotten a new heart. A lifelong worry, a lifelong dream were all solved with death of a single assassin. He'd done all but giftwrap the solution with a bloody bow. Flesh for flesh. A life for a life. For a person trained in the art of making order from chaos, silencing a thousand screaming voices with a single shot—it was hard not to admire the symmetry. Rarely were these things so simple. Rarely were they so clean.

But it was the aftermath that was troubling him. The aftermath that had his eyes fixed on that one open window.

He'd talked to Michael immediately after the surgery—heard him profess his faith. He learned about his son through the testimony of others, came to see it with his own eyes, shining through him like a beacon in the dark.

But now…?

The Michael he'd first met in Woodlands, was not the same Michael who was with him at camp. Not the same Michael he'd heard about all those years from Dr. Price. Something had changed inside him, and Vivian didn't, for the life of him, know what that change was.

And although it stunned him to admit it, Michael was not the only one changed.

Vivian couldn't shake the feeling he'd gotten that night at the bonfire. He couldn't escape the weight of it. The heavy sinking in his chest every time he tried to remember those names.

But for the first time in longer than he could remember, there was a light at the end of the tunnel. A possibility for reprieve. A chance to start anew. Just like his son had done, just four years before.

Yes, they'd both been granted a new life when Vivian had raced into Woodlands that night with a body bleeding out in the back of his trunk. But what was troubling him, the feeling he was trying so hard to shake…was that only one of them was taking it.

Why was seminary off the table? Why was politics being abandoned for crime? What exactly had Michael meant when he said, 'why not go right to the source?'

A knock at the door roused him from his introspection and he got slowly to his feet to answer it, his mind still a million miles away.

There were other reasons, other than spiritual reasons, for him wanting Michael to get as far away from Woodlands as possible.

Lucius Montana was a big name in his industry. A name that commanded almost as much fear and respect as Peter Canard. A death like his wouldn't go unnoticed by the other side. It was too big a slight. Too big a blow to go unchecked. The team that Michael had talked to in the park—the ones that were currently sitting in piles of ash at the bottom of an industrial-grade incinerator at the far end of town—would not be the last.

In fact, they were sure to be just the beginning.

And not every team would be so lenient. Not every team would be so restrained. If Michael, with this newfound 'clean up the streets' attitude of his, mouthed off to the wrong person? He'd get a bullet in the chest. And that new heart of his would all be for nothing.

The knocking started again, and Vivian called an irritable, "I'm coming," as he padded across the hardwood floor.

Maybe Dr. Price was right. Maybe he never should have come here. Or rather, he should have dropped of Montana's body and then run for the hills.

It had been selfish to assume that just because he loved Michael, he had any right to be in his life. There was a reason assassins didn't have families. The job implied that you cut ties. And now, for him to have brought those shadows with him back to Michael? All just to get to know his, son? It was unforgivable.

Vivian shook his head and smoothed down his skirt as he reached for the door.

And in what capacity did he really *know* Michael anyway? He was wearing a damn dress. He'd changed his name to Vivian. His own child thought he was a widow searching for a fresh start. A woman whose husband had died in Afghanistan.

Really, he thought as he unlocked the door. *Where did that leave them?*

*   *   *

"Are you sure this is okay?" Michael gasped as he and Alex half fell-through his front door. "What about Carly?"

"I texted my aunt to pick her up." Alex was having a hard time extracting her lips from his and she hitched her legs up higher around his waist. "She'll be fine."

"Okay. Good."

He started walking them backwards to the bedroom, kicking the front door shut while clumsily navigating his way across the carpet.

"What about you?" she asked breathlessly, kissing a wet trail up his neck. "Don't you have your church person coming over for dinner?"

"Shit." Michael glanced at the clock, before turning back to her. "No—I have a little time."

She shook her head as he started down the hall and pointed instead to the couch. It was closer. He immediately complied and lowered her down, holding his weight gently above her.

There was a reason doctors told you not to have sex too soon after a major surgery. He'd realized this after they'd done it the first time in the car. His entire body was aching with a pain and fatigue he hadn't known for a long time. The line running down his chest felt like at any moment, it might rip back open, and there was a dull throbbing in his head he was finding difficult to ignore.

Maybe that was just the booze, he thought, ripping off her jacket and throwing it on the ground.

Whatever the reason, he quite simply didn't care. Because while he was feeling all sorts of new kinds of awful—it had been years since he felt so alive.

A boiling mix of blood and adrenaline was flying through his veins, his new heart was pounding. When she slid off her pants and pulled the two of them together, it was like no time had passed. They were teenagers again. Their whole lives ahead of them. Nothing but time.

* * *

The door smashed in before Vivian could open it, splintering into his face at the same time that a small shadow hurled itself through the frame.

With most anyone else, Vivian's reflexes, stunned though they were, would have been enough to shield the blow. But with his mind sluggish with forbidden emotions and the newfound weight of a conscience holding him back, he wasn't able to raise his hands in time.

A sharp kick to the face sent him flying, landing on the ground amongst the shards. Then, before he could recover his senses, a pair of small hands was dragging him to the kitchen.

The lights from the clock on the VCR blurred before his eyes as his cheek slid roughly along the carpet. The red lines slowly wound themselves into numbers, which slowly translated into a single, panicked thought.

Oh God…Michael!

A flood of adrenaline coursed through him, as Vivian fell away and Peter Canard leapt suddenly to his feet. The young man went flying as Canard caught him behind the knees, but he was able to steady himself quickly, coming to rest upon the counter, perching atop it like a bird.

He chuckled softly, as Peter took a step back as he surveyed his attacker for the first time.

His first reaction was surprise. This kid was barely older than Michael. And while Peter might have taken notice if someone built like Michael wandered up to his door, the man in front of him didn't warrant a second thought.

He was tiny, by all standards. Fit, but small. With drooping eyes and a rather lopsided smile, one that widened exponentially when he saw Peter staring.

"Case 341," the man said softly. "It's an honor to finally meet you."

Peter blinked. 341? The kid was talking in case files?

An image flashed through his head—a man he'd met long ago. A headhunter of sorts, offering an employment opportunity that Peter had eventually passed on to chase after another. The man had gone on to do rather well for himself, however, building an agency of his own. In some circles, he was known as 'the Director.' In others, he was merely called, 'Germany.'

Either way, Peter had a nagging suspicion that this young man had met the Director before. That the case file in question, had German roots.

"I'm Geo," he said suddenly, extending his hand in a way that seemed almost normal.

Peter blinked again and cocked his head to the side, wishing for the millionth time in the space of just a few seconds that he wasn't wearing a dress. "Of course you are. I'm Peter."

Geo smiled again. "Of course you are."

He had an accent that Peter was finding hard to place. Somewhere in South America, surely. Maybe Bolivia? Peru?

Peter threw up his hands and gestured to his suddenly destroyed kitchen. "Well, I would have invited you inside, but it seemed you already made yourself quite at home."

Geo's eyes never left his face.

"The Director sends his regards."

Ah—so it was the Director after all. That was actually going to pose quite a bit of a problem. One that Peter would have to rectify the second this little bastard was in the incinerator with the rest of his friends.

He shook his head. "It's certainly been a while. Tell me— how long have you been working for him?"

Geo's eyes flashed almost defensively, and his voice took on the hint of a scowl.

"Long enough. Long enough to be assigned to you—the great Peter Canard." He smiled to himself again before shaking his head, keeping his eyes locked on Peter all the while. "The idiot, really. I mean, how stupid do you really have to be—to go and get yourself a kid?"

He dodged the knife Peter threw at him with the greatest of ease, sliding slowly off the counter as it clattered to the floor behind him.

"That's it? We're done talking already. I've been thinking about what to say for hours, you see. The whole way over on the plane. I've been wondering what I want to ask the man whose file is actually longer than my own."

Peter's eyes held no hint of a smile any longer. It had vanished the second Geo mentioned he had a child. "Well it takes a *big* man to admit that. Thank you."

Geo didn't rise to the bait, he merely looked at him curiously, staring intently through those droopy eyes. "And the question is obvious: why did you do it? Why did you have this, *Michael?*" He said the name with distinct derision, staring at Peter as though he'd done something embarrassing. "You had such an illustrious career. You were respected. Feared. And while your file doesn't state your age, I can only imagine how very long that must have taken to build." He cocked his head to the side. "So why did you do it, Peter Canard? Why Michael?"

The logic and reasoning centers of Peter's brain shut off as Geo said the magic word.

"Because Michael is the only thing that matters."

Then the two of them flew towards each other in the dark.

* * *

"*That* is the Michael that I remember," Alex murmured contentedly, leaning her head back against his chest. "Not this iced tea drinker."

He chuckled and wrapped her tighter in his arms. The two of them were nestled together on the little couch, using his long overcoat as a blanket. After the first time, there had been another, and another. By all accounts they would have continued right on through the night, if Michael had not fallen suddenly back in a blur of pain, clutching at his recently ravaged skin.

The second he had, she'd flipped like a light. Shifting from a raging sex tigress, into the gentlest of companions. She ran to the medicine cabinet and grabbed a handful of his pills. Then she pushed aside the remnants of the congregational casseroles with disgust and reached back in the fridge until she'd pulled out a bottle of water for him to wash them down.

The water was followed by two shooters of tequila she pulled out of her purse—leftovers from a bachelorette party she couldn't remember—and the two of them toasted all over again.

This time—to him. To 'coming full circle,' she called it.

"Seriously though," she rolled over to get a better look, careful not to place any weight on his chest, "I miss you Mikey. I don't want this to be the last time I see you again."

He swept back her hair with one hand, cradling her face with the other.

She was still so beautiful—despite all the horrors that had darkened her life. She remained bright. As bright as she'd been the day they'd met at the Y.

"I don't want it to be the last time, either," he murmured, hearing the words before he made the conscious effort to say them.

She grinned and he kissed the tip of her nose. There was no need to catch up—to fill each other in on everything that had happened in the last four years. That's why God made sex. So that none of that ever had to happen.

Her eyes closed and she leaned back against him, her light fingers tracing once more up and down his scar. "I'd ask if I could stay over, but I know you have that church friend—"

"*Shit!*"

The next second he was on his feet, looking around the sex-ravaged living room in dismay. She rolled onto the floor with a thud and a giggle as she peered up at him, still naked, staring wildly around.

"Alex, you've got to get out of here!" He glanced at the clock and paled, scooping up the empty tequila bottles and stuffing them back into her purse. "I can't believe she's not here yet!"

Alex pulled his jacket up around him and gave him a rather frosty look. "*She?*"

He rolled his eyes, tossing over her bra and panties. "*She* is like forty years old. She's been helping me with my rehab. Something that *you* worked very hard to undermine today."

Another giggle. "You need a little adversity in your life, or you'll never learn to grow."

"Yeah, I remember that poster from juvy. Get up—you need to leave."

She got lazily to her feet, pulling on her clothes in slow motion. "Why exactly do I need to leave? You don't want me to stay, so you can introduce me to your friend?"

She was teasing him, but he was too panicked to realize it—darting all over the room, picking up the evidence of their misdeeds, periodically clutching his chest.

"What? Uh—no, it's not that. You'd, uh, you'd actually probably maybe really like her…"

"Mikey!" She tossed a pillow at his face to stop his perpetual motion. "I'd *actually probably maybe really* like her?" she repeated with a grin. "After all that, I'd better."

He flashed her a pained look and she held up her hands.

"Relax—I'm gone. But know this, *Michael,* now that I found out your dirty little secret, you're going to have a hard time keeping me away from this place."

"My dirty little secret?" he asked, pulling open the door. "And what's that?"

She hopped up on her toes and kissed the tip of his nose. Then bit him sharply on the lips.

"You're not as good as you want everyone to think you are…"

Without another word, she winked and disappeared into the night, still glowing from the high of her victory and the promise of many more to come.

His eyes followed her until she rounded the corner and disappeared from sight. One hand came up automatically to his incision, while the other dabbed his mouth for blood.

That wasn't right, was it? It wasn't like this was some kind of act. This was his life now.

And furthermore, it wasn't like they had done anything wrong. Sure, he'd indulged in alcohol and Alex—two things he'd sworn to forever stay away from. But it's not like those things were sins. And he was a grown man. It was his life—to do with whatever he so desired.

A small nagging voice begged to disagree, but he silenced it without another thought and settled down on the couch to wait for Vivian's arrival.

He would be waiting a long time…

CHAPTER

14

"I have to give it to you, Canard. I'm impressed."

There was a slight scuffling sound and some water splashed out of the tub.

"Most men would have broken hours ago."

Under the cracked bulbs in the dimly lit bathroom, both men knelt upon a sea of broken mirrored glass. But while Geo was in full command of himself, Vivian was bound and gagged, head beneath the surface of the water, as a flood of narcotics circled his veins.

The pressure of Geo's hand let up for a split second, and Vivian was allowed to breathe.

The night wasn't always on track to end this way. In fact, until very recently, it had been Geo who'd been at the mercy of Vivian. The initial fight might have lasted longer than what was considered normal, but it was clear that one of the men had an upper hand. Vivian had simply been doing this sort of dance for years longer than his young counterpart, and his experience showed.

It wasn't until a missed call from Michael distracted him, that Geo was able to stab him with a syringe full of sedatives.

Now, the tables had turned. A fact that Geo was enjoying immensely.

There was an art to torture through drowning. The main objective wasn't to actually kill the subject, after all, only to induce fear. Therefore, a certain amount of oxygen was a requirement to get satisfactory results.

Whether Geo happened to know this or not, he had decided to take a different path.

The hand let up again, and Vivian collapsed on the shards of glass, panting as well as he could through the drugs and the gag. The suffocating pairing, combined with the water and Geo's heavy hand, had completely incapacitated him—stripping him of all usual sensitivity and making it hard for him to follow much of anything his captor had to say.

Compliments? Was that the part of the monologue they were on now? For all his efforts to prove himself as one-of-a-kind, Geo had shown a proclivity to first master the classics—the classics being what Vivian could only describe as a badly drawn villainous cartoon.

Who knows? Maybe the kid had grown up watching Brando films.

As if sensing Vivian's waterlogged judgement, Geo abruptly released his hold.

"This isn't my usual custom," he blurted, as if suddenly embarrassed. "But the Director asked me to make sure that your death was an…interesting experience. One that included not only you, but those ones that you hold dear. As payment for his friend." With surprisingly delicate hands, he leaned forward and wiped off Vivian's face with a dry towel. "I'm sure you understand."

Vivian blinked slowly as he tried to get on top of the sedative. He cocked his head as if to speak, and ever obliging, Geo removed the gag.

"Believe it or not, I do understand. I knew that Montana would have repercussions. I'd heard of his affiliation with the Director. I simply didn't have a choice at the time."

Every second he was talking, was a second he wasn't underwater. And another second his brain had to clear the sedative from his system.

Geo was more than happy to oblige—this honor amongst thieves' bit had obviously struck a positive chord. "I appreciate that. You wouldn't believe how many men dissolve to mere animals the second their life is on the line. I'd like to think we all have it in us to be better."

Vivian resisted the urge to roll his eyes, flexing his fingers instead—regaining that delicate muscle movement he would soon need. "Well, you never know. None of us do, I suppose, until we're in the position ourselves."

"You're handling yourself quite well. Won't even give me Michael's address."

There was a brief pause in the conversation as Vivian stiffened and Geo smiled.

"I don't *need* you to give me the address, you understand. It will be the easiest thing in the world to find him." He ran his fingers back through his damp hair. "To be honest, I just needed something to ask you whilst putting you under. It seemed improper not to."

Torture room decorum. How quaint.

Again, Vivian fought back the urge to scream at the deranged man and worked instead upon now moving his wrists. It was coming back—the physical sensation—slowly but surely. He only hoped he could keep Geo talking long enough for it to work.

Fortunately for him, Geo was on a roll…

"I'm assuming he's somewhere nearby—within easy driving distance so you can keep an eye on him. And since this entire area is depressingly low-rent, I'm guessing security won't be a problem." He grinned again and knelt down to be on Vivian's level. "Of course, I could always procure it from the hospital records…but I'd like to have a bit of a challen—"

A piece of glass slashed across his throat—just centimeters from severing his windpipe.

He went reeling back as Vivian went reeling forward, using the superior weight of his body to knock the little man off-balance. They came down hard upon the shattered tile, and twisting around, Vivian was able to get in three good punches.

But unfortunately, that was where his advantage came to a sudden end. He hadn't been able to put enough force into the glass to do any lasting damage, and Geo was too much of a professional to succumb to shock.

In a series of quick movements, Vivian was back against the door, knocked senseless by a kick to the face. His eyes blinked slowly up and down, watching in stilted pieces as Geo calmly located a new hand-towel from beneath the sink, doused it in sanitizer, and pressed it to his neck.

"Again," his voice was a bit scratchy now, but was no less controlled than before. "I'm impressed."

"I do what I can," Vivian panted, pulling himself up on the side of the tub. "Guess I'm not the gentleman we both thought."

Geo looked at him for a moment, before smirking at the dress. "No, I'm afraid that ship has sailed."

His fingers fumbled in his pocket for a moment, before he pulled out the same little glass bottle he'd used before and filled another syringe, plunging it into the crook of Vivian's elbow and pressing down the stopper.

"Time for some more," he murmured as he worked.

In spite of the adrenaline coursing through his blood, Vivian felt himself physically numb and relaxed as the new wave of narcotics entered his system. It was actually rather generous; he knew enough to admit. There were certain paralytics that did nothing to desensitize the nerves—these were the kind he traditionally favored himself. But Geo was allowing him a brief respite from the pain. Most likely so that they could talk some more.

As psychotic the young assassin might be, he wore his loneliness on his sleeve. Vivian remembered the feeling well. The life required almost total isolation. It was a rare opportunity indeed to be able to speak to someone on the same level.

"So tell me the story here," Geo said as he leaned back against the counter, dabbing occasionally at his neck. "You get some woman pregnant, abandon her and her son, and then come back years later with a stolen heart and a brand-new life as a cross-dresser."

Vivian's lip split open as he grinned in spite of himself. "Something like that." He licked away the blood and leveled the young man with his eyes. "Sounds crazy, doesn't it?"

Geo considered. "Not as crazy as some things. I knew a woman once who spent an entire year wearing the carcass of the leopard who killed her fiancé. Granted, most of us thought she had gone a bit unhinged at the time…"

Vivian hitched himself up higher, panting with the effort. "That's a sweet story."

"So this Michael," Geo continued, "do you still think it was worth it?"

Time seemed to slow as Vivian stared at him for a second more. Then his mouth stretched up into a slow smile.

"What kind of gun do you use?"

Geo glanced down at his shirt. "Actually, it's a…"

He stopped cold.

When he looked back up, his own gun was pointing directly at his face.

While the rest of Vivian's body may have been shaking, his hands were dead still, levelling the barrel at his opponent's face.

Stealing the weapon had been surprisingly easy, a simple lift made when he tackled Geo moments before.

As his finger stretched for the trigger, he graciously inclined his head.

"Let me take this time to say, Geo, that *I'm* impressed." His hand tightened on the grip in anticipation. "And I can't tell you how pleased I am that it's me who gets to do this."

He pulled the trigger.

Only…nothing happened.

The corner of Geo's mouth twitched up in a smile that didn't reach his eyes. Without breaking Vivian's gaze, he reached slowly into his pocket and pulled out the loaded clip.

"I never intended to kill you, Peter Canard. Not today. Not with that gun."

He got to his feet slowly, furious at having lost his weapon, but reining it in nicely.

"Not when there's so much more ahead…"

The door banged open, and then he was gone. A second later, the front door banged shut.

It was over. At least…for now.

* * *

Michael didn't know how early was too early, but when the ever-punctual Vivian didn't return his call by seven the next morning, he figured he should go over there. After all, she usually turned up at his house around that time to begin his therapy, and it wasn't like her to miss a dinner without so much as a call.

He pulled out of the driveway and headed down the street with his head still swimming with thoughts of Alex. Thoughts of Alex…and a great deal of accompanying guilt.

After waking up with a hangover for the first time in over four years, he was starting to see things in a sharper perspective. Alex was like a gateway drug. One that could lead down a slippery slope if he were to let it. He didn't like that he knew he would deliberately withhold the fact that he'd seen her to those people closest to him—the people who cared about him the most.

Already, the lies were quick to surface.

He'd gone to bed early. Passed out while reading a book. Supposed to have dinner with Vivian and lost track of time. How did the meeting with the seminary admissions office go?

Well…on that one, he could most likely tell the truth.

A little smile played about his lips as he remembered how charmed the representative had been by his story—like putty in his hands. He'd forgotten what it felt like to have that kind of power over people. Since 'the night,' he'd upped the general age demographic he spent his time with by about twenty years, and dropped it by another fifteen. He was immune to the influences of people his own age (in a town like Woodlands, it seemed like the best bet if he wanted to stay clean), and thus, they were immune to him.

Until yesterday. Yesterday was a re-awakening. Of so many, many things.

He was still absentmindedly grinning when he pulled into the driveway at Vivian's and turned off the car. Still smiling to himself when he jogged up the front steps to ring the bell, one hand drifting automatically to his recently battered incision. It wasn't until he realized that the door was slightly ajar that the first wave of chills ran up and down his spine.

All at once, his senses locked down and he was on his guard. This wasn't the first time he'd visited a house only to see the door lock jimmied or a screen ripped off its hinges. Each time, he hadn't liked what he'd found inside.

He entered slowly, silently—glancing around him all the while. He resisted the urge to call the police. He also resisted the urge to call out Vivian's name lest whoever had prevented her from coming to dinner was still on the premises. Instead, he picked up a fire poker without breaking stride and headed down the hall.

Amidst the waves of adrenaline pounding away in his head, he was vaguely surprised by how much he was picking up just by focusing on his surroundings. Had he always been able to hear the second-hand clock with such clarity? How had he never noticed that the wallpaper lining the halls was still intermittently raised with the occasional bubble?

Triaging each detail in order of importance, he had nearly made it to the bedroom when a sudden sound behind the bathroom door caught his attention. He whirled around, silent as a ghost, and raised the fire poker up behind his head.

Then, with a loud yell, he kicked open the door.

It was impossible to say who looked more surprised. Michael or Vivian.

"What the hell are you doing here?!" Vivian cried, at the exact moment that Michael shouted, "What the hell is going on?!"

Vivian, though startled, composed himself quickly, thanking his lucky stars that he'd already mopped up the majority of the blood from the floor.

"You first," he said sternly, eyeing the fire poker still raised in the air.

Michael lowered it slowly, paling as he looked around the room. "When you didn't show up for dinner yesterday, I thought I'd come here to make sure everything was okay. The front door was open, and…what happened in here?" His already dilated eyes widened even further when he saw the open cut on Vivian's face. "Oh my god, Vivian—are you alright?!"

"I'm just fine," Vivian answered calmly, wishing Michael would lower his voice before he woke the neighbors. "I was...robbed last night. I'm sorry Michael, in the commotion of everything that happened—I forgot to call."

As discreetly as possible, Vivian tilted his shoe to knock the empty syringe safely out of sight behind the toilet.

"Robbed..." Michael's eyes darkened with rage as he paced forward to examine the cut on his father's face. "And they did this to you? Did you get a good look at them?!"

"No," Vivian sighed, thinking of Geo's lopsided smile, "I'm afraid I didn't. But come on now, let's get you out of here—"

"*Me?*" Michael countered, resisting Vivian's hands as he was coaxingly angled towards the door. "I'm a little more worried about you right now. You say this happened last night? Why didn't you call the police?"

Vivian hesitated for a moment. The last thing he could ever do was call the police. Of course, that probably wouldn't make a lick of sense to Michael...

"Because this is Woodlands," he said shortly. "Things like this happen every day. I didn't get a good look at the guy, and even if I did, the police wouldn't be able to do a thing about it." He gestured around the house with a look of grim acceptance. "Let's face it Michael, I was due."

But Michael was shaking his head, pulling his phone out of his pocket and dialing at the speed of light. Vivian's heart stopped in his chest, and he almost yanked the thing away before he caught himself.

"What are you doing?" he asked warily.

Geo was still out there, patiently waiting to carry out his sinister plan. The last thing Vivian needed to do was involve more people—it was bad enough that Michael had showed up here in the first place.

"I'm calling a friend of mine—a doctor," he quickly clarified at the look on Vivian's face. "He'll be able to get that cleaned up for you."

Vivian's eyes closed for the briefest moment as he tried to keep his face clear of emotion.

Dr. Price. Of course Michael was calling Dr. Price.

Vivian himself had almost called him last night. The sedative Geo had given him was taking longer than usual to wear off and he was concerned that he might be headed over to Michael's next. But one look at the blood-spattered bathroom had made him pause. How many more times could he call Price to help him clean up his messes? How many more judgmental speeches could he endure before a part of him gave in and left town?

No, he would deal with this on his own. Make it look like a simple mugging. It was a task that he was making great headway on before Michael had showed up out of the blue.

"I don't need a doctor," he said quietly, but the phone was already ringing.

"Ray?" Michael asked quickly, picking up the nearest over-turned chair. "I need your help." There was a pause as a low voice on the other end said something unintelligible, but Michael quickly cut him off. "No, it's not me—I'm fine. It's a friend of mine. She got mugged last night and one of the guys hit her pretty hard on the head. If I text you an address, do you think you could come down here?"

Vivian sat down on the couch and pretended to be shaken. It wasn't that hard to do. He'd spent half the night being drowned in his own bathtub, and the other half scrubbing blood off the floor. Price was about to get here, who knew where the hell Geo was, and although it was a rather low priority at the moment—he was keenly aware that his strictly sober son smelled distinctly of tequila. All in all—not his best morning.

"He's on his way," Michael said, hanging up the phone. "Are you sure you don't want to call the police? They might post a squad car outside for a few days if you're lucky."

"No, no, it's fine," Vivian dismissed the idea quickly, glancing wearily around the room for effect. "They wouldn't catch the guys anyway."

Michael's eyes narrowed at the shattered mirror.

"No," he murmured, so softly it was almost to himself, "no they wouldn't."

The two of them got to work straightening out the house, but they only had to wait a few minutes before there was a knock on the door. Dr. Price was a busy man, but for the last fifteen years, he had never been too busy to take a call from Michael.

"Hey, Ray," Michael said as he pulled open the door, "thanks for coming."

"Sure Mike…anytime."

Price was wary as he stepped over the threshold. He had been to this house before. And the last time he was there, the living room was lined with garbage bags stuffed full with bits of butchered assassins. It was the last place he wanted to be now. And the last place he wanted to see Michael.

"This is my friend I was telling you about," Michael turned to make the cursory introductions. "Ray Price, meet Vivian

Knight. Vivian—Ray's going to take good care of you. He's been with me since I was a kid, handled my surgery and everything."

"You don't say," Vivian said hesitantly, holding out his hand. "It's a pleasure to meet you. Thank you for making a house call."

Price's eyes were hard, but he shook the hand as he was expected to. "Of course." His voice lowered in a thinly veiled accusation. "I'd do anything for Michael."

Vivian blushed and dropped the doctor's hand as Price glared at him accusingly. The entire exchange was lost in Michael, however, who was rifling through the doctor's bag. Having basically grown up in hospitals, he knew his way around, and it wasn't long before he pulled out a basic suturing kit, as well as some antiseptic and gauze.

"This good?" he asked, handing it over to the doctor.

Price took it without breaking eye contact with Vivian. "That will be fine, Michael. Why don't you head on home—we can handle it from here."

"Not a chance," Michael breathed, crouching down to his knees as he examined the trail of glass over the carpet. "Someone still has to find out who did this…"

The men shared a deeply disturbed look, before Price tried again.

"In that case, run out and get the topical disinfectant from my car." He tossed Michael his keys and began unwinding the gauze. "It's in the glove compartment."

"Got it."

As Michael vanished outside, the two men turned slowly to face each other.

"This has got to stop!" Price exclaimed the second the door closed behind him.

Vivian raised a furious finger to his lips and muttered, "I know. And for the record, it's not like I planned any of this. Michael showed up this morning of his own volition."

"Because why wouldn't he?!" Price countered. He was still having trouble controlling the volume of his voice. "You're his *friend*, now. You've implanted yourself in his life!"

"Ray…" Vivian caught his breath as he gazed around the broken living room. "I know."

The doctor sighed and began unloading his bag. "Well, I'm assuming you don't need help disposing of the body since I don't see any of your handy trash bags."

He soaked a cloth in alcohol and held it out to Vivian, but Vivian didn't move.

"There is no body."

Price froze.

"What?"

"There is no body. I didn't...I didn't kill him. He got away."

He got away.

Those three words would haunt the two men for longer than either one of them would like to admit...

* * *

Meanwhile, outside, Michael was having a few revelations of his own. He had most definitely not imagined the sudden and dramatic increase in his observational powers, for the first thing that he noticed upon walking down the front steps was the muddy half of a shoe print—quickly fading. He knelt down at once to examine it.

It was small. Much smaller than he would have guessed. Almost child-sized, maybe five-five or five-six. He followed the direction to where it angled up by the window, and ran his fingers over the frame with a frown.

Slight indentations in the wood. Splinter fragments mixed with bits of dried paint on the ground. And farther up, on the rain pipe, another trace of misplaced mud.

This robber, whoever he was, was clearly as nimble as he was small. He had shimmied up the size of the house and entered through the domed window by the ceiling—one that the police would never think to check.

Who was this man?

Michael's frown deepened as he stuck his hands in his pockets and looked up towards the roof with a scowl. Houses like Vivian's were a dime a dozen. If you wanted to break in, there was no shortage of ways you could try.

But this? This looked like a professional job. A regular hit— if you will.

A *hit?*

Michael shook his head quickly to clear it as he headed to the car.

What the hell was he talking about? Like he knew any of this? A professional job? Based on the angle of one muddy footprint that probably had nothing to do with the break-in?

Snap out of it, Michael.

He quickly rifled through the glove box and retrieved the disinfectant Price had requested. Maybe he was taking this transfer to the crime beat too seriously. He was starting to see things everywhere.

But as he walked back into the house, tube of ointment in hand, his eyes flickered once more to the rain gutter. He stopped dead in his tracks.

It had been pulled ever-so-slightly off its hinges, and then replaced with the utmost care.

A sharp prickle of realization lifted the hairs on the back of Michael's neck, and he glanced instinctively around to see if anyone was watching.

He had fixed Vivian's rain gutter just the previous week— gone over every single inch of it by hand. Those screws that were loose today had not been loose yesterday morning. He was sure of it.

The sound of two voices softly arguing inside caused his attention, and he quickly jogged up the front steps to deliver his package. But before he opened the door, he cast one final glance at the roof.

Vivian was right. The police wouldn't do anything, because they knew they wouldn't find anything. Not in this neighborhood.

But maybe, just maybe, someone else could…

CHAPTER

15

"I'm not sure...can I try another?" To most people living in New York City, Woodlands was a daunting place. Not so much in size, but in reputation. It was where criminals retreated when they got too hot for the streets in Washington Heights and Hell's Kitchen. It was the genesis of all the retired street thugs and hustlers—the single place they'd call home. Local law enforcement had a turn-over rate higher than eighty percent. The city was its own sovereign. One with a very strict set of rules, rules understood only by the inhabitants. One would not cross its borders lightly.

But to those people living inside Woodlands, to those people who had cut their teeth on the piles of gravel and rusted razor blades buried on the edge of the skate park—Woodlands operated very much like any other small town.

There was a movie theater that only showed pictures from before the 1940's. There was a bank with only three legitimate tellers—the rest traded their name for a series of less than savory jobs on the side. There was even a roller rink for the younger children. Or at least, there *was* until it burned down in a fire meant for the Woodlands Drug Store—one of the only places to keep its books completely above the line despite constant neighborhood pressure to fold. Many people suspected this was because it was backed by congregational members of the local church.

At any rate, as a boy who grew up in the heart of this town, there were very few places in Woodlands that Michael had never been. Truth be told, he could only think of three:

The vintage dress shop.

The local synagogue.

And the army surplus store with the rusted sign selling 'Knives and Tactical Gear.'

"Sorry," he apologized, "just one more?"

The knife clattered on the counter between them as the wearied clerk looked up with a strained smile. "Sure." He re-traced his steps for the twelfth time back to the glass display case where the weapons were held. "Anything particular in mind?"

Michael's eyes traced the rack, trying to latch onto anything of significance. "Uh…I'm not too sure what I'm looking for to be honest."

With his back safely to the customer, the clerk rolled his eyes. *You think?*

"What about that black one—can I try that?"

For the first time in the last forty minutes, the clerk showed a bit of life.

"That one? That's a decent knife. Call it a fixed blade combat knife. 55-57 RC. Seven inches long. Handle made of black canvas micarta."

"Seven inches," Michael repeated, running his fingers up and down the blade with a frown. "Is that good?"

The clerk flashed him a crooked grin. "How many inches do you need?"

The age-old question.

Michael rolled his eyes. "I'll take it," he said with no further discussion. He set the weapon carefully down on the counter before reaching for his wallet. "Cash okay?"

"Cash is great."

"How much do I owe you?"

"It's three-fifty even."

Michael paused, then looked up incredulously. "Three hundred and fifty dollars?"

"You want quality, you've got to pay for quality." The man rang him up quickly and handed him a receipt. "Besides, that shouldn't be anything for a guy like you."

There was a beat of silence.

"A guy like me?"

Michael looked up sharply, and both men found themselves in an awkward stare.

The cashier blanched apologetically. "You know, just…" He gulped. "Never mind—I'm sorry. Do you want a bag with that?"

"No, thanks," Michael said stiffly, slipping the case deep in his pocket.

He was out the door the next second, more stung than he cared to admit by the man's words. That hadn't happened to him in a long time—that someone would look at him and automatically assume he was some kind of thug. Of course, it made sense. In a town like Woodlands, any man beneath a certain age residing in a certain neighborhood received a similar treatment. And a man built like Michael? It was hardly even a question.

And it wasn't like the label didn't come with perks.

Most times, there was a healthy dose of fear beneath the sideways glances, a convenient layer of caution under the words. Enough fear and caution to get Michael pretty much whatever he'd want. It was an accurate and aggressive stereotype he had used to his advantage many times before, and whilst he was standing in the middle of a knife shop—he could hardly blame the man for making certain assumptions.

That being said, it was a stereotype he had worked very hard to overcome. In part, by avoiding places exactly like the knife shop.

It had taken several long weeks for Willy and the boys at the coffee shop to relax around him long enough for him to gain their trust. The YMCA had been loath to consider him for a position coaching youth sports. If it wasn't for his respectful persistence—as well as a good word or two put in by Pastor Jeff—they would never have given him a chance.

Point being, growing up in the neighborhood set you at a distinct disadvantage if you got the idea into your head that you wanted to live a clean life. You had to swim against the stream, beat against the current. It was exhausting.

It was also something Michael had grown exceedingly good at…until now.

What did I expect? Come in at ten in the morning, still reeking of last night's booze, to buy a blade?

He flipped up his jacket collar for warmth and leaned his whole body into the icy wind, heading for home. With every step, he felt the hard leather case pressing into his lower thigh.

A part of him couldn't believe what he'd just done. He hated weapons. Despised the very sight of them. He'd gotten his fill several years ago when one of them fired five bullets in his face. For two years running, he'd led an anti-gun rally at the school and manned an anonymous drop-off container in front of the Y.

Then again, a part of him couldn't believe he hadn't done it sooner.

The man who had robbed Vivian? The two thugs at the park?

It was the tip of the iceberg. He could tell you a million stories. Give you a million personal anecdotes. This wasn't a safe town. He knew that full well, yet somehow, he'd taken on the role of a bystander—watching as the strong beat down the slightly less strong. Watching as innocent people got caught in the cross-hairs. Watching as the police ran around chasing dead end after dead end. It was a vicious cycle, one from which he saw no escape.

But since the surgery, he'd started seeing things in a different light. As if this new heart of his had an appetite for something more.

He didn't have to stand by and be a passive observer, a symbolic pillar for good. The trick about symbols was that they didn't actually *do* anything themselves. They relied upon the goodwill and sentiment of those around them to take up the banner. And goodwill and sentiment were in short supply in Woodlands.

No, there were other ways of making a difference in this community. Other ways of combatting the little miseries he saw every day—the ones that chipped away at his fair town.

There were evil forces at work? Evil people behind them?

He could *make* them change.

He rubbed the tip of the knife in his pocket and quickened his stride.

Through force, if necessary…

* * *

Across town, Vivian was battling stereotypes of his own.

"Are you sure you don't want me to get someone to help you install that, ma'am?" the man behind the counter asked with a drawl. His eyes travelled slowly up and down Vivian's navy print dress, before meeting his gaze with a smile. "Little lady like you doesn't want to be lifting all this heavy equipment all by herself…"

An image of this *little lady* dumping two bullet-ridden corpses into a meat-packing incinerator flashed through Vivian's mind, and his face tightened into a hard smile.

"I'm sure I can manage, thank you."

A memory floated to the surface from many years ago—his wife, Joni, complaining after getting home from an electronics store shortly before Christmas. She'd gone in, knowing exactly what she wanted to buy—having researched it extensively—and had proceeded to be lectured by no less than three men about the shortcomings and limitations of her choice as they formed a tight circle around her and tried to up-sell her another.

'Man-splaining.' The first time Vivian had heard the term, and he remembered thinking the whole thing to be quite funny.

It didn't seem that way now…

"Why is it you need all this stuff, anyway?" the cashier asked again, loading several hundred dollars' worth of surveillance equipment back into Vivian's cart.

Vivian grabbed the heaviest bundles himself, angling them effortlessly inside. "I have my reasons. In this town, I suppose you have people in here buying security cameras all the time."

The man's eyes flickered to the muscles bursting through Vivian's dress, but he tuned it out as cognitive dissonance. "Sure do." He heaved in the last two cameras before flashing a sudden, roguish grin. "You think your man's cheating?"

Vivian just blinked. He couldn't be serious, could he? This couldn't be normal.

"I mean," he held up his hands innocently, "not that I'm one to judge—"

"My husband is dead," Vivian answered with finality, hoping the man would take the hint and hand over the receipt so he could get the hell out of there.

"Aw, well I'm very sorry to hear that," then in the same breath, "although in that case I'd love to come by some time and take you out for—"

Vivian was out the door as quickly as Michael, putting as much distance between himself and the cashier as possible—lest the man suffer the same fate as his imaginary husband.

The video cameras were absolutely meaningless—Vivian understood that. A superfluous show of caution meant only to appease both the neighbors and his son. Geo didn't give a damn about cameras. And if for some reason he decided he didn't want his face captured, it would be the easiest thing in the world for him to evade them.

But despite the precariousness caused by the hitman's arrival, appearances had to be maintained. Of all the things Price had shouted at him last night—and after Michael left, he'd shouted a great deal—he was right about two things.

First, Vivian was getting sloppy. Careless.

Two months ago, there was no way in heaven or hell that Geo would have been able to get so close—much less hold him temporary hostage in his own bathroom. He'd become distracted, slow. And to beat this strange little man the Director had decided to be the instrument of his fate—he'd need to bring the old Peter Canard back.

Second, he needed to seriously consider leaving for the sake of Michael.

While the first argument was easy enough to accept, he simply couldn't bring himself to consider the second. Thus, he fixated all his attentions on one simple task.

Resurrection.

When he got home, he slipped into a pair of feminine sweatpants and a loose jade sweater. Easy to move in; but keeping very much in line with his careful costuming thus far. He couldn't rely upon 'Vivian' to keep perpetuating herself. She would need to be thoughtfully attended to keep up the charade. That meant no more fixing cars and pulling young girls from a frozen lake. That meant security cameras and the occasional well-deserved spa day.

Thus it was in a state of feminine disrepair that Pastor Jeff stumbled upon Vivian at his house later that day.

"Vivian?" the pastor called as he made his way slowly up the front steps. Vivian, perched atop a ladder listening to Aretha Franklin in earbuds at top volume, didn't hear. "I was just coming round to—GOOD HEAVENS!"

Vivian fell off bottom three steps of the ladder with a shriek, but it was Jeff who jumped back in horror. A drip of toxic green face mask fell to the ground between them with a loud *clop*.

"Oh my poor dear…you've begun to mold."

Vivian turned his face away from the minister and raced to the bathroom to remove the evidence. At least the fluorescent green had masked the bright red flush of his cheeks upon having been discovered. When he returned a moment later, Jeff seemed just as determined as him to put the entire thing permanently from memory.

"I was just stopping by to see how you were holding up," the minister said kindly, similarly relieved Vivian had chosen to remove the sludge from his face. "Michael told me about the break-in…"

"Oh yes, well," Vivian tucked his hair behind his ears and glanced around at the half-opened boxes of cameras and tape, "these things happen, right?"

"I'm afraid they do."

Unfortunately for Vivian, Pastor Jeff knew firsthand that they happened a lot more than she realized. In fact, for a single woman new to the city, he was rather surprised it hadn't happened sooner.

"You putting up some cameras?" he asked conversationally, kneeling down to examine several of the opened boxes.

Vivian smoothed down his curls with a smile. "As best as I can. It's kind of a trial and error process right now."

Jeff smiled sympathetically. This was not the first time he'd visited the home of someone newly-wronged, to find a house full of boxes. It would not be the last.

"Well I'm here to offer my services in any way I can." His smile faded to a frown as he squinted at the tiny lettering on the side of a box. "Although I won't lie to you, I have just as little idea as to how to put this all together as you do…"

"Why don't we just take a break for a bit," Vivian diverted him quickly.

In the comfort and privacy of his own home, Vivian could have the system up and running in less than ten minutes. And while he was committed to keeping up appearances, he was in no mood to hold the minister's hand for the next ninety.

Instead, he led the way to the kitchen and poured them two steaming mugs of coffee before settling down at the table. Jeff accepted it gratefully and took a scalding gulp.

"Actually, I was also coming by to talk with you about Michael. I know it's been a bit of a mad house around here, but you haven't had a chance to talk to him about his meeting with the seminary advisor yesterday, have you?"

Meeting with a seminary advisor? It was the first Vivian was hearing of it.

"No..." his forehead creased to a frown, "I'm afraid I haven't. You said it happened yesterday?"

Jeff nodded. "Yesterday afternoon. I'm sure everything went great, I just haven't been able to get a hold of him since to find out. It took me two months to set up..." He sounded more excited than annoyed, but both emotions were definitely there.

"I'm sure he just hasn't had the time," Vivian defended quickly. "I was supposed to meet him for dinner last night—so I know he was getting that ready. And then this morning when he came by, the house was in shambles and I was hiding in the bathroom. Give him some time, and I'm sure he'll call."

Jeff nodded at once. "Of course, of course."

But the longer the two men sipped their coffee, the more troubled he seemed to become.

"It's just, do you think Michael has been acting a bit...strange lately?"

Vivian thought of the tequila, Michael's confession about doubts while going up the mountain, and the traces of lipstick on his neck the last time Vivian saw him. To say nothing of this new streak of vigilante justice he'd been raving about whilst gunning for the crime beat.

But he cleared his face to a curious frown. "Strange? How do you mean?"

Jeff shook his head slowly. "You know, I'm not even sure how to describe it. He just seems a little...off. I've known the kid for a long time, I can tell when he's distracted. It's just, he's so close to getting everything he's been working towards for the last four years, and now that he's finally here, he seems..."

"...distracted," Vivian finished, recycling the pastor's words from before. He couldn't agree more, and yet, he felt the need once again to defend his son. "Come to think of it, I think I know what you're talking about. He's been a little distant, unavailable at times." He shook his head sagely. "I've seen it countless times before in patients I was working through recovery."

Jeff's eyes flashed up as he immediately latched onto any kind of explanation. "You have? In the disabled vets?"

"Absolutely."

Lucky for Michael, lies came easy to both Vivian Knight *and* Peter Canard.

"Once they get past a certain point, their bodies begin to register the shock. Everyone handles it in slightly different ways, but Michael seems pretty a-typical in his reaction."

Jeff actually exhaled in relief. "That explains so much. Of course, it would be the recovery. I didn't even think of that. I can't imagine how frustrating it's been, having all those limitations. As if the kid needed another thing to go wrong in his life."

Vivian absorbed this quietly for a moment, lost in thought.

"One could say he came out stronger because of it," he reasoned softly, willing it to be true. "He didn't pause for a second before he barged into my house to make sure I was alright."

Jeff shook his head and looked around the room with a low whistle. "That's absolutely right. And a good thing he got here when he did. There's no telling whether the monsters who did this might have come back."

Vivian's face darkened, but he hid it skillfully behind his mug.

There was more truth to the minister's words than he cared to admit. And unfortunately, it wasn't a matter of *if*. It was a matter of *when…*

CHAPTER

16

When Michael first purchased the knife, he had no intention of using it.

He was going to keep the knife in a locked drawer in his bedside table, to be pulled out and waved around as a warning in case of burglaries. He was not going to remove it for any other reason, whatsoever. It was to be a silent security blanket—nothing more, nothing less.

At least...that was the plan.

Two days after Michael purchased the knife, the rationalizations began pouring in.

He was *not* going to carry it around with him wherever he went.

Except, how many muggings and random acts of violence had he seen nearly every day on the streets? Why buy a knife if you intended to continue walking around unarmed?

He was *not* going to remove it for any other reason than self-defense.

Except, why own a knife in the first place if you didn't know how to use it? And how was he supposed to learn to use it without putting in hours upon hours of practice?

Most importantly, he was *not* going to let this knife become a part of his identity. It would not define him, it would not compromise his beliefs, it would not influence his actions.

But the ship had already sailed on that one, hadn't it? He was a man with a knife now. It was time people stood up and took notice.

Four days after buying the knife, his leg already had the beginnings of a regular callous where the case pressed constantly against his thigh.

But dedicated or not, after locking himself in his bedroom for the last four days with nothing but a pack of energy drinks, a series of rotating icepacks, and a laptop computer opened to endless streams of instructional training videos, Michael was ready for some fresh air.

The knife went with him as he walked leisurely down the street to a fast food joint around the corner. He'd already grown accustomed to the feel of the grooved handle in his hands. He'd taken to twirling it absentmindedly around the house as he went about his days' activities—pleased with how naturally the movements seemed to come. Now, it was safely holstered in a hard leather case that he'd wedged into his belt and hidden beneath his jacket. A proper holster would have to come later. For now, he'd make do.

The greasy cuisine he craved was near the top of his 'things NOT to do after surgery' list, but he figured what the good doctor didn't know, couldn't possibly hurt him. And between staring down the barrel of a gun and surviving open heart surgery, it wasn't likely that something like a cheeseburger would scare Michael now.

Nonetheless, he kept a wary eye out for Nurse Franklin as he moved up another place in the outdoor line. This place wasn't that far from the hospital and he happened to know it was a favorite of hers. Not that he wouldn't welcome the opportunity to see her again, but unlike burgers and fries, and even the potential wrath of Dr. Price—Nurse Franklin *did* scare him.

The winter wind tossed his afro back and forth and he tilted his face to the sky with a contented smile. Finally, back where he belonged. The smells of car exhaust, industrial stream hurling up through the grates, bacon grease sizzling on the grill—they brought him back to another time. A less troubled time, ironically, considering how filled it had been with trouble. It felt lighter than the time he was living in now. Without the weight of the expectations and responsibilities that hung around his neck like a gentle noose. A part of him missed it.

Nothing wrong with that, was there? So he missed the carefree effervescence of his earlier youth? What person didn't? It meant nothing. Just simple nostalgia.

A sudden vibration in his pocket interrupted his thoughts. He checked the number and stifled a sigh. Pastor Jeff. Again. He'd been calling nonstop ever since Michael's supposed seminary interview a few days ago.

A part of him couldn't resent the minister for his excitement, and Michael had never failed so long to return a call. But for the life of him, he didn't know what to say.

This was his top pick for seminary. He knew he should be excited. He *knew* this. But try as he might…he simply couldn't bring himself to care.

He wasn't saying seminary was off the table. By no means. Only that he wasn't interested in pursuing it any further either now, or at any point in the foreseeable future. He had done enough research, knew enough about it to understand that it was more than a job, it was a complete overhaul of one's life. Talk about taking your work home with you! If one was to complete the required schooling and graduate into the profession, it would transform their identity as a whole. They'd have to eat, sleep, and breathe the Church from there on after.

Up until a few weeks ago, that had been more than a dream—it had been a craving.

But now…?

He didn't know where the newfound apathy had come from, he didn't know how it had slyly shifted his priorities in their entirety without him ever realizing. But the fact remained—it had. The only problem was, he had no earthly idea how to explain something like that to Jeff. Not after they'd worked so hard together to get Michael to this point.

He'd had the same problem when the admissions' representative had called him three days ago to reschedule. She was leaving the next afternoon and needed to see him before then if they were to finish what they'd started. Instead of answering her sweetly thought-out voicemail, he'd simply deleted the number and returned to his weapons training.

Seminary will always be there, he told himself firmly. Though there was a part of him that didn't believe it. *Until then, there was work to be done here.*

He had just moved up another space in line, when he heard the argument.

It started as something slight—a disagreement over the cooking of a burger, or a complaint about the length of the line—but quickly progressed to a heated war on pricing in general. Taking advantage of his height, Michael leaned forward to get a better view of what was going on.

It was two young men, versus the old man behind the counter. While the old man had most definitely seen his share of skirmishes, those days were decidedly behind him, and it was easy to see he had no means of combatting the force in front of him. As for the young men, they were no more than a pair of common street thugs. No special talent or skill—just a loud aggressive streak and the force of numbers to back it up.

Michael had seen a hundred of them come and go. Hell—four years ago, he could have easily been standing right there with them.

"What'cho gonna do old man?" one of them taunted, waving his bag of food in the air between them. "You gonna refund us our eight dollars or are we gonna to have to come back there and take it for ourselves?"

The old man was in a tight spot. The two upstarts showed no indication of backing off, he had no means of combatting them on his own, and Woodlands wasn't the kind of place you wanted it advertised that the police frequented your burger joint. With a grave face, he reached slowly into the open cash register. It appeared concessions would have to be made.

"Alright, alright, fine," he tempered them, hiding the overwhelming shame under a mask of annoyance instead. "Then you two get the hell on out of here."

The bigger of the two men leaned against the stand with a smirk. "We'll leave when we're good and ready, old-timer." He grinned stupidly and paced back through the frozen line of waiting customers, thoroughly impressed with his performance thus far. "In fact, now that we know you're so damn accommodating, we might be stopping by a lot more often."

His eyes darted through the stoic crowd, resting on each face to see how his commentary was being received. No expression was too trivial. No detail was too small to escape his roving attention.

That's why it was so strange he didn't see Michael's fist swinging towards his eye.

"Son of a…"

He looked up from the ground in a sprawled-out daze, squinting to make out the top of Michael's head in the glare of the white winter sun.

"WHAT THE HELL'S THE MATTER WITH YOU, FOOL?!"

Red hot adrenaline coursed through Michael's veins. His fingers traced the knife in his pocket as he stared down at the fallen culprit, sneering all the while.

"I think it's time you and your friend headed home."

He might as well have been caped.

The guy pulled himself back up to his feet, just as his companion was turning around to see what all the commotion was about. When he saw the smear of blood on the ground, courtesy of Michael's introduction, he forgot about his collection endeavor entirely and hurried back to join them.

"Oh, you're a dead man," the bigger man spat a mouthful of blood and what looked suspiciously like a tooth on the ground, before subconsciously positioning himself beside his friend for support. "You have no idea who you're messing with."

The corner of Michael's mouth turned up in a smile. "I'm guessing it's the two of you."

By now, the rest of the line had the good sense to walk away. No burger was worth all of this. The old man—casting a meek look of gratitude at the back of Michael's head—pulled shut the iron caging to close the stand and hurried out the back to his car.

"That's right, 'Holmes,'" the smaller man spoke for the first time.

Despite his size, he was confident—clearly the one in the pair who knew how to handle himself. But he looked Michael up and down with the cautious respect of one who knew enough about fights to know when it was better to walk away. As he took in Michael's impressive frame, it looked like he might have been considering just that.

Then his eyes fell on the bright pink scar poking out of the top of Michael's shirt. A look of confusion flitted across his face, before something clicked.

"Yo man—you just have an operation or something?"

Michael paused, thrown a bit off balance by the question.

When he didn't answer, the taller of the men followed his friend's gaze to the scar.

"Dude—that's some Frankenstein shit. Looks new."

The smaller man took a step forward with a grin. "Looks real new."

Michael braced himself as they closed in. Jaw clenched. Hands at the ready.

It was now or never.

The knife! Pull out the knife!

But something inside him froze. This was a fist fight, nothing more. If you introduced a knife to a fist fight? If you voluntarily engineered that kind of escalation?

Michael had seen enough friends die of stab wounds to know the cost.

So the knife stayed in his pants.

Hours later, from a bed in the ICU, he would come to rethink that decision…

* * *

Many years ago, when Ray Price was still in med-school and Peter Canard had been recently recruited for black ops, Ray had sent Peter an email from halfway across the world. It was a clip from a movie, only a few seconds long, depicting the film's stereotypical bad guy. He was sucking on the edge of a hunting knife, smoking, and stroking his twin Doberman's while he plotted his next nefarious move. The email had come with a simple message:

'Level with me, Pete—is this kind of thing basically your life now?'

It had been meant as a joke, and despite the horrors raging on outside his door, Vivian remembered thinking it was actually quite funny. Not remotely accurate, but a valiant attempt by his friend none the less.

He'd agonized as to what to send back that could match it. How did one explain to a privileged D.C. doctor, that not everything 'spy-related' was grandiose explosions and slow-motion walks into the sunset?

Eventually, he'd given up and just wrote 'yes' in Morse code. See if Price, with his two hundred-thousand-dollar education could figure that one out.

But right now, sitting in a makeshift bunker in the middle of his living room, hooded and cloaked with black-out curtains taped up to the walls—Vivian was beginning to suspect that all he was missing were the Dobermans.

The glare of no less than nine television monitors gleamed in his face, as he carefully studied every second of feed from each of his hidden cameras. The regular ones he'd nailed up beside the front door and under the back eaves were just for show. The real feed was coming from a handful of sleek Russian-grade cams set up strategically in the places no one would think to look. The places Geo would most likely be entering.

Ever since Jeff had left his house four days ago, he'd been on virtual lock-down. Siege mentality had set in hard, and although he was unaccustomed to being the one on the defensive, in this particular scenario, he saw no way around it.

The only times he deviated from his position were his daily checks on Michael. He'd sit low in the car, circling the neighborhood slowly before high-tailing it back to his house, trying hard to ignore the fact that for all intents and purposes, he was stalking his own son.

On any other occasion, he would have permanently planted himself outside Michael's house—never let the kid out of his sight. But in this particular situation, the more distance he put between the two of them, the better. For Michael's sake.

This was made significantly easier because, for whatever reason, Michael had chosen to hole up these last few days just like Vivian. His car hadn't left the drive, and a different series of lights was on every time Vivian drove by. Without being sure exactly why his son had taken this moment to channel Howard Hughes, Vivian simply thanked God that, for once, Michael had made his job that much easier—allowing him to return to his video monitors with a vengeance.

When his phone rang, he almost didn't pick it up. Just Jeff again, no doubt. He worried that he still hadn't been able to get a hold of Michael since the day he had blown off his interview. And while the incident worried him as well, as well as Michael's subsequent seclusion, he suspected the reasons behind both had a lot do with the aforementioned lipstick and tequila—nothing life threatening. Certainly not enough to make him leave his post.

But when the phone rang a second time, just seconds later, he pulled his eyes from the screens long enough to check the caller ID. What he saw didn't make any sense.

"Hello?"

"Hey, Vivian—it's Michael."

Vivian jumped to his feet in alarm.

"Michael—why are you calling from St. Andrew's Memorial?"

There was a nervous pause during which Vivian heard the telltale beeps and whirls of a dozen pieces of medical machinery.

"It's nothing serious," Michael assured him quickly, then continued rather vaguely, "I just...got into a little accident."

Vivian was out the door the next second, leaving the flashing monitors and impromptu bunker behind. "I'm on my way."

Geo would have to pick another day to make his move.

...if he hadn't just made it already.

* * *

Once Vivian got to the hospital, precisely twelve and a half minutes later, it took him no time at all to locate Michael's room. His charming son had become a favorite patient during his last stay here—a bit of a local star—and the place was already buzzing about his return.

"Is it his heart?" Vivian demanded of a nurse, cornering her in their shared elevator. "Are there signs of rejection?"

The young woman shook her head with a surprising smile. "Didn't you hear? He stepped right in the middle of a street fight. Pulled two huge guys off this little old man. Probably saved the guy's life! I heard there was a motorcycle involved…"

Vivian's eyes narrowed. He couldn't tell how much was fact and how much was exaggeration. Not to mention, with so little information, he couldn't tell at all if Geo was in any way involved.

He snapped his fingers in front of the woman's eyes and she startled to attention. "But he's going to be alright? There was no serious damage done?"

Thankfully, she was too enchanted to remember a little thing like HIPAA.

"Not sure, but he's stable for now. The doctor's coming by to check on him soon—run some tests." She swooned. "I can't even imagine. It's just such a brave—"

Yeah, yeah.

Vivian turned his face so she wouldn't see him roll his eyes, grateful when the elevator *dinged* and he was released into the ICU.

Brave was not the word he'd use.

Stupid. Reckless. Careless. Delusional. Ungrateful. Absurdly, unequivocally BAD.

But *brave?* Nowhere on the list.

He edged past a weeping family trying to guilt information out of a poker-faced nurse and headed up to the front counter.

"I'm here to see Michael Canard," he said quickly, slipping into the persuasive purr he found worked best when he was wearing a brazier and heels. "My name's Vivian Knight."

"Michael, Michael…" she said, scrolling down a list on her screen. "Are you family?"

Vivian's heart skipped a beat, aching just this once to tell the truth.

"No, but he just called me. I'm sure he—"

"Oh here you are," she said brightly. "His emergency contact."

Vivian glanced up in surprise. He was listed as Michael's emergency contact? Since when? That was a change Michael would have had to have made quite recently—in just the few weeks since Vivian had come into his life after the surgery.

And…why exactly had Michael chosen *him?* Why not Jeff or whoever it had been before his transplant—most likely Ray? Wouldn't they be a more logical choice?

Before he had time to properly assimilate this information, he had been guided to Michael's room at the far end of the hall.

For the second time, in just a little under two months, Vivian stared through the slats in the blinds at his fallen son.

How different this time was than the last.

Before, while Michael's condition had certainly been grave, physically—he had looked just fine. Pale. Scared. Strung out on painkillers—but fine.

Today could not have been more different.

At a glance, it looked as though his entire face was one giant bruise. Stains of dark blood pooled beneath his skin, making him look like some kind of failed art experiment. Where there weren't bruises, there were cuts. Lots of cuts. The kind of cuts that came from repeated kicks and hits to the face. And since the face was the universal thing that most people would instinctively protect, Vivian shuddered to imagine what kind of state the rest of his body was in.

But none of that was what troubled Vivian the most. What troubled him was the involuntary, almost subconscious way Michael's hand kept shooting up to his incision site whenever he moved.

It was brutal. It was morbidly thorough. It was a tough sight for any parent to take.

But Vivian didn't think it was Geo.

There was a sloppiness to the bruising. And a pattern of combat that didn't fit one of Geo's size. Perhaps the nurse in the elevator was correct. Perhaps Michael really threw himself into the middle of a street fight.

Vivian ground his teeth together as he pushed open the door.

Well, if Michael was expecting to be treated like some sort of hero for doing so, he had another thing coming...

"Hey," Michael looked up when he heard the door, "you came."

Vivian stared down at him for a long moment, before taking a seat beside the bed. He looked even worse close up.

"Of course I came," he said stiffly. Then he added, "I'm your emergency contact."

Michael blushed, adding even more color to an already overly-painted face.

"Yeah, about that..." His eyes ventured up, seeking forgiveness. "I hope you don't mind, it was always Dr. Price. But when they brought me in today—"

Vivian held up a silencing hand as the rationale behind the decision suddenly made sense.

"When they brought you in today, *after you jumped into the middle of a street fight*, you didn't want to deal with Price's lecture. So you called me instead."

Michael froze uncertainly, suddenly looking very much his young age. The cartoonish guilt written all over his face would almost have been enough to make Vivian laugh—on any other occasion than this.

"Well, then it seems you made two huge mistakes tonight," he said briskly, setting down his purse and turning to Michael with a stern glare. "Because Price's lecture couldn't possibly be any worse than mine."

Michael's face fell and he shifted painfully on the bed. "Look, can't we just—"

"*Absolutely not!*" Vivian interrupted, eyes flashing with anger. Only a life's worth of training kept him focused enough to remember to deliver the speech in a woman's voice. "What the hell were you *thinking*, Michael?! That four weeks after getting a heart transplant would be the perfect time for you to prowl the streets looking for trouble?!"

"I wasn't," Michael paused, editing, "I wasn't looking for trouble. I was just standing in line at Sully's when these two guys—"

"Oh you're off to a great start already," Vivian cut him off again, fuming. "Sully's. The greasiest burgers in town. Glad to know you're taking your recovery so seriously."

"Really? The burger joint?" Michael stifled a little grin. "That's the thing you want to get mad about?"

Vivian's eyes narrowed. "Oh, I think you'll find there's enough *mad* in me to go around."

The grin disappeared.

"Uh…well I was standing in line, and these two guys tried to hold up the old man running the stand. Right out in the open. Nobody did anything to stop them."

There was a pause and Vivian's face softened the slightest bit.

"Nobody except you."

For the first time, all the playful, apologetic charm was gone. Michael looked him straight on, eyes shining with the self-righteous validation of his actions.

"What was I supposed to do? Just let it happen?"

Vivian sighed. "You were supposed to call the police. You were supposed to avoid *at all costs* getting into a physical altercation that could have caused damage to your new heart."

"So the old man pays the price?" Michael asked heatedly. "Those two bastards deserved a beating for what they'd done. Or worse. They're lucky I didn't pull out my—"

In hindsight, it was very fortunate for Michael, and very unfortunate for Vivian that Vivian interrupted that sentence when he did.

"And who the hell are you to make that call?" he demanded. Whether Michael liked it or not, this caped crusader phase of his had to reach its end. "'God alone, who gave the law, is the Judge,'" he quoted from the Bible. "'He alone has the power to save or to destroy. So what right do you have to judge your neighbor?' James four verse twelve."

He might not have spent as much time in a church as his son, but he was a quick study.

Michael's eyes flashed. "'Learn to do right; seek justice. Defend the oppressed.' Isaiah one verse seventeen!"

"Learn to do *right*," Vivian leaned back with a hard laugh. "You think what you did was right? Christ, use a whole lot of street fights and violence back in the day to get things done?"

"I had to—" Michael bowed his head stiffly to his chest, as his shoulders fell with a little sigh. "I had to do something."

At once, Vivian's anger dissipated, and he leaned forward to take Michael's hand.

"Michael, I know you…I know you *think* you were doing what was right. But jumping into the middle of a street brawl to save an old man a few dollars? That isn't you."

Michael bit his lip, and for a split second, the conversation slowed to a halt.

All the walls and banter fell silently away to reveal the battle going on just below. This was hurting Michael just as assuredly as it was hurting Vivian. Sitting there, bloodied on another hospital bed, he looked as if he was literally being torn in two.

The uncertainty, the doubt? The struggle to find a moral center? The pain of it danced in his eyes, but in the end, he merely shook his head, unable to do any more.

"Isn't it?" he asked quietly.

For a moment, neither he nor Vivian looked entirely sure.

Then, before Vivian could answer, the door swung open with a loud *bang*.

"Funny seeing you here, Mike."

Ray Price was in no mood to be trifled with. In one hand, he still held his car keys, while the other clutched a hastily procured replication of Michael's chart. Both were shaking.

Michael leaned back, looking suddenly pale. "I thought you weren't on call tonight."

Price's eyes narrowed. "Did you now?" He dropped the clipboard with a loud clatter on the tray by Michael's feet. "Seems as though one of the nurses saw fit to call me anyway. She thought it was strange that I hadn't been informed, but when I got to the hospital minutes later, it all suddenly made sense. Why would I have been informed? *When I'd been removed as your emergency contact?*"

Michael leaned even farther back into the pillows while Price towered over him in a paternal rage.

"Ms. Knight," the doctor said shortly, "if you're finished here, I suggest you go. Michael and I have some things we need to discuss…"

CHAPTER

17

The tongue-lashing Michael had gotten from Price was as severe as he'd ever seen. While the doctor couldn't believe things hadn't gone worse—considering Michael was still sporting the sutures from a major surgery—his relief at this fact had done nothing to dissuade him from giving his patient the speech of a lifetime. He even went so far as to shut the blinds and lock the door, giving them complete privacy and removing the opportunity for Michael to catch the eye of a sympathetic rescuing nurse.

But it wasn't the argument with Price that gnawed away at Michael's stomach.

Even worse than the thirty-minute lecture, which ended with pain-meds and lab work, even worse than the knowledge that he had disappointed a man who'd come into his life as a child and basically raised him as family—even worse than all that, was the talk Michael had with Vivian right before.

He couldn't tell you what exactly unnerved him so much about their conversation. He didn't know if it was the conflicting Bible verses, or the fact that—no matter how many times he later apologized for what he'd done—he felt absolutely no shame. Was it the furious look on her face, or the fact that when he looked at his own reflection, he didn't recognize who he saw?

Maybe it was that for the first time in Michael's recent life, he didn't have the answers.

He had no idea why he was feeling the way he was feeling. He had no idea how he had ended up in a hospital bed listening to Price's medical sermon in the first place.

More importantly, he had no idea why it felt *so good* to hit those guys on the street.

Lying on his cot in the ICU, he relived every second of it. Every swing of his arm. Every muffled connection as bone hit bone.

It was a rush. One just as strong as the nostalgic connection he'd had with Alex a few days before. One he hadn't felt in just as long, but that hadn't lessened at all in intensity with distance or time.

He was hooked.

It didn't matter that he didn't win. It didn't matter that the two men were able to take advantage of his recent medical trauma and knock him to the ground.

The fight, the blood, the vengeance—all of it. He wanted more.

It was that simple. Consequences be damned, it felt good, and he wanted more.

When he walked out of the hospital later that day, he found himself occupied with a single all-consuming thought. And it wasn't gratitude to the dozen doting nurses. It wasn't shame and contrition when Price refused to meet his eyes.

He wished he'd taken out his knife…

*   *   *

"Hang on—I don't understand," the connection cut in and out, crisscrossed over several continents, "you say you had him there on the floor…but he got away?"

The Director wasn't used to taking these calls in person. He wasn't used to checking in on an operation until after its completion. These things were cut and dry. In and out. Bang, bang, you're dead. As cliché as it might sound, murder was a relatively simple operation—you got them, or they got you. There wasn't a lot of middle ground.

Peter Canard had been one of the few exceptions. He and Montana, both. Their long-standing feud had often been gossiped about in sound-proofed basements and empty parking garages around the world.

'The one that got away.' Both men laid claim to the phrase. Both men saw the other as a strike against their perfect record.

Both men were right. But that did nothing to dissuade the stereotype. These things simply weren't designed to drag on past their expiration date.

On the other side of the world, Geo leaned back with a silent sigh, absentmindedly shredding the edges of a paper napkin with his fingers. "You said I should get…creative."

The Director closed his eyes and placed his hands over the receiver.

The second the word had come out of his mouth, he regretted saying it. While he had worked with well over a hundred agents in his time—death dealers, everyone—Geo was a slightly different situation. He had to be handled carefully. Kept on a tight leash.

"Creative, Geo. Not sloppy."

Geo flinched, fixing his eyes on a group of co-eds on the other side of the diner.

Sloppy was right.

In truth, while he'd planned on a lengthy demise for the great Peter Canard, he hadn't actually intended either of them to leave his house that night. His 'creative' plan had been a bit of a mouse trap, scenario. He would hold Peter hostage—in varying amounts of agony—as one by one, all the concerned people in his life slowly showed up at the house seeking answers. As the week progressed, Geo would dispose of them, one after another, before finishing with Peter.

At least...that had been the plan.

He still had no idea how Canard had been able to secure his gun, and that unsettled him greatly. In all the time he'd spent pouring over the man's illustrious file, it had never once occurred to him that he might be outmaneuvered. That it was possible he could be beat.

Of course, Peter hadn't beat him. He'd only stolen an empty gun. But it was a mere coincidence that Geo had emptied the clip. If it weren't for that fact, he would most likely be in the trunk of a car right now, bumping along an unlabeled road on a trip to meet the first team sent out to recover Peter.

"Geo—are you still there?"

The Director was impatient. He trusted in his young protégé's talent and ruthlessness, but his strategies...sometimes lacked the necessary finesse. The last thing in the world he needed was for Canard to be onto their trail. The fact that Geo had left him alone…? It didn't bode well.

"I'm here."

Geo's eyes were still locked on the co-eds, tracing the tight curves of a young twenty-something as she flirted and angled for the attention of a man he deemed unworthy.

"Canard knows who you are? He knows why you've come?"

Why was it that girls like that were always attracted to the bottom of the barrel? Nothing but an inflated ego attached to a pair of biceps. Geo doubted this one could string together a complete sentence.

"He knows."

There was another pause as the Director reined in his temper.

"So tell me again why it is you aren't driving to his house right now to finish the job?"

A waiter bumped into the dunce in question from behind, causing him to spill a generous helping of Dr. Pepper down the front of his shirt. The girls scattered. Geo smiled.

"Canard isn't going anywhere. He can't. He's too afraid to leave behind his son."

This time, the silence between them was high charged.

"His son? You were able to confirm that he does, in fact, have a son?"

Geo took a small bite of his sandwich, leaning out his booth so he could watch the girls walk away. "Michael. Same last name. Twenty-six years old. Lives on the other side of town."

The Director's eyes sparkled. "You'll use the son, then? To get to Peter?"

"At this rate, he should walk right into my hands. Bit of a knife-crazed vigilante. I followed him to a surplus store the other day. Less than a week after he bought a blade, he charged into a street fight and ended up in the hospital. He should be released later today."

"Sounds like my kind of kid," the Director chuckled.

"I thought you'd like him. Actually reminded me a bit of Montana, back in the day."

A pair of nervous looking aides knocked on the door, and the Director was suddenly in a hurry. "Just get him, Geo. Take care of this for me. Will you do that?"

"Consider it done."

* * *

When Michael finally got home that night, there was a shadowy figure sitting on the front porch. He approached it cautiously, watching as it slowly unfolded itself and stood up upon seeing him. It wasn't until he had gotten halfway up the walk that he recognized who it was.

"Didn't think I'd see you again so soon."

Alex stalked towards him with a sly grin.

"I hear you've been picking fights with old men over at Sully's?"

He laughed, rather painfully, and wiped a fresh spot of blood from his newly opened lip.

"Not exactly the way it went down."

She stood up on her toes in front of him, soaking in every bruise and break with an almost critical eye.

"I would imagine it shouldn't be 'going down' at all—not with you fresh off a major heart surgery, right?"

He took a step back and she put her hands on her hips.

"Michael, am I right?" she demanded.

"Come on, not you too," he grumbled, fumbling around in his pocket for his keys. "I already took it from Ray over at the hospital."

"Well yeah—I would think so." She stood right beside him at the door, refusing to be shaken off. "What were you thinking, Mikey?"

"Alex—"

"I'm serious! What—you're too torn up for sex, but not for a random street brawl?"

He rolled his eyes, jamming his key into the lock without aim or success. "I'm so sorry that after round twelve, I thought maybe I should stop before my stitches ripped out—"

"I'm not talking about that. I'm talking about you jumping into the middle of something you knew you couldn't finish, just so—"

He finally whirled around, staring down at her under the fluorescent porch light.

"—so that they wouldn't mug some old man right in front of me? Yeah. I jumped in."

She chewed on her lip for a moment before snatching the keys from his hand and slipping them easily into the lock. "I bet Price was pissed…"

Michael tensed at the memory. "That…would be understating it."

He followed her inside, dropping his jacket and his second round of discharge papers on the messy coffee table while she vanished into the kitchen.

"I've never heard him yell like that," he continued, cringing as unwelcome stirrings of guilt begin churning in the pit of his stomach. "Remember when we crashed his car down by the canal? Tried to tell him we'd been kidnapped to cover it up?"

Alex poked her head back into the living room. "Yeah?"

"It was worse than that."

"Shit. Glad I wasn't there to see it." She vanished again and began rummaging in the refrigerator. "Although, you know on second thought—I wish I was. You and I both know how happy Ray would have been to see me."

Michael chuckled and sank down onto the couch, running his fingers back through his messy hair. "Of course."

It could not have been farther from the truth.

Even the name 'Alexandra Morales' had been formally banned long before the girl herself stopped climbing through Michael's window in the middle of the night. She was a pariah, Price had often said. A cancer to everything she touched—constantly undermining every good thing that came into Michael's life.

Of course, Price wasn't exactly wrong. Their juvenile joy ride in his prized Mercedes SUV was hardly the worst of their crimes.

When Alex had been busted for coke at fifteen, she'd taken Michael down with her. The night she was arrested for drunk driving, she'd said it was Michael behind the wheel.

While Price found this unforgivable, Michael didn't really mind.

Alex liked things to be even. No matter how high or low life got—it had to be square on both sides. It was one of the few things she had control over, growing up in a chaotic, rotating door of foster homes and abusive men. This sense of forced equilibrium was her therapy. Her serenity. And unfortunately, during the time Michael was dating her, his sentence.

They'd shared a holding cell on more than one occasions, simply because she didn't think it was right that she be sitting there alone. Whether he had been present or not at the crime in question—Michael had certainly done everything she'd done and worse. It only made sense to her that they would both serve the time.

On the flip side, when he got busted for selling drugs, she'd been his alibi every time. It almost became a joke with the local precinct: if ever they brought in Michael Canard, they knew it was only a matter of time before Alex Morales showed up—banging on the door and swearing up and down on the cross that he'd been with her the whole time.

The second they took off the cuffs, she was always his first call. Well, she or Price. It depended on the severity of the crime and whether or not Michael thought he could get out of it without his guardian 'conscience' getting wind.

It had created a strange sort of competition between the two—Alex and Price.

Both felt as though they had certain claim to Michael. Both had earned his devotion and trust. And yet, while Michael remained willfully oblivious, both understood that neither one could inhabit the same world as the other. It made for an unsettling truce, at best.

"Hey, you got beer since I saw you last. I'm impressed."

Michael glanced towards the kitchen, roused from his sudden nostalgia. "Yeah, I did. Grab me one?"

She flipped off the lights and edged around the corner of the wall, holding a pair of bottles in both hands and inching forward with a particularly mischievous look on her face.

"I grabbed you two."

Michael watched her curiously, a question in his eyes, until she tossed back her long hair and stepped out of the shadows. His face broke into a grin.

"Alex, where's your shirt?"

She pretended to look confused. "My shirt? I…must have lost it in the kitchen."

He shook his head dismissively. "Don't worry about it. Happens a lot with that kitchen, it's why I get a discount on my rent."

She giggled and climbed carefully onto his lap, popping the lids off two of the bottles with skilled fingers. "So?" she asked, placing one in his hand. "What should we drink to?"

"You got the beer—you propose the toast."

She grinned. "Is that how it works?"

"That's how it works."

"Hmm…" She shifted around and took an absentminded sip as she considered. "To dodging bullets. It could have gone a lot worse for you today."

His eyes travelled up and down her slender body, before coming to rest on her face.

"Let's drink to the kitchen."

* * *

Since the day that Ray Price had handed Michael his first phone on his thirteenth birthday, he had yet to miss a call. It didn't matter if he was in surgery, on a date, driving home to see his ailing mother—he would always, *always* take Michael's calls.

Today, he had missed three.

'Ray, please pick up. Look, I…I'm *very* sorry. You know how much having this surgery and the recovery mean to me. I would never do anything to jeopardize that. I just…I couldn't stand by and see this guy get mugged. And about the emergency contact— I freaked out, okay? I knew what you'd say, but I'm telling you, if you'd been there…hang on…I think your phone is deleting my'

Ray rolled his eyes as the line went dead. He might have bought Michael his first phone, but that certainly didn't mean the technically illiterate kid had ever mastered it.

'—sorry about that. This thing's a devil. Anyway, I just wanted to tell you that I'm sorry and I'll never do anything so reckless again. I wouldn't even have jumped in this time if it wasn't for…wait…*damnit*, it keeps cutting me—'

Fighting back a smile, Ray deleted the second message and moved on to the last.

'I'm sorry. Okay? I'm sorry. That's all I'm going to say. That's all I have time to say, because this phone you got me is a piece of—'

The final message cut off with a loud *beep* just as Price pulled up into Michael's driveway. As much as he wanted to let the kid stew in the repercussions of his actions, he had never been able to stay angry with Michael for long. He was incapable. And the fact that this whole mess began when Michael had jumped in to save an elderly man from a mugging…?

Well, try as he might, it was hard to stay angry at that too.

He was still chuckling to himself about the slew of failed voicemails as he walked up the front steps and knocked softly on the door. He was too preoccupied to notice the familiar car parked a little further down the street, or to hear the soft noises coming from inside.

When a second knock got no answer, he walked with a frown to the front window and shielded his eyes as he peered inside.

"MICHAEL CANARD!"

Michael and Alex fell off the couch in a flurry of profanities and desperate grabs for clothes. While she high-tailed it for the kitchen, he turned to the window, pale as a sheet, and held up a supplicating hand to Price.

"Ray, I can—"

Price took a step back and glared, deliberately crushing the row of tulips Michael had planted the previous year under his boot.

"You can what? Explain this?" he growled, as Michael shifted the pillow shielding his waist and hastily pulled on some pants. "You're going to have to."

"Yeah, I—" Michael tripped on the empty beer bottles littering the floor, grimacing apologetically as Price noticed them too. "Let me just unlock—"

"You know what?"

Price took a sudden step back. Between the street brawl, the emergency contact, and now Alexandra Morales with a six pack of beer—he'd simply had enough.

"Don't bother."

Michael ripped open the front door—tugging a shirt clumsily over his head—as Price stormed back to his car.

"Ray—wait!" he called, running outside barefoot after him.

But Price was already pulling down the driveway and out of reach. Before he left, he rolled down the window and paused a moment, glaring back at Michael's desperate face.

"I came because I got your messages. Thought that maybe we could grab some dinner and have a talk." He shook his head in disappointment as Alex appeared uncertainly in the door frame. "But it seems you already have company."

"Ray..." Michael's eyes searched the doctor's, silently pleading with him to stay. "It's not what it—"

Price scowled. "It's not what it looks like?"

Michael sighed. "Will you please come in and talk with me? Please, Ray. Don't just leave like this. I'm *sorry*. Please. I need you to—"

"What you *need* is to take a good long look in the mirror, son." Price pulled slowly down the street, leaving Michael standing there on the curb. "Because the man I see in front of me, is not the Michael I know."

Michael's face tightened and he dropped his eyes to the ground.

"I know. You're right. If you could just—"

But by the time he looked up, Price was gone.

"—stay."

CHAPTER

18

Michael sat outside on the front porch the next morning, watching as the sun peeked its way slowly through the trees. Hardly anyone was out at this time of day—just the occasional jogger or the last of the party stragglers, still trying to make their way home. This was the unofficial safe zone. A neutral time, just at dawn, when for a moment—just a moment—Woodlands liked to pretend like it was just a normal town. Not some strange dystopian wasteland.

"Good morning, Michael."

Michael lifted his head, forced a smile, and waved politely to the McCutchens as they hobbled along past his driveway. As long-time residents of Woodlands, they were well aware of this calm before the storm, and they took advantage each morning to take a brisk stroll.

"I heard you ended up in the hospital again yesterday," old Frank McCutchen called, squinting across the wet pavement. "That true?"

Michael shook his head dismissively. "Misunderstanding. Everything's fine."

Frank's wife, Joyce, took over as her husband dissolved into a fit of coughs. "Well you just be sure to call us, dear, if you ever need anything. You know we're right around the corner."

Michael smiled again and nodded. "Will do. Thanks, guys. Enjoy your walk."

His eyes followed them as they limped on down the street and around the corner. He'd always liked the McCutchens. Ever since he first moved here, six years ago, they'd always gone out of their way to be especially kind—bringing him cookies on the holidays, stopping by after every winter power outage to make sure he was alright.

Must be 'orphan-syndrome,' he'd always told himself. People tended to use the parentless as a means to make themselves feel better.

'What did you do today? Oh, today I hand-delivered oatmeal raison bars to an orphan—a regular Oliver Twist in the flesh.'

Growing up in the foster system, he'd seen the effects of 'orphan-syndrome' too many times to count.

But looking back through older eyes, he decided he had to reassess the McCutchens.

Some people were just born good. Solid to the core, there was no corrupting them. The McCutchens ran with the best of them. Well…they hobbled.

"Was that the super old couple you told me about?" Alex asked, wrapping her arms around him as she knelt behind him on the stairs. "The ones with the Dalmatian?"

"Daisy," Michael recalled, nodded. "She died."

"Mmm." She kissed the side of his face, pretending not to notice when he tensed slightly beneath her hands.

Since Dr. Price's unexpected visit last night, Michael had been flat and out of reach. She was quite familiar with that side of him—it was the same remote aloofness that had always presented itself when he was high—but it had been years since she'd seen it, and she wasn't particularly eager to stick around for it now.

"I'm gonna run," she said abruptly, pushing off his shoulders to her feet.

He glanced up in surprise and a flicker of guilt flashed across his face. "Are you sure? I could make some coffee or…" He sighed softly. "Sorry I wasn't much fun last night."

"Hey," she shoved him with her foot, coaxing a smile, "it's Ray. My nemesis. I get it."

The corners of his lips twitched, and she chuckled before suddenly sobering.

"Mikey?"

He looked up again, unable to keep the hint of sadness from the smile. "Yeah?"

"He's going to get over it. Promise."

With that, she kissed him abruptly on the cheek and trotted down the stairs to her car. It made a violent shrieking sound when she first started it, then shot off down the street in a cloud of smog and dust.

Michael stared after it, wishing very much for those words to be true.

Knowing, in the depths of his heart, that they were not.

* * *

The sun slowly rose and drifted across the bright sky, trailing long shadows down from the rooftops and chimneys on the street. The McCutchens returned from their walk. Kids left on the bus and eventually returned from school. The sky began to darken.

Michael sat and watched it all from the front porch. He hadn't moved from the spot where Alex had left him.

His face was still and expressionless as he gazed out at the street. His hand would rise in automatic greeting to anyone who called his name, and when necessary, his mouth even turned up in the expected smile.

But anyone who knew him even slightly better would quickly see that all was not well with Michael Canard. There was a fierce battle raging on just below the eyes. A battle that hadn't subsided in the least since he'd walked out that morning at dawn.

He'd debated a million times calling Price. He'd even pulled out his phone and started dialing once or twice. But until he knew what he was going to tell him, he didn't want to make the call. He hadn't been lying when he shouted his apologies the previous night—when he'd begged Ray to stay and talk. But it probably wasn't the talk the good doctor was expecting.

Michael needed…help.

His face sank into his hands and he winced as his fingers pressed against the new bruises.

Because the man I see in front of me, is not the Michael I know.

Price had put words to the exact problem Michael had been struggling with these last few weeks. A problem as simple as it was terrifying.

His own reflection.

It was as if, suddenly, his internal compass had been turned upside-down.

What had once been moral certainties, now blurred to disturbing shades of gray. Rules and resolutions were questioned. Boundaries were stretched. The Michael he used to be, and the person he'd worked so hard to become…they suddenly didn't seem all that different.

He forgot exactly what he'd been aiming for in the first place. He didn't feel whatever internal pressure it was that had made him want to change. And most importantly, the most disturbing thing of all—he was having a hell of a lot of trouble making himself care.

He cared about Ray, though. That much would never change. He'd cared about Ray, ever since Ray had made the inexplicable and monumental decision to care about him all those years ago. Without the doctor's influence in his life, in all likelihood, Michael would be dead already.

It hurt him to see Ray so upset. A hurt so deep in his chest that it shook loose some of the casual rationalizations that had taken up residence there.

He couldn't call him. That much was clear. He had transgressed beyond the limits of a mere phone call. But perhaps, just perhaps, if he could talk to him in person…

With a quiet sigh, he pushed stiffly to his feet, climbed into his car, and headed off to the last place in the world he ever wanted to see again.

* * *

"Hi there," Michael leaned across the registration counter with a smile, "I'm looking for Dr. Price. He should be on call today."

The receptionist sucked in a quick breath as she blushed bright scarlet.

"Dr. Price, you said?" she squeaked, fingers flying as she typed into the computer. "Is he expecting you?"

"Um…not exactly, but—"

"Michael?"

Michael's eyes shot up to see Nurse Franklin heading towards him from across the lobby floor. He said a silent prayer of thanks and hurried to meet her, flashing the receptionist a parting wink as he left.

"Mrs. Franklin—hey!" he greeted her warmly, grinning as she pulled him in for a motherly hug. But warm as the embrace might have been, her eyes were stern as she leaned back.

"Honey, you better not be here because you jumped in the middle of another street brawl," she warned. "And what's this I hear about it being at Sully's—"

"I'm not here for me," he said quickly, flashing that same, disarming smile. "I was hoping to see Ray, if he was still in?"

"Oh, Dr. Price? He's stuck in a long surgery—O.R. 4."

"Oh…" Michael's eyes flickered to the elevators, before returning to the nurse. "Do you think there's any way I can wait for him in the gallery? I think he wanted to check on my incision when he was done," he added quickly.

Not that he needed a medical reason to be granted access. After his now famous transplant surgery, the familial connection between the two had become well known throughout the hospital.

"Sure, honey, that would be just fine." She checked a buzz on her pager. "You know the way, don't you?"

"Fifth floor, second door on the right?"

"You got it." She squeezed his arm with a smile. "You stay safe, Michael. You know I love seeing you, but I don't want to be seeing you in here—you got it?"

"Got it."

He saluted and headed off to the elevators, riding them up to the fifth floor.

As he stepped out into the surgical wing, an eerie chill ran across his skin. He'd virtually grown up here—doing puzzles as a toddler, and later, doing homework as a child—waiting for Ray in the observational gallery above the operating rooms. By the time he was seven, he'd seen each of the major organs sitting in metal pans on the table, and had witnessed more flat-lines and resuscitations than most EMT's did in their entire careers.

He'd never thought it was at all strange—it was simply where he went most days after school. It wasn't until later, after he'd grown, that he recognized it was a rather morbid place to stash a child until dinner.

But none of that accounted for his sudden discomfort. None of that was the reason the hair on the back of his neck was standing on end.

The last time he'd come here…it had been him on that table.

And he'd almost died.

He stifled a shudder as he pulled open the door to the viewing gallery, eyes adjusting to the dim light as he peered down to where Price was working on stitching a severed artery below.

The room was so dark and quiet that it took him a moment to realize he wasn't alone.

"*Shit!*" he gasped, clutching his chest as the man sitting at the other end of the gallery turned his way. "Sorry—I didn't see you there."

The man grinned, a lazy lopsided grin, before shrugging a shoulder.

"It's no problem."

Michael grabbed a chair at the opposite end, and the two sat in rather awkward silence, watching Price do his best to stem a never-ending tide of blood.

Finally, when the weight of the stillness became too much to bear, Michael took a stab at breaking the ice.

"Do you know him?" he asked quietly, gesturing down to the middle-aged man lying on the operating table.

The man's eyes flickered down to the flurry of activity racing on beneath them, and once again, he smiled that same lopsided smile. "Yep—that's my guy."

"I'm sorry."

The man looked up in mild surprise, fixing Michael in his drooping eyes.

"You're sorry?"

"For your…" Slightly confused, Michael glanced down at what now appeared to be a gun-shot victim, before back-peddling quickly. "Sorry," he said again, dropping his eyes to his lap, "I didn't mean to pry. I'm sure he's going to pull through."

Much to his surprise, the man started chuckling. He stared intently through the glass, following Price's every move, before scooting suddenly across the gallery to take the seat beside Michael—the crooked smile still lingering on his face.

"I'm Geo."

He extended his hand. After a moment's pause, Michael shook it.

"Michael."

Up close, the two men assessed each other for the first time.

They were approximately the same age, that much was clear, but the similarities stopped right there.

Michael was tall. Handsome. Desirable. A testament to youthful physique and vitality.

Geo was none of these things.

If they had been standing, he would most likely have come up to Michael's chin. Instead of Michael's radiant hazel eyes, his were a dull brown. Instead of the grace and poise, apparent even while sitting, Geo appeared to be mistakenly assembled—a series of ill-fitting parts that had just happened to luck together into making a whole.

But the one thing he didn't lack was confidence. An unsettling, in your face kind of confidence that was difficult to understand and made Michael the first one to look away.

"What are you doing here?" Geo continued with that same, uncomfortable smile. "Do you know Malcolm too?"

"Malcolm?" Michael glanced down again at the bleeding man before quickly shaking his head. "I'm waiting for Dr. Price."

"Dr. Price..." Geo followed his gaze. "Is he the attending surgeon?"

"Yeah."

They lapsed back into silence once more, each one keenly aware of the other, although only one of them understood the reason why.

Finally, Geo leaned back with a shudder. "I hate hospitals," he said abruptly.

Michael looked over with a trace of a smile. "Me too."

"Looks like you've been to one recently, though." Geo reached over and pulled down the neck of Michael's shirt with one finger to reveal the scar beneath. "Heart surgery?"

Michael stiffened and pulled away, the hint of a warning in his eyes. "Yeah."

His arms crossed deliberately over his chest as he leaned back in his chair, creating a casual barrier between them.

Geo grinned again, before pushing abruptly to his feet.

"Well, it was nice meeting you."

A second later, he was already at the door.

Michael's eyes shot up, following the lithe movements with surprise before glancing back down at the man lying on the table with a frown.

"Don't you want to stay and find out what happens?"

"Oh no…" Geo flashed him a parting smile, eyes lingering on Michael's face. "I already know what happens."

He disappeared without another word, leaving Michael sitting alone in the dark.

* * *

"Michael? *Michael?*"

Michael jerked awake, lifting his head from his arm as his eyes struggled to adjust to the dim light. Price was standing over him, streaks of blood covering his white jacket.

"It's four a.m. What are you doing here?"

"I was…" Michael's eyes flickered to the now clean and darkened operating room, before returning to Price. "I was waiting for you. Guess I fell asleep."

Price folded his arms across his chest, gazing down sternly, all other emotions held safely at bay. "Well?"

Michael combed his fingers through his hair and stood up quickly. Now that his moment of reconciliation was finally here, he could not have felt less prepared.

"I wanted to apologize again—in person," he began quietly. "What you saw last night, I didn't—"

"Michael—"

"No Ray, please. Let me explain." He looked up beseechingly before dropping his eyes to the ground. "I ran into

Alex at random the other day when I was coming out of a meeting with my seminary advisor."

"Your seminary advisor?" It was perhaps one of the only things Michael could have said to soften the doctor, and Price looked up with interest. "How did it go?"

Michael shifted nervously. "With Alex? Or—"

"With the *seminary advisor*, Michael."

"Oh. Right." He cleared his throat. "It went...well."

All day, sitting on the steps, he had told himself he wasn't going to lie. *All day*, he'd promised that he was going to come clean, lay all his cards out on the table, and turn to his oldest friend for honest counsel as to how he was feeling and what he should do.

But Price wasn't just a friend. He was a father—or at least, as close to one as Michael ever had. He was an elder. A doctor. Someone who held Michael accountable. Someone whose opinion meant the world. And having disappointed him once already...

As Michael looked into his eyes, he simply couldn't bring himself to do it again.

"Yeah, it went really well," he continued, trying to bolster his story. "The woman said I should think about whether I'm interested in a four-year program or two."

Price nodded, studying his young friend carefully, before bringing him back on point.

"So you ran into Alex?"

"Yeah, she was—" Michael edited quickly, sensing that recounting how Alex was picking up her little sister from juvenile holding might be the worst thing to say, "she was just going out to lunch. I went with her, and…"

His eyes flickered up, desperate for forgiveness.

"Ray, I know I shouldn't have been drinking—"

"*Damn right you should not have been drinking,*" Price fired back, enunciating every word. "With how much you've wanted this, I don't know how you could have been so stupid!"

His medical clipboard came up between them, a long-standing prop to divert his gaze when frustration threatened to overpower. Michael's shoulders fell with a silent sigh. He'd been on the other side of the clipboard many times.

"But even more than that," Price continued, "I simply cannot, for even one second, understand how you let that girl back into your life."

"I wasn't planning on it—"

"It doesn't matter, Michael, *you did!* Do you even remember the last time the two of you were together? Are you even thinking about what life with Alex is actually like? Or are you so caught up with your lunch dates, you can't even tell?"

Price held up his hand, to stop Michael from answering. He was full-out yelling now, causing the nurses and passing orderlies to scatter and take the stairs.

"Because I remember! I remember the whole colorful experience! Can't even choose which part was my favorite. Maybe the night I had to stitch up your forehead because she hit you with a tape recorder. Or the time I had to bail you out of jail after she was drunk driving. Or the time I found you passed out in my backyard after almost overdosing on cocaine!"

"None of those were Alex's fault," Michael countered. It might have been unwise to contest any part of this, but he felt the need to try. "It was my decision to do those things, my terrible judgment at fault. You can't blame her for everything, Ray. Most of it was squarely on my shoulders." He lowered his voice persuasively, "She's been taking night classes, living with her aunt and sister. She's trying to turn her life around, Ray, just like me—"

"No, not like *you*, Michael. Alex Morales may be a lot of things, but she is not like *you*."

The clipboard was back again, dancing in the air between them.

"You are special. You are talented. You are thoughtful. And you are kind." Price shot each word out with a vicious glare. "But do you know what you are that's best of all, Michael?"

Michael hung his head and remained silent.

"You're *unsatisfied*. You don't want to spend your entire life living in this hell-hole, you want something bigger for yourself, something better. A future."

Price took a step back, panting as if he'd just run up the hall.

"I am *so proud* of everything you've overcome to get to this point. I am *so proud* of how hard you've worked to turn your life around."

The hallway echoed into silence between them.

"And that's why I won't stand by and watch you jeopardize it," the doctor concluded abruptly. "As long as Alex is in your life, I won't be. You'll simply have to decide."

Michael finally looked up and met his gaze. "Ray, you can't—"

"I just did, Mike. It's that simple."

Without another word, he turned and began walking away.

If he saw the way Michael took an automatic step to follow before catching himself, he didn't let on. He just forced himself to keep going.

He was almost to the door before Michael called softly, "Did Malcolm make it?"

The elevator dinged open and Price glanced back with a frown.

"Who's Malcolm?"

CHAPTER

19

"I'm in the market for some concert tickets." There was some static on the other side of the line, before a cheerful voice answered.

"Oh yes, sir? And which concert would that be?"

Vivian closed his eyes with a pained grimace, saying each word with deliberate care.

"Is there still a chance to see the Black-Eyed Peas?"

The sound of muffled laughter.

"Well that all depends on your favorite member of the—"

"Cut the crap, Chase," Vivian snapped. "Consider me 'coded in.'"

"Alright, alright, line secure. Let me just transfer you over…"

Vivian sat down at the kitchen table and rubbed his eyes. Ever since the job of safe-guarding the lines of communication had fallen to the interns, the specific recitations to be chanted back

318 | ANTHONY WILLIAMS

and forth at the opening of each call had gone from awkwardly uncomfortable to downright absurd. Chase Simmons, self-proclaimed king of the assassin subordinates, was the worst offender, and considering his circle of notoriously unstable co-workers, he wasn't likely to survive to the following year.

There was another electric crackle before a woman's voice answered the phone.

"Canard."

It wasn't a question. It was never a question. It was usually a summons. Sometimes a reprimand. Often a commendation. Never a question.

"Brandt."

In this call, there were no awkward pauses. No wasted words.

"Don't play games with me, Peter. There had better be a damn good reason why you didn't check in after Budapest or—"

"I'm out, Brandt."

He heard her take a breath.

"You're out," she repeated without inflection. "Out of what?"

"Out of this, Brandt—out of the whole business. Consider this my formal resignation."

"Your formal resignation..." There was a ceramic *clink* as she set down her coffee. "You know, most people give thirty days' notice."

She was stalling now, and it was most unlike her. But Vivian knew better than to break the silence. He would wait and let her work things out on her own.

People got into his business for a variety of reasons. Some were coerced, some volunteered, some were recruited and groomed. He'd even heard of a select few being kidnapped and brainwashed into it. It all depended on your level of talent. And in a world flushed with guns and people willing to pull the trigger, *talent* was something you had to prove.

Miss a couple jobs, you were considered as expendable as your targets. Survive long enough—and certain favors would be granted to you.

Vivian had long enjoyed the perks of these kinds of favors. He'd horded them greedily while watching as his lessers fell along the wayside or eked out a mediocre living struggling to do what he did best.

He had seen more people come and go than he, with his perfect memory, had the heart to recount. He'd seen Directors replace Directors, over his years of service. He'd been standing there, in a conference room in Austria, when the woman on the other end of the phone had been handed the keys to the castle.

He knew where he stood in the scheme of things.

He just didn't know if they'd be willing to let him walk away.

"Peter...this is most unusual."

Vivian nodded patiently and continued to wait in silence, surprised by how surprising it was to hear his own name. In a way, it felt like it had always been Vivian.

He figured that right now, Brandt found herself facing three options.

She could—*one*—have him killed.

This was an interesting solution, and, despite their history, probably the first that jumped to her mind. Assassins did not just 'leave' the profession—did not ask to leave. While most were killed long before this would ever be a problem, the ones who survived long enough to consider making the request would have accumulated so much confidential information that they would simply be too great a liability to be allowed to go. A very, very slight percentage of them might be offered 'higher management' positions—like Brandt. But both she and Vivian knew that's not what he was talking about.

She could—*two*—stall and/or blackmail him to continue.

Although just as effective as the first option, this one proved trickier to actually follow through. The agency didn't have much dirt on Peter Canard. It was a testament to how well he'd covered all his tracks, that his own handlers didn't know he had a child. His record was spotless for a reason, and he suspected that even now, as she was undoubtedly running through these options in her mind, she was unable to think of anything weighty enough to change his mind.

Which left option three.

She could let him go.

"Thirty years, Miranda," he said gently, slipping past the formalities as he used her first name. "After thirty years, I'm ready to call it a day."

"May I ask why now?"

She was fishing, but also genuinely interested. An agent like Peter Canard only came around once in a blue moon, and he was one of the few people who might actually be considered for such a request—granted that his information was in order.

"I killed Lucius Montana."

He had timed it perfectly—rehearsed it beforehand.

It was the perfect answer, he'd realized. A cosmic sort of symmetry, and an undeniable high note on which to end his career. Furthermore, although he couldn't see it all the way in Vienna, he was sure Miranda Brandt was smiling.

"I thought it was you. We'd heard unconfirmed reports that Montana had gone missing, presumed dead. When you fell off the grid this last month, I put two and two together."

"That's why they gave you the big office."

"Congratulations, Peter. I mean it. It's well done."

He bowed his head, clutching the phone to his ear as he took a deep breath.

"Which brings us back to my request."

Brandt cleared her throat. "Was it a request? I heard it more as a statement."

Stalling again. She must truly have no idea what she was going to do.

"It was both." Vivian sighed and decided to lay all his cards out on the table. Well—most of his cards, anyway. "You and I both know that if you wanted, you could make it very difficult if not downright impossible for my retirement to happen. I'm *asking* you not to do that, because I'm *telling* you I want to leave."

The words were clipped but respectful—of both her authority and her time. But Vivian also knew his own worth; he did not let it go unnoticed.

"You would be hard-pressed to find any ten agents who have done more combined for the agency than I have, and you and I both know, I'm getting up there in age. If you're worried about a leak, about someone coming after me for information..."

He couldn't help but smile.

"Let them come."

There was a long pause after his words. A pause in which he knew, halfway around the world, a woman sitting behind a desk was deciding the course of his fate. He found himself holding his breath. Then, finally, there was a barely audible sigh.

"Where will you go?" she asked.

He exhaled in relief, beaming at the kitchen wall.

"Here and there. I have a small retirement fund saved up, and I've always liked to travel."

She laughed. As much of a laugh a woman like her was capable of making.

"You'll be missed," she said shortly. "I'll have to find someone to replace you."

"Good luck," he teased, suddenly feeling nervous to hang up and set down the phone.

This would be his last phone call to Austria—all he'd ever known. This would be the last time he and the woman behind the desk would ever speak. A part of him was almost sad.

324 | ANTHONY WILLIAMS

"You too."

He pulled the screen away from his face to disconnect, when he heard her add,

"Sincerely, Peter. Good luck."

The line went dead.

He stared at it for a moment, unable to believe it was true. Then he set it down slowly on the kitchen table and stared at it some more—a part of him half-waiting for it to ring.

But it didn't ring. It would never ring again.

That chapter of his life was closed. Permanently. For good. A new life was calling, a fresh slate with a chance to start over.

His eyes flickered to the pile of television monitors stacked in the center of the living room and a small smile crept up the side of his face.

There was just one little thing standing in his way...

* * *

Michael didn't arrive home until late the following evening. He'd spent the entire day driving aimlessly around the city, speeding past the same sights that had inspired and haunted him as a child, no clear destination or direction as to where he should go.

How apropos, he thought bitterly as he pulled into his drive.

The little excursion had been meant to clear his mind—to help him focus and pick a side following Price's chilling ultimatum.

It wasn't a choice—he kept telling himself.

Price was telling him to pick life with a future. To pick friends who would look out for him, who had his best interests at heart. To pick a job he believed in, a God he believed in, and a whole host of other things that came from life outside the dark confines of Woodlands.

That wasn't a choice, he repeated. That was what he wanted.

What he was supposed to have wanted.

But another, angrier voice rose up to combat the first—growing louder and louder as Michael tore through residential neighborhoods and cruised along the interstate.

That wasn't a choice Price had the right to demand he make.

Michael might be alive because of the good doctor's efforts—from keeping an eye on him as a child, right down to the actual surgery that came just in time. But the point was, he *was* alive. This was *his* life. Every choice, every decision—it was *his* to make alone.

Price didn't get to make ultimatums. He didn't get to pick and choose the ways Michael was allowed to spend his time. And he certainly wasn't in any position to insist he stop seeing Alex.

Of course, a part of him understood Price's reasons—understood that his insistence was far greater than just one girl. That it was an entire future he was advocating. A part of Michael might have even known, deep down, that Price was right.

But he couldn't see that part now. He couldn't see anything.

Everything was blurred—relegated to infuriating shades of gray. A color which he aimlessly meandered through until finally just giving up and returning home.

"Hey Michael—everything okay?"

Michael jumped in his skin and whirled around to see Frank and Joyce McCutchen walking past on an evening stroll. He had never seen them out so late—they always took their daily walk in the morning. For a moment, he just stared.

Then he remembered himself and smiled quickly. "Yeah, everything's fine. You two enjoy your evening."

He turned around and headed quickly into the house before they could say anything further or draw him into a conversation. As fond as he may be of the pair, he was in no mood to uphold casual pleasantries right now.

He was in such a hurry to get inside, that he didn't even notice the door was unlocked. It opened beneath his hand as he strode purposely through the living room and to the kitchen. He was halfway there before he realized Alex was sitting on the couch.

"You were out a while."

For the second time in less than a minute, Michael whirled around and clutched his heart.

"*Shit—Alex*! How did you get in here?"

She didn't move from her position on the couch.

"Still have a key."

As his pulse returned to normal, he slowly lowered his hand. "I swear, you people are going to short-circuit this thing before I even get a chance to use it." He squinted at her through the dark, eyes struggling to adjust. "Why didn't you turn any lights on?"

It wasn't until he flipped on the overhead, that he saw Alex wasn't alone. She had brought a little party with her.

"Why did you disappear four years ago without a word?" she countered.

A half-empty pint of tequila was on the coffee table next to her—smeared lipstick around the rim—and a fine white powder was dusting the dark wood.

Michael looked at each carefully, before slowly lifting his eyes to her.

He had seen Alex drunk before; he had seen her chasing. He knew her body's limits probably better than she did. Tonight, she had clearly exceeded them.

"How much of that stuff have you had?" he asked lightly, sinking down next to her and easing the bottle from her hands. Her face tightened in defensively, and he took a quick drink.

He understood the rules of this game, he had played it many, many times himself.

Rule number one: no one drinks alone.

"You didn't answer my question," she slurred, her bright eyes fighting to focus. "Why did you leave me? Why did you disappear?" A choked sob caught in her throat and she wiped at the dried streaks of mascara on her face. "You didn't even call me—you just...left."

His throat tightened, and he took another quick swig when she reached for the bottle, keeping it causally out of her hands.

How could he explain what happened?

It wasn't like he hadn't thought about it before. Send her a call, send her a text. Tell her that he couldn't do that kind of life anymore—that it was killing him. Tell him about Ryan, and Steve, and Jake and the other guys that were lying dead beneath the bridge. Tell her that it could have been him.

But that was the problem that stopped him every time. The moment when his story spun completely off the rails.

It *should* have been him. There was no explaining why it wasn't.

So what was he supposed to say?

'Sorry Alex, some guy emptied a clip into my face—don't worry, I'm fine—but I'm not going to meet up later? I'm going to church instead?'

He couldn't see that going over well...

"I wanted to," he admitted softly, stroking back a long strand of her hair as she swayed drunkenly on the couch. "I wanted to a lot. I just...didn't know how."

"That's no excuse, Michael!"

She pulled another hit of something out of her purse and snorted it up her nose before he could stop her. He watched with worried eyes, then discreetly dug his nails into her bare ankle, curled along his leg. She couldn't feel it.

"Hey," he reached for the purse with a coaxing smile, "I think that's enough for now."

Her hand flashed out faster than a snake and grabbed the other end.

"Leave it, Mikey."

"You've got to save some for me," he countered charmingly, still playing the game.

But even in a chemically induced trance, Alex could still spot the lie.

"Yeah?" she challenged with a little smirk. "Then do it." Her hand slipped inside, and she pulled out a little tube, filled with the white powder. "Do a line, baby."

His breath caught guiltily in his chest as she dumped some onto the table and scraped it into shape with an old driver's license.

He wasn't going to do it. For a lot of reasons. On some things, at least, he was still clear.

"Naw—I'll stick with tequila," he countered, lifting another shot to his lips in a desperate attempt to appease her.

Her head tilted back in wild, hysterical laughter. A familiar sound that sent chills running down his spine. "You haven't actually changed at all. Not at all. You're still an iced-tea drinking, son of Jesus. Just slumming it here with me."

"Hey, hey—" he caught her hands as she reached again for the bottle, "that's not true. You know that's not true. Come on— talk to me here."

She yanked her wrists free and glared. "What's there to talk about? You. Left. Michael."

Each word fired in the air between them, wounding them both.

"You left *me*," she continued, scooting forward on the couch. "*I* wasn't enough."

It felt as though a slow vice was squeezing Michael's ribs. He couldn't seem to take a full breath. Couldn't seem to look her in the eyes.

"Alex, that's not true. Things just got...complicated. It had nothing to do with you. It never had anything to do with you. And I'm...I'm sorry. I really am."

He ran his fingers back through his hair—his head already a little fuzzy with the tequila. It felt like all he was doing lately was apologizing. Apologizing to Ray for not being good enough, apologizing to Alex for not being bad enough. What the hell was he supposed to do?

"You're sorry," she repeated, her face still frozen in that dangerous smile. She leaned down to the table to take the line herself. "Well that's something, I guess."

"Babe, wait—"

In a flash, Michael brushed the cocaine off the table, catching her gently around the waist as she slipped forward. But occupied as he was, he was unprepared for her retaliation.

"What the hell did you do that for?!"

In a drunken rage, she picked up the tequila bottle and smashed it over his head.

The room spun as a warm stream of blood ran down his face. Then the sterilizing sting of the alcohol hit, and he brought up his hand to his temple with a cry.

"Oh—*Mikey*! Shit, Michael, I'm so sorry! I didn't mean to—"

He held up a hand to silence her, pointing her to the kitchen. "Just get me a paper towel."

But direction of any kind was no use. The second she saw the blood, her hysterical rage vanished into hysterical apologies.

"I can't believe I just—" her breath cut off with a sob, "I didn't mean to—"

"It's okay, it's not your fault," he said.

The same thing he always said when she was like this. He grimaced and uttered a silent profanity as he pulled a piece of glass delicately from his face.

"Please, can we just…"

She couldn't stop crying. She couldn't stop shaking. And she couldn't seem to slow down. The mix of uppers and downers had proven a devastating combination, and before Michael knew what she was doing, she grabbed his bloodied hand and slipped it under her shirt.

He tried to pull back. "Alex, what are you—"

"Can we just forget about this?" she begged, tears still running down her face as she clumsily tried to undress. "*Please?* Can we just go back, like old times?"

"*Alexandra.*" He took her firmly by the shoulders, holding her in place. "You need to take a second and breathe. Just calm down. We're going to get this cleaned up, and—"

She twitched suddenly in his hands, and he stopped cold.

"...Alex?"

For a second, both of them were still.

Then her eyes rolled back, and she went into convulsions.

"ALEX—NO!" he cried, grabbing her off the couch and dragging her into his arms. Her skin was burning up and her pulse was so quick it was a mere flutter under his fingertips. "You will NOT do this to me again!"

The next second, he was sprinting with her to the car. The crisp night air bit into him as he darted down the driveway, freezing the blood and tequila as it ran down his skin. Colors blurred around the edges, and as he yanked open the door and threw her inside, he realized the whole world was tilted slightly on its side. She must have hit him harder than he thought.

A second later, they were flying down the center of the road. He drove as fast as his broken-down car would allow—racing through stop signs and red lights. Every few seconds, he would glance at her—still twitching in the passenger seat—and squeeze her hand.

"Alex—stay with me, okay? Keep your eyes open, honey, we're almost there."

The sound of a sudden siren made him jump in his seat. The inside of the car flashed red and blue as a squad car pulled out behind him, signaling for him to pull over.

"You have got to be kidding me!"

For a second, he almost kept going. But his little car couldn't out-run theirs, and after a moment's consideration, he realized that they could probably get her to the hospital a lot faster than he could.

He pulled over the next instant, tires screeching to a halt on the gravel beside the road.

"Officers!" he called, throwing open the door and running to meet them. "Officers, there's a girl in here who's over—"

"DON'T MOVE!"

Michael froze cold, as for the second time in his life, a gun was pointed in his face.

"TURN AROUND AND PUT YOUR HANDS IN THE AIR!"

Still stunned, he rotated slowly around, lifting his arms. As he turned past the car, he got a glimpse of his reflection.

Of course...

The side of his face was drenched in blood, bits of glass were still stuck in his hair, and his skin was dripping with tequila.

The next second, a heavyset man slammed into the back of his knees and knocked him forward over the hood of the car. Michael complied instantly, putting up no resistance, but gestured wildly to where Alex was slumped against the passenger window.

"Young man, you want to tell me what the hell is going—"

"My friend's in the front seat of the car," Michael interrupted with a broken gasp, "she's overdosing. Please—"

The officer left him immediately and went around to the passenger's seat. In Woodlands, 'overdosing' was the magic word.

"What's she on?" he asked routinely, yanking open the door as he knelt by Alex's side.

"Cocaine," Michael replied instantly, still panting as bits of blood and liquor dripped off his hair onto the hood of the car. "I was trying to get her to the hospital. Please—"

"Unit Nine, we've got a Signal 44," he said into his radio. Then to Michael, "What happened to your face?"

Michael paused only a fraction of a second. "An accident. Please, can we get her—"

"Yeah, yeah—we're going." With surprisingly delicate hands, the officer lifted Alex into the back of the squad car as his partner patted Michael quickly down. "You'd better come along too—get that cut of yours checked out."

"Sir," the partner said suddenly, "he's armed."

"What?" Michael cried, trying to turn around against the hands that held him. "No I—"

His voice trailed off when he saw his knife, sitting in the palm of the officer's hand.

"Yours?" the first officer demanded, looking slightly betrayed as he jammed his keys into the ignition.

Michael just stared, unable to think of a single thing to say. He hadn't realized the knife was still even on him.

The officer registered the silence as an admission of guilt. "Cuff him. And put him in the back of the car with her." He glanced at Alex nervously. "We need to get going."

The lights went back on. The sirens screamed to life. And the squad car went racing up the street, taking Michael back, yet again, to the hospital.

CHAPTER

20

It was like a bad dream. One Michael couldn't wake up from. A team of doctors and nurses crowded around them, barking incoherent orders as Michael was shoved unceremoniously to the side. A tangle of wires was strung from Alex like Christmas lights as they pumped her full of liquids and anti-seizure medication. At one point, she flat-lined and a pair of paddles shot a bolt of electricity through her chest. The room went silent for a moment, then snapped back into action as they heard the first tentative *beep*.

As for Michael, the cops didn't seem to think he was any kind of threat. Most likely because of the traumatized, shell-shocked look about him. They left him sitting on the floor in the hall, still cuffed, as they returned to the front desk to begin filling out the proper paperwork.

From where he sat, he had a full view of Alex's room, of the battle waging on to save her life. He stared with wide, haunted eyes. A silent stream of tears running down his face.

He didn't realize anyone was talking to him, until Price sat down by his side.

"Hey, kid."

He looked over in surprise. Those were the first words he could remember Price ever saying to him, in a hospital back in Washington D.C. He had only been about four years old at the time—it was one of his first memories. But the phrase had stayed alive between them, surfacing at odd moments or memorable occasions.

Running to the car after his first day at a new kindergarten in Woodlands. Years later, when he got picked up from the same school office after being suspended for setting off illegal fireworks at the prom. The day he'd walked into Price's office and abruptly invited him to church.

Always the same.

"Hey," he echoed back, his voice shaking.

Without saying anything else, Price reached out and squeezed his knee. Together, they watched the chaos in Alex's room for a long time.

She looked so small, lying there on the bed. Michael could barely stand to see it. So small and helpless compared to the world around her. As the doctors stuck her with needle after needle, he wished they would be more careful with her arms.

"She's going to pull through," Price finally murmured. Michael glanced at him, almost afraid to hope, and he nodded at the window. "Vital signs are stable. She's leveling out. You got her here just in time."

It was like someone had pulled the plug on a drain. All the air rushed out of Michael's chest as his shoulders dropped in exhaustion.

"You're sure?"

"I'm sure."

He lifted his hands to his face and Price noticed the cuffs for the first time. His eyes tightened, but he didn't say anything about them directly, he just glanced around the empty halls searching for the arresting officers.

"You have an escort somewhere?" he asked quietly.

Michael wiped his face and nodded, remembering them for the first time. "Yeah," he cleared his throat, suddenly aware of the fact that he reeked of tequila. "Here somewhere."

Price gave him a long look, before he finally shook his head and sighed. "Come on, Mike. Let's get you cleaned up."

He helped lift Michael to his feet, and together, they walked into the exam room next door. Without stopping to think, Michael hopped up onto the table—same way he'd been doing since he was a toddler—and tried to take off his jacket. Then he remembered the cuffs.

"Sorry," he murmured, "I can't—"

"Look up here," Price instructed, ignoring him as he shined a light into his eyes.

Michael did as he was told and followed it to the right and to the left—a little unsettled by the trouble he had in doing so. It felt like it was moving very fast—he was having a hard time keeping pace.

"Well, I could do a head CT to confirm, or I could just tell you. You have a concussion."

Michael nodded at the floor. "I figured."

After scribbling something down, Price ran his hands gently over Michael's scalp, pulling back suddenly as if something bit his finger. "Is that—" he parted Michael's hair, "is that glass?"

Michael couldn't meet his eyes. "Yeah, it's glass. But I'm sure it's clean."

"I can smell that."

Either to be medically thorough, or for his personal satisfaction, Price decided to sterilize the wound anyway—pouring a generous helping of antiseptic onto Michael's scalp before securing it with a pad of gauze. Michael flinched and bit his lip, but stayed perfectly still.

He deserved this. He deserved this and more.

But still, he had to explain.

"She was waiting at my house when I got back," he said softly. "Everything that happened—she'd already done by herself. I didn't take anything she took."

"You were arrested, Mike," Price replied robotically, as he pulled a syringe from a nearby drawer.

"For speeding to the hospital to get her here. I wasn't going to—" He cut off with a gasp as Price angled the needle beneath his hair, numbing the scalp before stitches.

"Breathe," Price reminded in a voice just as mechanical as the first.

He was having no better luck meeting Michael's eyes than Michael was with meeting his. There was simply too much anger there. And too much pain.

Again, Michael did as he was told, watching silently as Price returned to the same drawer to retrieve a suturing kit.

"You feel anything?" Price asked, tapping him twice around the wound. He shook his head, and the doctor began stitching.

It wasn't until halfway through, Michael realized he was crying.

Price realized it at the same time and dropped his hands at once.

"Mike?" He knelt down so they were on eye level, examining him with alarm. "Is the lidocaine not working?"

"I don't want to do this anymore."

It was barely more than a whisper. But both men heard it, loud and clear.

"I don't want to live like this."

It was dead quiet. Even the clock seemed to have stopped ticking.

Price hesitated—hesitated for what seemed to last an eternity. Then he got to his feet and gathered Michael up in his arms. Michael stiffened in surprise, taking a second to catch his breath, before burying his face in the doctor's shoulder.

Price wouldn't care that he was getting blood all over his starched white lab coat—he never had. All he'd ever wanted was for Michael was to be safe and happy. A man loved by those around him. A man with a future.

That's all Michael ever wanted too—he saw it now, clear as day. There was no decision to be made. No sudden ultimatum standing between them. They were on the same side.

He would have embraced him if it hadn't been for the cuffs.

"Ray, I—"

There was a loud noise behind them.

"Michael Canard?"

The door burst open and both of the officers from before came storming in. They paused a moment when they saw the suturing thread still dangling past Michael's ear, but then moved right on forward to pull him to his feet.

Price stepped deliberately in their way.

"I think you're going to want to take a step away from my patient."

The officers scowled but paused their advance.

"I'm sorry, Dr. Price," the one who had cuffed Michael answered, "but there are certain protocols we have to follow—"

"And that protocol was to leave my patient unattended and bleeding on the floor?"

Perched on the table behind him, Michael stifled a smile. Growing up around the hospital, he had seen Price go head to head with the police countless times. It always seemed to end the same way.

"He's sedated, cuffed, and there's a needle hanging out of his head. If you really think he's going to make a run for it, then you can stand outside the door. Either way, gentlemen, get the hell out of my examination room."

They lingered for another moment, trying desperately to save face, before sauntering back towards the door as if it had been their idea all the while. Ray and Michael watched them depart with twin satisfaction, smirking in the silent win.

Everything would have been perfect, if it had ended with that. Indeed, Price and Michael could have continued their tearful reconciliation in peace if the arresting officer hadn't turned around and said one final thing.

"Just to let you know, Mr. Canard—under the circumstances, we're not going to book you, and you're not being formally charged at this time. We will, however, be confiscating your knife. Have a good evening."

Have a good evening.

Michael's stomach fell to the floor as the door closed, leaving him and the doctor in awkward silence. When it could go on no longer, Price stepped deliberately into his line of vision, wielding the suturing needle like a blade.

"Your *knife?!*"

Michael sighed. The evening wasn't over yet…

* * *

It wasn't until about an hour later that Price finally thought to call Vivian.

After the police left, he and Michael had another miniature explosion about the knife. But the dust had finally settled, and the doctor had finished suturing his head in peace. The fact that he wasn't being officially arrested helped a good deal. He was in recovery now with Alex, assumedly saying goodbye, before he headed home.

Upon pulling his phone out of his lab coat, Price looked down to see he had seven missed calls. All from the same number. He dialed it back quickly, and waited with a frown. Vivian answered on the first ring.

"Ray—where the hell have you been?!"

Price raised his eyebrows, caught off guard by the panic in his friend's voice. "Whoa there, slow down. What's going on?"

"I can't find Michael!" There was the sound of a car accelerating in the background, followed by an impatient honk. "I went to his house earlier tonight to check up on him, and there's a trail of blood leading down to where his car should be."

"Peter, hold on—"

"I found the car, abandoned on the side of the interstate. Blood and glass littering the front seat. Price, I think they took him."

"That's what I'm trying to tell you, it's not—"

"I'm heading to JFK now. If they were in a car, Geo must be trying to leave the city. I swear to God, Ray, when I find him—"

"*Vivian!*"

346 | ANTHONY WILLIAMS

Only the shock of hearing his oldest friend call him by a woman's name, snapped Vivian out of his rant.

"Michael was here with me at the hospital, he's headed home now."

There was a mechanical groan followed by the screech of tires as the car assumedly spun around in the opposite direction—heading back to town.

"The hospital?" Vivian asked, still worried but sounding remarkably calmer. "Again?"

Price rolled his eyes. "Welcome to my life."

"What was he doing there?"

"It's a long story," he wiped his hands on his coat, trying to rub out a stain of Michael's blood. "Short version—he was arrested for speeding while trying to get a friend of his to the hospital after she overdosed. The friend survived, and all Michael got was a slap on the wrist."

There was a slight pause.

"He was arrested for that?"

"Well, he was covered in blood and tequila at the time—not to mention the fact that he was armed, so—"

"What the hell do you mean, *he was armed?!*"

Price sighed again. "He had a knife on him. Like I said, it's a long story."

"I'd like to hear it."

"Later—we can meet up tomorrow. Everything's fine, Pete. Everything's fine and it's already been a long day. Let's call it a night before anything else can happen, okay?"

"Fine." Vivian was still tense. "But I'm coming over first thing in the morning."

"Yeah, yeah." Price stifled a yawn. "Don't forget your purse."

The line disconnected.

Price wandered down the hall with a faint smile. Considering how badly it started, he'd have to say the night had ended on a high note. He had defeated the police and Alex had survived her cocaine-induced meltdown. But by far, the most important victory lay with Michael.

Price was confident, that after the events of tonight, Michael had gotten back on track.

He had seen that same repentant, almost transcendent look on his young friend's face before. It was the morning after the worst night of his life. The day that he'd walked into Price's office at the hospital and declared he was going to dedicate his life to Christ.

It was the same sort of confidence. The same look of steely determination. Although, this time, Christ had been noticeably absent.

Price was still smiling as he signed out Michael's paperwork by the front desk. The nurse sitting behind the desk glanced up, looking tired, but smiled as well when she saw the doctor.

"Checking out?" she asked.

"At long last," Price replied, scribbling his name on the bottom of a dozen identical pages. "Busy night."

She chuckled. "It always is. Hey—I thought I saw your friend in here again. Michael? I hope everything's okay…"

Price set down the pencil with unnecessary relish. "He's going to be fine." The words warmed him through and through. "In fact, I don't think you'll be seeing him back here."

She took the files off the counter and added them to the top of her stack. "That's good to hear—and I'll enter these into the system right now."

"Thanks, Lydia."

Price was just turning to go when another paper caught his eye. It was sticking halfway out of her pile, the only folder askew in a perfect stack. But it wasn't the odd angle that caught Price's eye. It was the name written on the side.

"What's this?" he asked, pulling it out.

"What's what?" Lydia glanced up. "Oh—that's the log for the observational gallery this week. Kim sent down a memo from upstairs saying that each name has to be recorded on the previous week's log. Makes a whole lot of sense, right?"

She rolled her eyes and went back to her typing. But Price was frozen in place.

It wasn't Michael's name that now held his attention—it was the name written directly above. Written in nearly illegible chicken-scratch, but written there, nonetheless.

Geo.

*   *   *

Price was in his car a minute later—flying down the interstate at a speed that was sure to get him arrested as well. He yanked his phone from his pocket and dialed Michael for the hundredth time in less than a minute.

"Come on…pick up…" he growled under this breath.

It went straight to voicemail.

When Michael didn't answer, he called Peter, honking the horn furiously as he flew out from behind a slow-moving semi.

"Hey Ray, didn't think I'd hear from you until—"

"Geo was with Michael, Peter! He could be heading there right now!"

It was one of the marks of a true assassin that in times of undeniable, undisputed danger, there was no explosion. No trace of panic. Not a single wasted movement.

Vivian was calm.

"How do you know this?"

"Geo was signed into the visitor's log at the hospital last night. He was in the gallery with Michael, watching my surgery—he knows where he is and what he looks like." He swerved around another truck and struggled to catch his breath. "And I can't get Michael on his phone."

Vivian's voice dropped an octave. "I'm headed there now."

"Me too, I'll see you—"

But another call beeped in and Price's blood ran cold. Aside from Peter's, it was the only other number he ever dreaded to see. The only other number that gave him a mild stroke every time it called. He clicked over at once.

"Yes?" he answered tentatively.

"It's me," came the reply. "A man just walked into Michael's house. I think… Ray, I think this time it's the real thing."

Price veered off the freeway and onto a side street. He was almost there. If the world could just pause for another second—

"Is Michael home?"

The voice hesitated, and the sound of a wheezing engine faded in from the distance.

"Ray—he's just pulling up. Do you want us to go inside?"

"No!" Price answered quickly.

From everything he'd heard about Geo from Peter, he was the last man on earth to be trifled with. His mind raced a million miles a minute as he shot through a stop sign and pulled onto another street. Almost there.

"Just keep Michael from going inside. I'll be there in two minutes." A cold sweat broke over his forehead and he wiped it with a shaking hand. "No matter what happens—"

"Don't let him go inside. Understood."

* * *

Michael pulled into his driveway feeling like an actual weight had been lifted from his shoulders. Of course, that might have been the lingering effect of the pain meds Price had loaded him up on, but he felt it was something deeper than that.

For the third time in his life, something profound had changed today. A door had opened, and he, Michael Canard, was about to walk through.

Yep—things were definitely changing. He could feel it.

"Michael?"

An aged voice crackled out of the darkness and Michael turned around in surprise.

"Mrs. McCutchen?" he asked curiously, squinting into the night. "Is that you?"

The second she spotted him, she and her husband walked swiftly up from the sidewalk to stand between him and the house. Michael frowned. Swiftly was understating it. He didn't think he had ever seen the two move so fast.

"What's going on?" he asked quickly, hoping beyond hope that he didn't still have blood and tequila smeared down his face. "Is everything alright?"

Mr. McCutchen reached out with a deliberate smile and took him by the arm, leading him casually but firmly in the opposite direction, towards the street. "Everything's fine, Michael. We were just hoping you might have a minute to—"

The three of them looked up in unison as a car came screeching around the corner. At the same time, a hand lifted back the curtains in Michael's window. The smell of burning rubber filled the air and Michael instinctively pulled his arm away from Mr. McCutchen.

Something…wasn't right.

He opened his mouth to speak, but at that moment, several things happened at once.

The door to his house flew open at the same time that Ray Price jumped from the car. He was yelling something, but Michael couldn't hear what it was. A strange buzzing had filled his ears, as if someone was holding their hands over his head.

There was a loud gasp from behind him and he turned around just in time to see the gun.

Just above it, stretched a lopsided smile.

There was a blur of movement, and a single shot fired.

Then all was quiet once more.

CHAPTER

21

The service was beautiful. Wasn't that the thing you were supposed to say in moments like this? That everything around you was beautiful?

Michael certainly heard it enough times as he stood in front of the coffin, hands tucked in his suit pockets, a hollowed-out expression on his face.

The flowers were lovely.

The eulogy was heartfelt.

Dr. Price would have loved it.

Except that Ray Price would not have loved it. Ray Price would not have found it beautiful. Because Ray Price didn't want to be lying in a wooden box, about to be lowered six feet into the ground.

"Michael," a faceless hand squeezed his shoulder, "it was a beautiful—"

"Please go," he answered shortly. The hand disappeared.

One by one, the people sitting in the chairs behind him began to get up and leave. There was a small reception scheduled for later, the time for mourning Ray at the graveside service had apparently passed. Michael could see a man with a shovel hovering impatiently in the wings.

"Michael?"

It was Pastor Jeff this time. The man who had conducted the lovely service.

"Michael, I'm having the rest of the flowers moved to the sanctuary for the wake. Is that alright? Would you like to take an arrangement for yourself?"

Michael kept his eyes fixed on the grave and said nothing.

"Do you…do you need a ride to the church?"

"No."

It was the first time he'd spoken all morning and the word stuck in his throat.

Jeff braced himself for more. "You…already have a ride, or—"

"I'm not going to the church."

Of course he wasn't.

The minister glanced helplessly around and found himself locking eyes with Vivian Knight. She was standing at the far edge of the proceedings, watching them closely. Despite her fixed attention now, she had been rather absent these last few days—a lapse that was both as bewildering as it was infuriating given their young friend's fragile state.

Jeff gave her a long look, before he returned his gaze to Michael.

"I know this isn't what you want to hear, son, but the first step to healing is through the Lord. I don't know if you've found a moment in these last few days to pray, but—"

Michael's expression darkened so abruptly that Jeff almost stopped talking.

"I think you're going to regret it if you don't come," he concluded gently. "I know how close you and Price were. You're going to want to have that kind of closure. To say goodbye—"

Without any warning, Michael spun on his heel and started marching back across the little cemetery towards the street, leaving the beautiful proceedings behind him.

"I said goodbye."

* * *

Why did they have the funeral on a Saturday, Michael wondered as he walked. Why not have it on a Tuesday, or a Thursday—some day when the evening wouldn't be concluded with two hours of cognitively-dissonant, yet high-spirited football? Some day when everyone wouldn't go on to church the

358 | ANTHONY WILLIAMS

next morning like things were as they should be—delighted to have seen each other just a few hours before and complimenting everyone's choice of graveside clothing?

Why did people make casseroles? Or jello? Why did *anyone* think that *anyone* liked casseroles? Or jello? How had it become a custom to pile on layers of industrially-processed guilt atop layers of grief?

These were the types of questions he would have usually laughed about with Ray.

A sudden gust of wind whipped his hair about and lifted his jacket halfway off his arms before he caught it. The day was as cold and icy as they come—Woodlands was zeroing in on Christmas. It was the kind of day that kept most people strictly indoors, but Michael found that aside from the erratic bursts of wind, he barely felt the cold.

What would happen to Ray's house, he wondered as he rounded a corner, stepping carefully on the slick ice. What would happen to all his Christmas lights? Would someone in his family come and put them up for him? No—of course they wouldn't. It was a stupid thing to think. But Ray always went all out for Christmas and Michael couldn't help but wonder.

He lifted his eyes and spotted the familiar rooftops of his neighborhood just up ahead.

The cemetery had always been a close walk from his house. Maybe a little too close, he thought now, as he made his way slowly down the street. Maybe he'd like a little distance.

He rounded the last corner, and it was all he could do to keep moving. His feet kept trying to stick to the ground, protecting him maybe, from the idea of home.

He hadn't been there since…anyways, he'd been staying in a motel.

It hadn't been his idea, but he hadn't put up any fight when it was suggested. The police had to quarantine the place for a specific amount of time anyway, and that amount of time just happened to coincide with the day of the funeral.

So Michael had stayed in an inn near the hospital. He'd taken a cab to the cemetery.

It was the 'For Sale' sign on the McCutchen's house that triggered the first of the flashbacks, a silent catalyst that quickly escalated into more.

He paused in front of their lawn, eyes flickering between the sign and the house. It might not yet have sold, but it was clear that the McCutchens no longer lived here. The car was gone, the welcome mat had been removed from the door, and all of Mrs. McCutchen's prized miniature rose bushes had been dumped by the side of the house.

The images started with no prior warning, hitting him like a punch to the gut.

'Get down, Michael! Get down!'

Michael sank to the ground under the weight of Price's body, as Frank and Joyce McCutchen pulled two semi-automatics from their jackets and opened fire. The police hadn't been able to explain the shower of bullet holes sprinkling the side of the house. When Michael had told them, wide-eyed and covered in Price's blood, that it had been his two old neighbors that lit up the streets—they had looked at him like he was crazy.

Not that they hit anything. Despite the forty-five bullets the local sheriff's department had picked out of Michael's walls, not one of them had managed to hit the target.

That crooked, lopsided smile flashed through Michael's mind and he doubled over where he stood, panting with his hands on his knees.

It had been the last thing he had seen before Price leapt out in front of him. He was still staring, mouth ajar, when the doctor grabbed him by the shoulders, then went suddenly limp in his arms as the bullet entered his back.

At first, Michael simply didn't understand.

Who was this man in his house? Why had Price followed him back from the hospital, and how had he gotten there so fast? What person in their right mind had seen fit to give the old McCutchens a pair of Berettas?

Then Price coughed a mouthful of blood into his face, and all those questions suddenly didn't matter anymore.

His mentor, his father, his oldest friend had died in his arms that night—gasping and choking for breath. There was nothing beautiful about it. Nothing a tasteful flower arrangement or heartfelt eulogy could begin to repair.

Because Ray didn't want to be buried in a frozen cemetery today.

He'd only wanted to save Michael's life.

A wave of nausea overtook him, and he vomited the remains of a casserole on the ground.

* * *

"Ray, I'm so sorry."

Vivian sat on the grass beside the coffin, peering down into the hole that was to be his friend's final resting place. The rest of the funeral goers had long since departed, scurrying off to their separate cars to join the procession to the reception back at the church. Some of the busier doctors, after sneaking guilty glances at their wrists, had quietly veered off in the other direction, heading back to the hospital.

Death waits for no man, Vivian thought ironically. *Ray might be dead, but there were still others to save. Time to scrub up, gentlemen.*

No one had paid him any mind as he'd hovered quietly in the back, watching the service unfold. No one except Pastor Jeff had even registered his presence. No one noticed him now, as he sat with his back against the carved walnut, resting a gentle hand on top of the wood.

No one except the impatient groundskeeper who had finally given up on waiting and was sitting in his car with a cigarette and a dirty magazine.

Finally satisfied that he had no possibility of an audience, Vivian reached into his purse and pulled out a silver flask. When he unscrewed the top, the unmistaken stench of scotch filled the air, whipped about by the angry wind.

After first raising it to his own lips, he poured out a dash into the grave, patting the side of the coffin as he did so. Just like they'd done since they were kids, passing it back and forth.

Of course, it hadn't been scotch then—but a selection of cheap beer.

And they hadn't customarily done it in a cemetery.

"You saved…my son."

Vivian tilted his head back and let the words flow out of him. Despite the freezing temperatures and the fact that he was sitting outside in a dress, he suddenly found it was very easy for him to drop all pretenses and just be honest. A steady stream of tears slid down his face, though his face remained thoughtful, calm.

"But why stop there? You *raised* my son. Looked after him while I was away. Gave him a future when all I'd ever done was sabotage what little chance he had to begin with."

Another swig of scotch, and another splash in the ground.

"If we're being honest Ray, *saving* him was hardly the most impressive thing you'd done."

Vivian's face hardened as he played back the words, recognizing their dark truth as a thousand phone calls, emailed pictures, and broken images flashed through his head. The life of Michael Canard, as told from a distance, with Ray Price as the guiding hand.

After that, there were some more recent images...

Vivian tipped the flask to his mouth and drained half of it in one gulp, his eyes fixing on what already felt to be lifetimes away.

The second he'd gotten Ray's call on the freeway, he'd turned around, tearing back to town like the devil himself was riding behind him. But fast as he'd driven, it wasn't fast enough.

He'd pulled onto the street just in time to hear the gunshot. Just in time to see Price dive forward and then sink into his son's shaking arms. He'd been close enough to feel the aftershock, to smell the powder and blood. To hear Michael's hysterical cries as he tried his best to put pressure on the wound while the old couple standing above him opened fire.

He had been so close, *so close* to stopping it all. But he hadn't. He'd failed.

Now here he was, sharing a flask with an empty grave.

The McCutchens had been a surprise—he wasn't expecting them. When he cornered them at the police station later the next day, he learned that Michael hadn't been expecting them either. In fact, the more Michael tried to piece them into the story, the more he began to doubt his own eyes.

They had been Price's idea, and something he paid for from his own pocket. A pair of unsuspecting ex-army rangers to keep an eye on Michael when Price himself wasn't around. This was something he had neglected to tell Vivian, halfway around the world, although, at this point, Vivian really should have seen it coming.

That was Ray—making the tough call, pulling the strings—keeping Michael safe.

To his dying breath.

Vivian's throat tightened and he spilled what was left of the flask into the soil, lifting the corner of the coffin and slipping the childhood memento inside.

He might not have been able to save Ray's life, but he would damn well make sure he hadn't died in vain. Geo's days on this earth were numbered.

And as for Michael…neither one of them would ever have to worry about Michael again.

*   *   *

It had taken Michael longer than he expected to make it off the street and back into his house. Once he'd finally made it past the McCutchen's, he'd found himself standing in the middle of a huge red blood stain at the base of the driveway. He'd thrown up again. Then there was the matter of the caution tape and the wooden police barricade nailed over the door.

When he finally made it inside, he found no comfort there. The place was exactly how he and Alex had left it. Smears of powder, drops of blood, broken bits of glass. Everything was just as it should have been, expect for one little thing.

A half-empty bottle of Corona sitting on the windowsill over-looking the lawn.

Michael stopped cold when he saw it.

He didn't drink Corona. Neither did Alex. And since they were on the clock, neither did any of the police officers who had set up residence in his house after the shooting.

It was Geo's.

He walked slowly towards it, hands shaking with rage as he picked it up.

This was where the bastard sat, waiting for Michael to come home. Seeing Price show up there instead. This was what he'd left for Michael to find.

With a blood-curdling scream, he hurled it against the wall— watching as it exploded in a thousand pieces and a cloud of spray.

Geo.

The name had taken up some sort of dark residence inside of him—echoing in the farthest recesses of his mind, whether he was awake or asleep.

He couldn't shake the feel of him. The look of him. The devastating aftermath of what he'd done. What was more, he didn't want to.

No, he didn't want to shake Geo loose.

In fact, there was nothing Michael wanted more in the world than to find him.

The next second, he was pacing down the hall, fumbling around until he pulled out his camera from where he stashed it under the bed. It might have taken him forever to make it back into the house, but he didn't stay there long. Less than a minute later, he was back out the door and heading to the interstate to hail down a cab.

There was somewhere he needed to go.

* * *

"I'll give you twelve-hundred for it."

Michael set the bag down carefully, glaring across the counter at the little cashier.

"It's listed for over two thousand."

"It's used," the man countered.

"It's *lightly* used."

Unwilling to back down, both men stared without blinking, both determined not to be the first to break.

Unbeknownst to Michael, he had stumbled into the very pawn shop where Peter Canard had made his official transformation into Vivian Knight for the first time. The man he was shooting daggers at, had actually complimented her wig before offering it at half price.

"Fine," the cashier finally relented, far more frightened than he'd let on by the expression on Michael's face. "I'll give you two thousand. But that's it."

Michael handed over the camera without a second's hesitation. "That should do it."

A part of him wept as the man extracted the gorgeous piece from the bag and turned it over with greedy fingers. His baby, his most precious thing. A part of him wanted to snatch it back and

368 | ANTHONY WILLIAMS

take off running—run straight out of this town and never look back.

But all those parts were silent now. They'd been silenced the moment Geo had fired that gun. There was one thing, and one thing only that occupied Michael's mind. And to accomplish it, he would have to say goodbye to his beloved camera.

In fact, he'd have to say goodbye to a lot of things.

"So what?" he said tersely, looking deliberately away as the man jammed it incoherently back into the velvet case. "We have a deal?"

With a sly smile, the man opened the cash register and gave Michael what he wanted. He had been in this situation many time before. Guy comes in with something special, guy is clearly beside himself and not thinking clearly. Guy will take whatever price he can just to get whatever it is that's driving him.

This one hadn't even remembered that there was a trio of high-priced lenses still partially gift-wrapped in the pocket of the bag.

"Have a nice day," he said sweetly, slapping the money into Michael's hand.

Michael took off without a second look and piled back into the cab that was idling outside. "Fourteenth and Mission."

As they shot off down the road, he leaned his head against the window, still drowning in horrific images and half-formed plans of revenge.

He had yet to make the connection between the little man he met in the gallery—the one who had taken away his entire family with a single bullet—and the under-sized footprint that had damaged Vivian's rain gutter as the man broke inside. That connection would be made later, eased out after unhealthy amounts of whiskey.

But before he could sit down with a bottle—the only thing he'd wanted to do since he got up that morning—there was one last stop he had to make.

"Here?" the cabbie asked, gazing up at the shop front.

Michael looked up in surprise, he'd completely lost track of time. The rusted lettering of a familiar sign stared back down at him.

'Knives and Tactical Gear.'

He pushed open the door and stepped outside. "This is it. Can you wait here— I won't be long."

"It's your money, friend," the man answered, and pulled out a newspaper.

The store was relatively empty—Michael was pleased to find. The only others were a pair of old men lingering near the back, pouring over what looked to be an ancient battle axe. He had learned not to discount the elderly lately, but that was an issue for another time.

"You again." The clerk looked up in dismay, remembering Michael's forty failed attempts to find a blade of his liking. "What can I help you with today—"

"Give me the kind of knife that kills people."

The man laughed nervously and glanced around. "You know, that's exactly the kind of thing you're supposed to avoid saying to people in my position—"

"Just do it."

After giving Michael a curious once-over, he walked slowly to the glass display case on the back wall. But as soon as he opened the lid, he seemed to rethink it and set it back down. He turned instead to another display case—this one buried behind a locked door in a cabinet.

There were only a few options to consider—probably about five or six in all—but he selected one quickly and laid it on the counter.

"N690 Tanto Combo Blade. Forprene handle, seven-inch blade. Weighs about fourteen ounces. Sells for six hundred even."

Michael froze for a moment, clenching his jaw as he looked at the blade.

"Is it good?" he asked quietly.

The man gave him a long look. "It will…get the job done."

Without a word, Michael peeled off the bills and lay them down on the counter. For a second, the man looked almost hesitant to take them, but a guy had to make a living. A moment later, he slipped them into the register and handed the holstered knife to Michael.

"Thanks." Michael was almost out the door, before he turned around. "Hey, do you know where there's a liquor store around here?"

This time, the cashier laid his hands down deliberately on the glass.

"Look man, maybe you need to—"

"Just tell me."

They shared a look.

"Up two blocks and around the corner. You'll see it on your left."

Michael nodded and slipped the knife into his jacket. "Thanks."

"You…you have a good night."

The door slammed shut as Michael vanished into the darkness, but the cashier found himself staring after him for a very long time. He almost didn't notice the two old-timers until they slammed the battle axe down on the counter.

* * *

Vivian stepped carefully around the red stain at the end of the driveway. His dark eyes took in every inch of it and he felt as though his heart might burst right through his chest.

A scattering of shell casings the police had missed were glinting softly in the tall grass. Casings that Vivian had counted and categorized before he'd even made it up the front steps.

Not that he needed to piece together what had happened. Although no one had seen him at the time, he had been standing right here—not twenty feet away, behind a parked car.

The entire thing played out before his eyes like a dream. He could see, in slow motion, the trajectory of every bullet. He could hear each casing as it echoed off the driveway and bounced into the lawn. He could sense, the exact moment, when the life left Ray's eyes.

Michael was home, that much was clear. There was fresh vomit in the garden and the light in the kitchen was on. Vivian made his way slowly up the steps, suitcase in hand.

The door was unlocked but he gave it a cursory knock anyway.

"Michael?" he called softly, pressing his ear to the bullet-ridden door.

"Come on in," came the reply.

Vivian stepped inside, ready for anything his son needed, ready for any new madness the world decided to throw their way.

But nothing in the world could have prepared him for what he saw.

Michael was crying.

Not ostentatiously. Not with the slightest bit of sound. In fact, Vivian would be surprised if he even realized he was crying at all. Yet, there he sat. A half-empty bottle of Jameson on the table, a broken Corona all over the floor, just crying.

Crying...and twirling a combat knife slowly on the table.

Vivian's eyes fixed on first the knife, then the bottle, before coming to rest on his son.

"Hey," Michael said quietly, pushing out a chair as he took another shot. "Didn't expect to see you here."

Vivian set down his bag and joined him at the table, making a quick study of his face before lowering his eyes to the table. "Well, I didn't get a chance to talk to you at the funeral..."

Michael flinched at the word 'funeral' but said nothing. Just took another drink as a silent stream of tears poured down his face.

374 | ANTHONY WILLIAMS

"And I wanted to…" he trailed off, trying to find the words, "…I wanted to make sure you were alright."

"I'm great." He raised the bottle to his lips. "Just great."

They sat in silence for a while. Each one staring at the wall.

Then Michael suddenly spoke. "I know who did it, you know. I know who killed him."

Vivian held his breath; unsure how much was the alcohol talking and how much was Michael. "Who?"

"A guy named Geo. My age. Tiny." He twirled the knife again and caught it with the tip of his finger, wiping the tiny dot of blood that followed on the table. "I'm supposed to go see a police line-up tomorrow to identify him. But he won't be there."

Vivian kept his eyes on the knife. "He might be."

"He won't."

The bottle came up again, and this time, Vivian grabbed hold—trying to ease it away as best he could. Michael held on with a little smile.

"I don't think so, Ms. Knight. We all grieve in different ways."

Unable to do anything else lest he give something away, Vivian let Michael tug the bottle out of his hands. "This doesn't look like grieving to me. It looks like something else."

"Oh yeah?"

Michael spun the knife in a quick orbit around his fingers, mesmerized by the soft glow.

"What kind of blade is that?" Vivian continued carefully, aching to pull it away before Michael lost a finger in a drunken accident.

"It's a N690 Tanto."

He lifted it up with shocking speed, looping it around his fingers with a flash of skill that made Vivian's head jerk up in alarm.

"A M690 Tanto, you said?"

Michael nodded, spinning the thing faster and faster until it was a silver blur.

The hairs on Vivian's neck stood up as his blood ran cold.

He was familiar with the blade. Intimately familiar. One just like it had been used to slice a hole in his lungs.

His eyes travelled slowly from where Michael was twirling the knife expertly through his fingers, to the bottle of rye whisky sitting on the table.

"Since when do you drink Jameson?" he asked quietly.

Michael let the knife fall with a loud clatter.

"Since now."

It was as if a dark fog descended over the table. A cold chill swept over Vivian's body and he lifted his eyes in horror. He remembered the mental comparison that had run through his head just a few weeks before:

Six foot four. Muscular build. Same blood type.

A good match—he'd thought. A perfect match.

The knife was in the air again, slicing a circle with a quiet hiss, as Michael's eyes fixed on the table. There was a look in them Vivian had never seen before. A look so monstrous and out of place, it didn't belong anywhere on Michael.

It belonged on someone else. In fact, it was the exact look he'd seen in the eyes of an old rival, just before he'd plunged a knife deep into his stomach. A rival that had died not far from here, not long ago. Behind a dumpster somewhere, mourned only by a girl and her dog.

But it wasn't the rival that concerned Vivian.

It was the fact that he'd given that rival's heart to his son…

Are you sure you don't recognize anyone, Mr. Canard? I could have them step forward again if you'd like a second look?"

Michael raised his eyebrows sarcastically. *"Mr. Canard?"*

The officer rolled his eyes. "Just, answer the question, Michael. I'm trying to do this by the book."

Michael sighed, clutching his cup of government procured coffee. "No, Billy. It was none of these guys. I told you, it was a little—"

"—a little guy with an ugly smile. Maybe Mexican. Yeah, you told me. About half a dozen times."

Michael dropped his eyes and shrugged. He hadn't expected for one second that the police might have actually found the perpetrator. Between their elusive encounter at the hospital and the fact that Geo had been able to flee the scene of the crime amidst heavy gunfire and without a single scratch—Michael had built him up in his head to almost epic proportions. No run-of-the-mill beat cop would be able to take him down. It was much bigger than that.

In his heart of hearts, he was sure it would come down to something involving capes on a rooftop. A regular comic book stand-off between Geo and himself.

Not that he hadn't checked out the line of suspects with vague interest. It had been a long time since he'd been down to the station for something like this. And it was the first time he'd done it from this side of the glass. Some of these guys, he actually used to know.

"Kind of weird to see it all from this angle, huh?"

Michael couldn't help but smile. "I was just thinking the same thing."

"You know what we used to call you down here?"

"What's that?"

Billy's teeth flashed with a wide grin. "Perp Number Four."

Michael thought about this for a moment, before chuckling softly. "Because you guys always stood me in the middle?"

"Because you were always the tallest."

Both men laughed again, oddly reminiscent for more complicated times. They had gone to school together, back in the day. Even played basketball until Billy rolled his knee and had to quit the team. It wasn't until after graduation, they'd gone very separate ways.

When they finally quieted down, Michael got to his feet and waved the cup.

"Thanks for the coffee."

"Michael," Billy's hand shot out to catch him, and Michael turned back in surprise. "I was really sorry to hear about Dr. Price," he gestured around the station, "we all were. He was a really good guy, ever since we were kids. He'll be missed."

Michael's eyes flickered around the station, before he nodded and flashed Billy a quick, but grateful smile. "Thanks, Billy. See you around."

"On the outside," Billy teased lightly.

Michael grinned. "On the outside."

Instead of going out the main gate, he headed around the back of the sub-station with a slip of paper to pick up his car from the impound lot. Given the life or death circumstances involved with his arrest, including his subsequent hospital stay, the city had graciously not charged him for a tow—he merely had to come and collect.

He climbed inside quickly, brushing bits of glass off the driver's seat, eager to leave this place behind him. His head was still pounding from a vicious hangover, and before making him look at the line-up, Billy had sat down with him and forced him to pour through hundreds upon hundreds of photographs in the precinct's old crime books.

He was exhausted. He was depressed. And what was more— he had a pushy, self-righteous, overly-concerned houseguest who refused to leave.

That's right. Shortly before going to sleep last night, Michael had realized what the suitcase Vivian had brought with her was for.

She was moving in.

Apparently, Michael had no choice in the matter.

"It makes perfect sense, Michael," she had said, spreading out a pair of sheets and a new pillow on the couch. "I haven't felt safe in my home since the break-in, and you're obviously in no state to be alone. The two of us can stay here together—at least until the end of the week.

He hadn't put up much resistance, at least, not that he could recall. He'd simply warned her that the white powder on the cushions was cocaine and advised her not to put her fingers in her mouth. Then he passed out.

Of course, in the cold light of morning, he couldn't think of a worse thing to have happened. At least, not right now. Not with what he had in mind. A dozen brilliant arguments and rebuttals leapt to the tip of his tongue to combat her, but by now, it was too late.

She was in. The couch was made up. The spare key was in her wallet. And while he might resent the intrusion, he didn't have the heart to turn a frightened woman out of his house.

Although, to be honest, he suspected Vivian might have guessed that and used it to her advantage when she pled her case the night before. She didn't exactly strike him as the type of woman who could get scared...

A hundred different faces were still flashing through his head as he parked in the driveway and walked up the front steps. The door opened before he could lay a finger on it, and he squinted against the bright lights inside.

"Thank god, Vivian, I—"

But it wasn't Vivian. Not by a long shot.

Michael's mouth fell open as all the countless images racing through his brain suddenly came together and melted into a single face—the one staring back at him with a lopsided smile.

Geo.

* * *

Michael was pulled inside before he knew what was happening, the cold cup of coffee slipping from his fingers and splashing on the welcome mat as he was yanked through the door.

He opened his mouth to yell, but before he could make a single sound, Geo leapt into the air and kicked him across the side of the face, felling him to the floor.

A host of blinking stars flashed behind his eyes as he looked up in a daze, wondering how such a small man could have used so much force. How had he even reached his head—

"Michael." Geo smiled down at him, nudging him with his foot as if in a greeting. "I wasn't sure when I was going to see you again. You haven't been home much. But I do sincerely hope you enjoyed the motel."

The world flashed in and out of focus as Michael lay there, trying to catch his breath.

"Where's—"

"*Vivian?*" Geo guessed suddenly. A very peculiar expression kind of amusement flashed across his face and the whole thing lit up with a beaming grin. "You were going to say *Vivian?*"

"Where is she?" Michael repeated with a glare, raising a hand to his bloody temple.

Much to his surprise, Geo erupted in fits of broken laughter—pacing back and forth in front of the door, actually clapping his hands with glee.

"You *were* going to say Vivian! Oh Michael, this is…this is almost too good to be true."

Michael watched him carefully, replaying the words in his head as he pulled himself into a delicate sitting position.

What the hell was this guy talking about? Was he just flat-out crazy?

But before he could make sense of it, a sharp kick caught him right in the chest, barreling into him with the force of a truck directly on his incision line. He doubled over with a silent cry, winded speechless, feeling as though his entire body might rip in two.

Geo watched impassively.

"That is a nasty scar you have there. You seemed a bit hesitant to let me look at it before, and I can see why. It must be very painful."

Involuntary tears sprang to Michael's eyes as he struggled to pull in a breath. Already, a thin streak of red was lacing its way up the front of his shirt, like someone had caught him with a rogue paintbrush.

"You didn't—" he gasped again, clutching at his pounding heart, "—you didn't come to the hospital for Price? You came there for me?"

Michael had gotten this wrong. He'd replayed every moment of his conversation with Geo up in the gallery. Many times over. And he'd come to certain conclusions.

The way he'd been there already when Michael walked in…? The way he'd gazed down at the doctor with a smile and said, 'Yep—that's my guy…?'

Michael had been sure that Price was the target, not him. That Geo had somehow known Price was going to Michael's house that night and had waited for him there, sipping Corona.

Now…it seemed as though Michael had been the target all along. That Price had just gotten in the way.

"Yes and no," Geo answered, sinking down into a crouch. His lazy eyes watched Michael's every move with unnerving, almost ravenous attention. "I went there that afternoon to see Price, and happened to run into you. And I came here that night to see you and happened to shoot him." His young face brightened again with another wondrous smile. "Strange bit of coincidence, don't you think?"

Michael's blood boiled over in his veins, as his fingers curled into trembling fists.

"Where is Vivian?" he asked again through gritted teeth.

"Ah yes," Geo got to his feet, looking down with a trace of amusement, "*Vivian*. I'm sure, wherever Vivian is—Vivian is just fine. At least for the time being."

Michael tried once again to sit up and got another quick kick to the chest.

"I didn't say you could get up," Geo said quietly.

There was a muffled cry, as Michael's head fell back against the floor. There was much more blood now. A veritable waterfall that cascaded down the center of his white shirt, as one by one, the stitches holding his chest together, snapped in two.

"Why are you doing this?" he panted, wrapping his arms around his torso as if he could literally hold himself in one piece. "Why Price? Why—"

His voice cut off with a sudden cry, and Geo sank instantly to his knees—squeezing Michael's ankle as he tried to soothe.

"Just breathe," he said softly. "It's easy to forget that."

A sudden image of Price saying the exact same words echoed through Michael's mind, and with a mighty effort, he reeled back and kicked Geo squarely in the face.

Geo flew backwards without making a sound, landing somewhere by the front door. But as hard as Michael kicked him, it was safe to say it did more damage to him, than his attacker.

His arms and legs had begun shaking with the pain radiating out from his chest, and he was beginning to lose feeling in his lower extremities. Instead of taking the opportunity to get up and run, he simply lay there, trying to keep himself together.

On the other side of the room, Geo picked himself slowly off the floor, lifting a hand to his bloody nose in shock. His eyes flickered twice between the blood on his fingers and what was left of Michael, before his lips turned up in an appreciative grin.

"Like father, like son."

Then he paced forward and hammered his foot down in the center of Michael's ribs.

This time, Michael screamed aloud as he slammed back into the floorboards.

Geo winced sympathetically. "I do apologize for harping on the chest. I had surgery myself once, back in Belgrade, and I know exactly how painful it is. I'm just trying to make it a bit easier on myself."

"What the hell is that supposed to mean?" Michael gasped, hands twitching against the floor as a cloying numbness began snaking its way up his legs.

Geo stuck his hands in his pockets, gazing down at the proceedings with a clinical eye.

"Well I know this isn't your fault, Michael, but it seems that something was given to you by mistake." He paused thoughtfully as his eyes travelled to the bright red stain blossoming over Michael's shirt. "I'm afraid I'm going to have to take it back."

The next second, there was a hunting knife in his hand. He'd moved so fast; Michael hadn't seen him reach for it.

"Wait, you have to…?"

He trailed off in horror as Geo walked slowly towards him—his mind unable to reconcile the nightmare. Then all at once, panic set in and he understood.

"No…" he breathed. Then much louder. "*NO!*"

He scrambled backwards as best as he could, but all his lower extremities had locked up with blood loss and shock, and he wasn't working with much. Geo out-paced him easily, catching him by the ankle and dragging him back.

"I had planned to do this a bit differently," he murmured, wiping the knife carefully on his palm. "But I think it will make a statement either way."

The last thing Michael saw was Geo gently removing his stained shirt.

"You might want to close your eyes," the assassin advised.

The tip of the knife grazed Michael's skin, and he offered up a silent prayer.

Then all at once, they were not alone.

There was a loud *bang*, and Michael's eyes flickered open and closed as what he could have sworn was a woman in a blue dress flew in between them.

The next second, Geo was airborne, smashing into a bookcase on the other side of the room. He landed with a muffled shout and lay still.

"Michael?! MICHAEL?!

Cool hands stroked back his hair, and Michael struggled to open his eyes.

He was right. It was a woman in a blue dress. His hand reached up towards her, as if to gauge whether or not she was real, and closed around her sleeve.

"Vivian?" he murmured, a little scared by how soft his own voice was.

"It's me," Vivian answered quickly, "I'm here."

There was a sharp pain as she pressed her hands firmly over his chest.

"You're going to be just fine," she assured him, "you just need to—"

His eyes widened in fear. "Behind you!"

A shower of glass rained down upon them, as Geo burst a heavy paper weight over Vivian's head. Bits of it tangled in her hair and fell into Michael's eyes, before she was caught by the shoulders and yanked away from him into the air.

Then the game was away.

The world blinked on and off, like a frayed wire, as Michael fought to stay awake. He managed to heave himself up against the bottom of the sofa, but what he saw didn't make sense.

Geo and Vivian locked in fierce combat.

His mouth fell open and his eyes struggled to keep pace as they rocketed around, smashing through furniture and pounding with their fists, blurring to mere shapes and colors as they battled each other across the room.

But it wasn't the viciousness of the fighting he couldn't understand—it was the skill.

It looked like something out of a movie. Something that didn't possibly belong in his living room, spiraling away as he bled out slowly on the floor.

Was this real? Was he even conscious?

The pair of them tripped over his legs with excruciating force, and the room sharpened back up into painful focus.

Yes—definitely conscious!

He wrapped one arm gingerly around his ribs and pulled himself up even higher on the couch. He was almost sitting now, and although his legs had apparently given up the ghost, the rest of him was still moving.

If only he could get to his phone. He scanned the room and saw where it had fallen out onto the floor. If he could just pull himself a little farther, he could call the police and—

But just then, almost as if it had a life of its own, a different solution pressed against his leg with a little nudge.

What little color there was left in his face drained right out, as he reached down slowly and picked up his knife. Despite the spasms of pain shooting through his body, the blade felt strong and sure in his hand. With a look of pale determination, he anchored himself against the coffee table, lifting a hand slowly behind his head.

Meanwhile, Geo and Vivian were locked in the battle of a lifetime. It was a battle of wills. Geo's will to prove himself, against Vivian's will to protect his son. Neither man would surrender even an inch of ground, and by now, they were both paying the price.

There was a muffled crack and Geo stumbled a few steps back, cursing under his breath in Spanish. His leg was twisted out at a bizarre angle, and no matter how many times he tried to snap it back into alignment, it refused to budge.

Any other day, Vivian would have leapt at the opportunity to strike, only now, he was struggling to do the same thing with his dislocated arm, fighting back profanities as he shoved it back into the socket.

"I have to hand it to you, *Vivian*," Geo shot him a bloody grin, "you certainly don't make it easy."

Vivian spat out a mouthful of blood. "Did you expect it to be easy?"

Geo considered, flinching every now and then as he tried to put weight on his leg. "I expected it to be done."

"Well I can help you there."

With a final cry, they collided together in the center of the room.

They swore and shouted and twisted around—both trying to get the upper hand—when Geo's fingers wrapped suddenly around Vivian's neck. He clamped down as hard as he could, twisting around so he was angled behind the damaged shoulder, with his back to Michael.

"I want you to know," he growled, squeezing impossibly tighter as Vivian choked and gasped for air, "the second you're gone—I'm finishing Michael." He leaned forward with a bloody sneer. "I'm going to carve out that heart you—"

But whatever Geo had been going to say next, they would never know.

His drooping eyes widened for a moment and he took a step back, releasing Vivian at the same time. At first, he looked merely surprised, staring down as a thin trickle of blood dripped from the corner of his mouth. Then his face went completely blank and he crumbled to the ground—never to move again.

Vivian fell back in shock.

His eyes slowly travelled from the knife sticking out of Geo's back, up to where Michael leaned weakly against the couch—one hand still raised in the air.

It had been a perfect throw, slipping seamlessly between the ribs to pierce his heart.

Worthy of Montana himself.

"Michael?" Vivian said tentatively, limping forward. "How did—"

"Is he dead?" Michael interrupted, never taking his eyes off Geo's body.

Vivian stopped cold, staring down at his son with a very strange look in his eyes.

"Yes, he's dead. You killed him."

The words seemed to echo in the suddenly silent room, hanging in the air between them.

"I killed him," Michael repeated faintly.

His eyes latched onto the bloody knife as the rest of his face went completely blank.

Then he passed out.

CHAPTER

23

"And you're sure that this is the man who assaulted you?" Officer Ned Torsel asked for the fifth time. "This is the man who broke into your house?"

Vivian couldn't blame him for being excited. It was one of the few burglary cases the Woodlands Police Department could say they actually solved.

Even if it hadn't been an actual burglary.

Even if it hadn't been them who actually solved it.

"Yes, that's the man. The same man who broke into Michael Canard's home just a few days later."

Vivian handed back the coroner's picture, his eyes flickering down to Geo's small, scarred body lying on the autopsy table with a bit of a twinkle. He'd like to get it framed.

"You're sure?" Torsel pressed.

"Absolutely," Vivian said with perfect confidence.

To be honest, it was one of the few times he could recall ever having told the truth to the police, and a part of him was tickled pink with the idea.

"After the break-in at my place, I asked Michael if I could stay with him for a while."

Torsel nodded and whipped out a paper to begin taking notes.

"Why Michael?"

Vivian shrugged. "He and I go to the same church and Bible study. I was also helping him with his physical therapy after his transplant surgery. It seemed to make sense."

The officer nodded again, stringing together a shaky timeline. "As I understand it, you were the one who brought him in to the hospital the second time, after the…incident."

Both men winced. Then Vivian nodded and Torsel scribbled another useless note.

The 'incident' was one way of putting it.

By the time Vivian had raced Michael to the ER, almost every stitch Price had put back in after his street brawl had popped wide open, and his entire chest was being held together with nothing but a pair of trembling hands and a prayer.

He'd almost bled out several times on the way there, but fortunately, once he actually made it to the hospital, the surgeons there were able to fix him up in a surprisingly short amount of time. As horrific as it might have been, breaking open the incision was about the only thing Geo had really done to hurt Michael, and once the doctors had sutured him back up and given him a blood transfusion, they felt comfortable discharging him the very next day.

Vivian had given him a ride home, watching him closely all the while.

It was unclear how much, if anything, Michael actually remembered about the fight with Geo. Vivian's both paternal and professional prodding had yielded few results. But given how much blood he had lost, and the fact that he wasn't asking a flood of impossible to answer questions, Vivian suspected that most of it had been lost to shock and mild exsanguination.

But, while the bulk of the story might have remained elusive, Michael definitely remembered the ending.

When Vivian had finally been let through into recovery, he'd found him sitting up straight as an arrow on his bed, staring impassively out the window.

"Hey kid," Vivian sat tentatively on the mattress, "how are you feeling?"

Michael gave him a very peculiar look, before he turned back to the glass.

"Like I killed a guy."

Vivian sucked in a quick breath. An old saying popped into his head, one that he'd heard circled around in Austria, and had followed him around the world.

They say that when you killed enough men, their spirits lingered in your eyes. You were a marked man after that. People could just look at you and know. Some people said it happened after only one man.

Vivian had always been of the persuasion that your eyes revealed only ever as much as you wanted them to. The weight of lost men had no place there, let alone just one.

Now, looking at Michael, he wasn't so sure.

"You killed a guy to save my life," he answered softly.

Again, Michael flashed him a strange look, before nodding slowly.

"That's right. He was very determined to kill you, wasn't he? And me."

Vivian had nothing to say to this. Perhaps he had been wrong about how much Michael remembered? Perhaps things were starting to come back?

But before he could go much further down that line of thought, Michael stretched his arms painfully and leaned back against the pillows with a sigh. "They have me on some pretty strong meds."

Vivian smiled in relief. "Is that right?"

"Now's the time you want to ask me all those personal questions."

Vivian chuckled as a nurse came in, followed by a doctor he didn't recognize. The doctor glanced down at the chart he was holding, before looking up with a smile.

"Well, good news is—we're releasing you. Bad news is—you need to come back in seven days so I can take a look at those stitches."

Michael dropped his head against the pillows with a contented sigh. "Deal." The doctor left and he turned to Vivian as the nurse bustled about, removing his IVs. "Think there's any way you can take me back home? You're still my emergency contact, after all. And my roommate."

Vivian had paused, studying him carefully. "I am?"

As the nurse wound more tape across his bandages, Michael sat up and winced.

"Yeah. Why wouldn't you be?"

"*Ms. Knight?*"

Torsel cleared his throat. Vivian jumped in his chair as he returned to the present. He had spaced out for a while there, and it was clearly not the first time the officer had said his name.

"I'm sorry—could you repeat that?"

The officer smiled kindly. "I'm sorry, I can only imagine how difficult this is for you. I was just asking if there was anything else you'd like to add, before we officially close the file."

"Close the file?" Vivian repeated, eyes flickering once again to Geo's autopsy.

"I'm happy to say so." Torsel slid the photograph back inside the manila folder and placed his folded hands on top. "Actually, of all the investigations I've seen in my time here with the precinct—this one is pretty self-explanatory. Open and shut."

Vivian stared at him for a moment, before his lips parted in a wide smile.

"Open and shut."

* * *

Across the hall, Michael was getting a similar speech from another officer.

"So that's when he began strangling Ms. Knight?"

"Yes."

"And that's when you threw the knife."

A slight pause.

"That's right."

Officer William 'Billy' Hardy leaned back with a whistle. "Well it's a good thing you did, Michael. Otherwise, I think we'd be carting off a different body to the morgue."

And on that note…

Michael leaned forward with sudden interest. "Billy, were you able to get anywhere with those hospital records?"

"I was." He slid the picture of Geo back in the file. Michael had refused to look. "It looks like your donor was just an average John Doe. No identification. No hits in the data base. When no one showed up to claim him, his remains were created and laid in the county plot."

"But what about fingerprints?" Michael asked, trying to mask his frustration. "I mean, everyone gets printed for something along the line. What about the DMV? They couldn't find a single match—"

"Actually, Michael, that's the only thing that was interesting about your John Doe."

"What was that?"

"He didn't have any fingerprints."

Michael leaned back in his chair, blinking slowly as he registered this.

"He didn't have any fingerprints?"

"Nope."

An almost manic smile crept up the side of Michael's face. Of course he didn't.

"And how the hell is that possible?"

Bill gathered the papers scattered across the table and placed them neatly back in his file.

"They were burned off. Must have been in some kind of fire."

"Were there burns on the rest of his body?"

"No, listen Michael, I'd love to stay and talk, but I gotta get this stuff to the chief." Billy grinned rather proudly. "They're making a special mention of it in the morning paper."

Michael stared at his simple friend with a trace of pity, before getting up with a smile.

"Of course. Thanks again for checking, Billy. I'll see you around."

He met Vivian out in the hall, and together, the two of them pushed through the double doors and headed back outside.

Once they were on the sidewalk, they turned to each other at the same time.

"Listen, I've got to—"

"Yeah, I was actually—"

They both stopped short with a pair of matching smiles.

"Crazy couple of weeks, huh?" Michael asked.

Vivian looked at him fondly. "Crazy."

"Not exactly what you were expecting when you moved to Woodlands?"

"Oh no, Michael," Vivian chuckled. "This is actually *exactly* what I was expecting when I moved to Woodlands."

Both men laughed quietly, until they were standing again in silence.

"I'm going to go pack up my things and move back to my house," Vivian finally said.

Michael glanced up; his face inscrutable. "You don't have to, you know. You're welcome to stay as long as you like—"

"I think it's time I moved on." Vivian looked at him fondly, his eyes soaking in every detail—every line, every scar. Committing them all to memory. "After everything that's happened, I'm sure you're going to want a little space anyway."

Michael said nothing, he merely smiled—staring at Vivian with the same kind of thoughtful reflection.

Finally, when he'd had enough, he stepped forward and the two embraced.

"Take care of yourself, Michael."

Vivian placed a hand on the back of his head, holding on as long as he dared. Michael closed his eyes as his arms tightened.

"You too."

They held on for a second more, before finally letting go. With a parting nod, both men headed off in separate directions. One going to a cemetery. One going to a church.

Michael was already halfway down the block, when Vivian called suddenly.

"Hey kid!"

He turned around and saw her standing there on the sidewalk, the wind blowing back her chestnut curls. He took a final look. A parting snapshot to file away for later.

"Yeah?" he called.

Vivian paused for a second, before her face lit up with a radiant smile.

"See you around."

Michael stared for just a second longer as the image burned its way into his mind. His lips curled up as an uncertain emotion flickered in his eyes. Too quick to identify. Too faint to remember. But it was there, nonetheless.

Then he lifted his hand in a parting wave and turned away. Walking off into the sun.

Epilogue

'Massive Explosion Shakes
Neighborhood to the Core'

The headline ran across the top of the Woodlands Chronicle the next day. It took up the entire front page, complete with a picture of the burned-out crater underneath.

Local police couldn't explain it, neither could the local fire department. Not only were all the gas and power mains unharmed, but the explosion had been meticulously contained, as if somehow designed to consume one single house—eliminating all trace of everything inside.

"I couldn't believe it, when I heard the news," Officer Ned Torsel was quoted saying. "I just spoke with Ms. Knight the other day. She helped us close a case we were working on, and now... I just don't understand how such bad things can happen to such good people."

Pastor Jeff didn't understand it either. In fact, when he'd picked up the newspaper that morning, he'd been completely shocked.

He had seen Vivian, just a few hours before the explosion. She'd shown up at his office at the church with a simple, yet urgent request. She wanted to be baptized.

He read through the article with tears in his eyes, trying to make sense of the tragedy.

The Lord worked in mysterious ways, but this fire, he simply couldn't understand. Nor did he understand why there wasn't a single mention of how her husband was a war hero killed in the line of duty. Seemed like shabby reporting, didn't it?

As unlikely as it would seem, news of the explosion travelled all the way across the ocean and ended up on the desk of a stern-looking man in Germany, illuminated now and then by the soft glow of perpetually blinking lights.

The man's eyes travelled from the picture of the crater, up to a picture on the corner of his desk. Under the frame, he and another man clinked glasses, toasting the fire's success.

"And justice be done," the man muttered.

He stared at the picture another second, before slipping the newspaper at the end of a thick file which he then locked with a stack of others in the bottom drawer of his desk.

"Francis…bring me that report on Tokyo, will you—"

* * *

Michael didn't see the headline. Nor did he hear about it on the news. He was a bit unreachable at the moment, sitting on a bus headed for Michigan.

The seminary was waiting. And after a long, troubled road— he was finally ready for it.

He leaned his freshly, cleaned shaved head against the window, tracing absentminded shapes in the steam.

Like father, like son.

His eyes twinkled as his lips turned up in a soft smile.

Maybe. Maybe not.

Maybe he would find out someday, piece it all together. Or maybe he would spend the rest of his life holding onto that frozen snapshot—curls blowing in the wind.

It was in the Lord's hands now. It always was.

And as every other would-be minister would be quick to tell you:

The Lord worked in mysterious ways…

About the Author

Anthony Williams is a first-time author that knows how to move a storyline. He grew up in a ghetto in Manhattan, NY, in the 60's, and draws on those experiences to radiate his audience. Upon graduating H.S., he joined the Air Force in August of '77. Although he didn't enjoy city life, he is grateful for the lessons it taught him, the life-long friendships and his acquired street-smarts.

Anthony ventured back to college in '91 as a music major, voice and piano. He later changed his major to Biology pre-med with an emphasis in cardiovascular surgery. He is fascinated with the heart and loves surgery. However, he didn't pursue a medical career for personal reasons.

As a priority, Anthony loves reading the bible daily and in chronological order (very important). "The best book I've ever read", he says. Anthony is a Christian and one of his favorite bible verses is: Jeremiah 17:9 – *The heart is deceitful above all things, and desperately wicked: who can know it? (KJV)*

Anthony is the youngest of seven children and has two children of his own, Michael and Timothy. He also has two grandchildren, Jasmine and Winter. Anthony currently resides in Mesa, AZ but identifies himself a Floridian. Clearwater, Fl to be exact!

In keeping his memories fresh, Anthony has made a habit of writing down his thoughts and dreams as they occur to 'freeze those moments in time'. This freezing the moment, has led to his affinity for photography. He believes that photography, captures life pieces that change moods by referencing times past and reminds us that we still matter. We paved the way. We were the trailblazers. Those frozen images are parts of a sum, pieces of a dream.

Anthony has now embarked on the journey as an author. *Canard,* a novel, is Anthony Williams' first published book. For a display of Anthony's works please visit his website at www.canardphotos.com

CPSIA information can be obtained
at www.ICGtesting.com
Printed in the USA
BVHW040216050421
604204BV00017B/1311